THE EARTH IS MY MOTHER

JOSEPH: THE NEZ PERCE

G. Freeman Webb

January, 1973
Revised December 2011 – May 2012

Front Jacket Illustration:
University of Washington Libraries, Special Collections, NA613
Rear Jacket Painting:
Antowine Warrior – *Young Warrior Dreaming*

THE EARTH IS MY MOTHER

G. Freeman Webb

Edition 1.10
Hardback ISBN 978-0-61549-285-8
Paperback ISBN 978-1-62154-871-3

Ularity Publishing Group
Contact www.ularity.com as needed.

TABLE OF CONTENTS

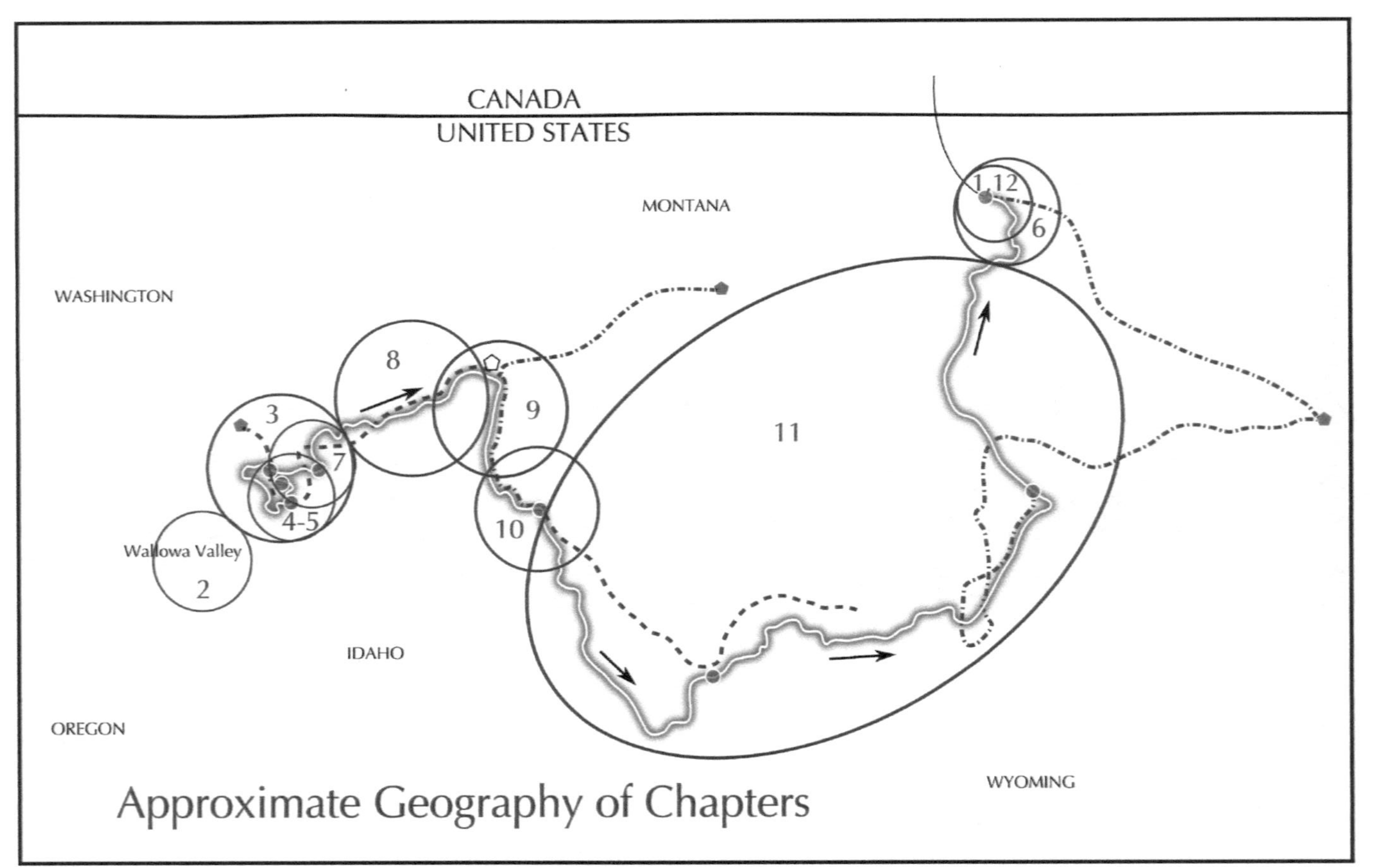

Approximate Geography of Chapters

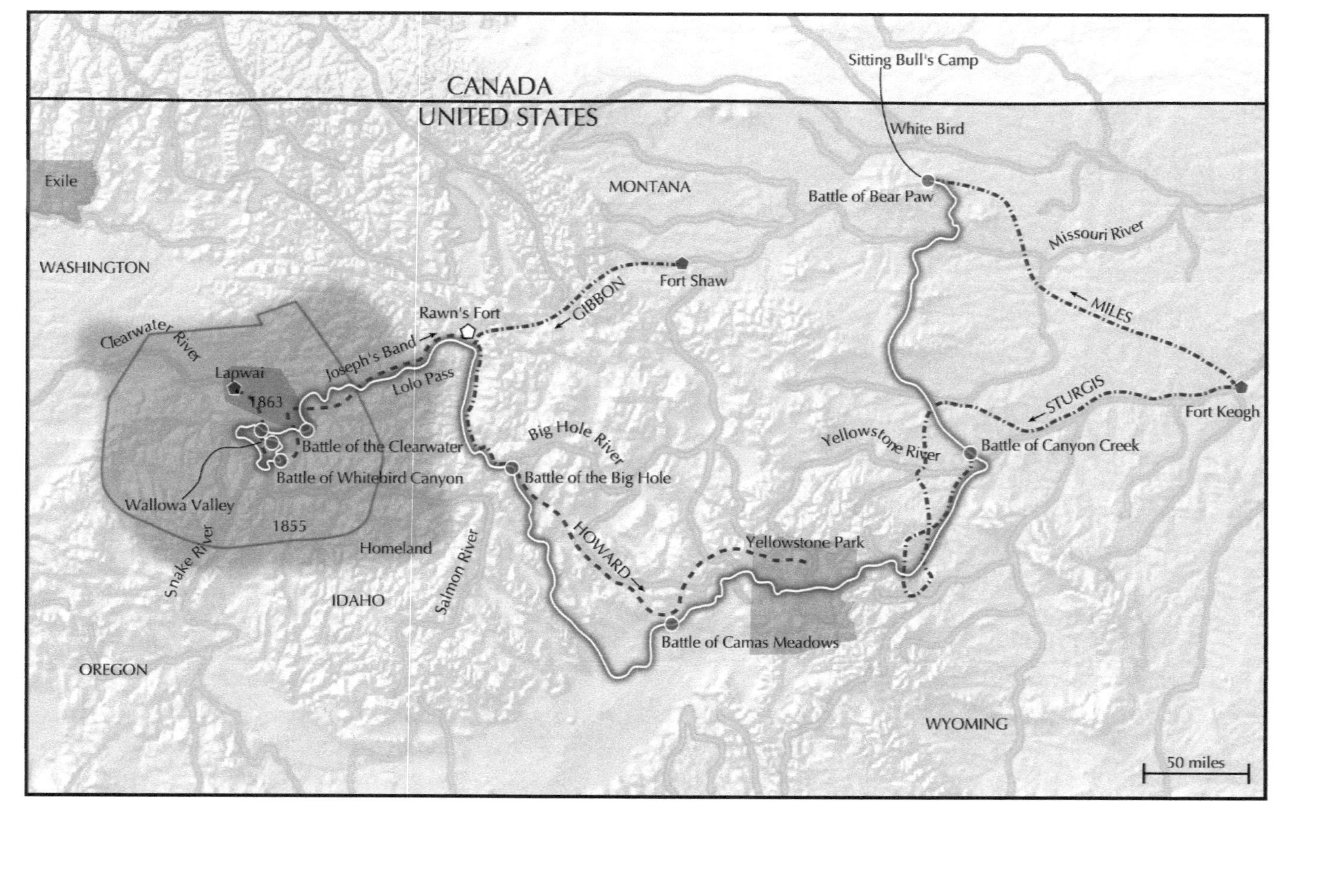
CANADA
UNITED STATES
Sitting Bull's Camp
White Bird
Exile
MONTANA
Battle of Bear Paw
Missouri River
WASHINGTON
Fort Shaw
GIBBON
MILES
Rawn's Fort
Clearwater River
Joseph's Band
Lapwai
Lolo Pass
1863
STURGIS
Fort Keogh
Battle of the Clearwater
Big Hole River
Yellowstone River
Battle of Canyon Creek
Battle of Whitebird Canyon
Battle of the Big Hole
Wallowa Valley
1855
HOWARD
Homeland
Salmon River
Yellowstone Park
Snake River
IDAHO
Battle of Camas Meadows
OREGON
WYOMING
50 miles

Dedicated to the courageous Native Americans who are identified here by name, and to the many unnamed, whose way of life, freedom of movement, and freedom of spirituality were taken from them.

Foreword

The history of the Nez Perce is a sombre one of abuse and displacement, unfortunately a common experience in the history of Native Americans, and other indigenous peoples.

The Earth Is My Mother attempts to present the displacement of the Nez Perce as accurately as the written and oral histories allow. However, written history is an inexact exercise, perhaps more art than science, always a reflection of an individual writer's perception, always influenced by his place and time.

Oral tradition presents a broader, more seasoned base. The incongruities of history may be ignored and transitions and amplifications provided in seeking "the heart of the matter," which is to say "truth." Leslie Marmon Silko said "the story is the story"—which might be paraphrased: "the story is the truth" for the story is a time-distilled product, stripped of randomness and irrelevant moments and events.

So, story, and truth are as one. A poet of epic statue, such as Homer, may embellish and refine the story, but it is the inherent truth alive in the story which lives and grows in the telling and retelling.

The truth inherent in the story of the Nez Perce feels obvious to me. I only hope that my labored effort to share one perspective of this story increases awareness and careful, measured, response in a reader—even as we sit together on the hard stone bench.

In the sharing of this story I have attempted to combine both written and oral traditions. I have attempted to adhere to known "facts" of written history, yet taken the liberty to depict action and events not documented in current written history. On one or more occasion a character is cast in an extended time frame. Cause and effect relationship has been extrapolated where enhancement of the core of the story seemed to call for such extension. Thus, while *The Earth Is My Mother* is filled with historical names, my depiction is one of fiction, in Stryon's words a "meditation on history," and in no way implies that the personal traits or relationships depicted herein are facts of history.

I have not included a bibliography. There are many works available on the Nez Perce. Most are of merit. Especially valuable are the records accumulated by Lucullus Virgil McWhorter. My principal reference source is *The Nez Perce Indians And the Opening Of The Northwest*, by Joseph M. Josephy, Jr. I consider Mr. Josephy's work the seminal study of the Nez Perce in their homeland. Errors or oversights in my work are mine, not Mr. Josephy's.

I am the Story Teller, pale shadow of my people the Nimpau, whose Mother is the Earth from whence we came. Procreated by the spirits which foster and protect us: the Earth, the Sun, the Wind, the Water, and the Fire. Descendent of Coyote who rendered the monster from the east and placed the people upon this sunlit plateau of beauty and bounty. Descendent of the ancestors who watch and wait to return to cleanse this land from those who consume and corrupt.

Receive this story as truth, for it is true. That which is remembered and told is truth.

This is a story of a free people of peace whose fate is war and confinement, a story which originates in harmony in the highland plateaus and swift flowing rivers of the Salmon, the Snake, and the Clearwater, a story which reflects the desperation of a people now surrounded by troops led by Nelson A. Miles who commands a detachment of the U.S Army forces the Nez Perce warriors have out-fought and out-maneuvered for seven months and 1700 miles—only to be intercepted in the foothills of the Bear Paw Mountains within sight of the Canadian border they sought.

Hin-mah-too-yah-lat-kekht, Thunder Traveling from Lofty Mountain Heights, called Joseph, has come to the camp of Miles to seek terms of surrender. His white flag of truce is ignored and he is seized, bound, and held in a frozen, snow-covered mule corral to await the general's convenience.

THE EARTH IS MY MOTHER

I. The Mountain and the Sty:
The Bear Paw Mountains, October 4, 1877

The subdued camp sounds float piecemeal to distinguishable patterns; individual objects slowly regain recognizable forms, silhouettes cast against a veil of inconstant light. Nearby, mules shuffle futilely against the cold. Beyond them soldiers squat almost motionless around a fire of buffalo chips. From time to time one kneels, chants, casts, and most often curses. Slowly, almost systematically, an individual guard shifts from haunch to haunch, rotating a roasted side to the cold again. In front, to the side, is the outline of a light, speckled horse—my horse-tethered with the camp mules. Far to the other side, barely visible in the flickering light of the fire, are saddle and blanket, dumped carelessly on the frozen ground. These sounds and sights are, however, but passing visions, subordinate to the consuming numbness, the death-like rigidity of my back, the pulsating throb somewhere near the top of my head which resonates pressure until it seems the skull itself must burst. With the pain is nausea. And mingled with the smell of man-sickness is the odor of mule dung—an odor like the medicine of long ago in the mountains above the valley of the Wallowa where the Nez Perce seeks his Wyakin, the vision which will direct his life and sustain his spirit.

Images of present fade as strongly now I glide over faint trails as have the deer and hare and coyote before—through the valley into the mountains. Crossing the shining Clearwater, swimming with trepidation the treacherous Snake, wandering, desolate and fearful, to the still Wallowa mountains, I seek in my origin, manhood and confidence of mind, the visitation of the Spirit which is all, which permeates and is this great plateau, the home of my fathers, this god-touched land which is the Nez Perce.

Slowly now the veil is lifted. The sky grows lighter. The moisture-laden cold penetrates body and soul, dissolves like ephemeral fog as the early sun touches the quiet mountain. Nature's living hush cloaks and stills, sealing off the body and spirit of man, freezing and rendering immobile his vain-glorious intrusion into violence-patterned harmony.

Alone now upon the quiet mountain, in the sunbathed, time-frozen moment of youth and strength I am afraid. I fear the earth will open and with gentle arms fold me back into its bosom. Dull now are my legs and heart, but I must continue outward, away from the valley of my father's camp. I must not stop here—nor soon—for I fear the earth. To rest, to sleep, to lie prone upon the earth our mother would now be fatal, for the earth draws against the strength of man ever beckoning him to return to rest and peace. Here, in the hush and force of nature, no man may resist. Fear only sustains and drives him erect.

Gradually fear passes. The sun floods life-warmth into me as I continue forward. A cow moose stands partially submerged in a small cove lake grazing unhurriedly upon some water plant. Nearby her half-grown calf tries the weed himself, finds it unsatisfactory, and attempts to nurse from submerged teats. Frustrated, he bellows, calf-bull, blowing, coughing, flinging water from his nostrils, head, and mouth. Butting, bullying, he succeeds in pushing the cow into shallower water where he nurses, the cow now standing tranquilly, placid shallow brown eyes reflecting but seeing nothing as young Tuekakas stands and watches, silent participant, quiet beneficiary.

The day fills. My body noon-day ripened, swells with the physical confidence of youth and strength. Here I walk where no man has walked before. Here I stand where Nez Perce have stood since the earth and the mountains and the sky came to be.

Yet there is no vision. Sixteen days have passed in cold and hunger and now in exhaustion and fear. For sixteen days I have sought the vision of life and manhood, the vision to sustain me and to sustain my people when I become the one, leader of the Wallowa Nez Perce, headman, chief, as is now my father, the great Tuekakas —the man called "Joseph" by the Missionaries even after he reft the great black book Spalding and Whitman and the beautiful Whitman woman brought into our land.

The world must now be apart from me. The Spirit which resides in all nature is of this mountain and will come to me if I am receptive, if I am pure in heart and intent. The strength and vision of the Spirit will sustain and gird man, will bind him to his mother the earth so that no man may lead him apart from what is true.

The world of present emerges about me. Captive, bound, in passive and involuntary transition between consciousness and dream-cloaked delirium on the snow-covered, dung-littered ground of an army camp

1700 miles from the valley and mountains of youth, the dream is all that remains—the dream and memories of the days of youth in the still plateau of diligent bounty, the silent and peaceful Wallowa where the grass stood belly high to the muscled stomachs of the Nez Perce ponies. Even in those days the old ones named me Tuekakas, or, as some insisted: "Joseph," after my beloved father who saw in his youth the goodness of the men called Lewis and Clark, who saw in his age the invidiousness of the man called Sherman.

Tuekakas, my father, the chief, a strange man, a powerful man. Because of him the eyes of the old ones followed me. In the beginning I did not know why and little cared. But soon the eyes of the women too went with me as gradually the young warriors came to ignore me and finally I could see that the companions of my own age stood apart from me, sometimes hushing in mid-conversation as I approached, sometimes forcing a boy's game with violence against me, sometimes falling away to let me win a hollow victory.

And so even in early youth there was isolation. Isolated from, first, the man himself: father, sire, in whose image the guarding spirits, Fate, seemingly had cast me, an old man even when I was a boy, a kind man perhaps but an unapproachable one, a man already obsessed with death or something like death, who squatted, and stared to the mountains. Isolated, in fact, from the woman who was my mother, tender, evasive, and for almost my entire memory fretful and ill at ease when we were alone. Separated, apart from all around me but two. Three with the grandmother, the bird-like, resolute spirit who followed no precedent, who knew no boundaries for the human spirit, the maternal spirit which in fact created my childhood. With the grandmother, was Ollokot, brother, a man, a warrior, and a friend even now being mourned in high-pitched woman's dirge in the desolate, grassless camp of the Nez Perce while I a useless woman-man touched by the hand of age at thirty-seven lie fettered like a horse colt at gelding time in the camp of a man and an army that two days ago no man of the Nez Perce knew existed—nor cared as we were a day's forced flight away from the land of the Gros Ventres, a land of safety and refuge for even the strong if treacherous Lakota, a land forbidden to the horse soldiers. Ollokot, brother, stood with me, and once there was Toma, the wife of my youth.

Images of the past:

In the dark center of the eyes is the soul itself. The eyes first illusive, shy, instinctively avoiding, protecting. Eyes which yet turn to my own, opening deeper and deeper, face pressed upward, long soft hair flowing downward, eyes which pour out self until the moment when the body arches, moves involuntarily, the moment when the eyes darken and close, and the soul escapes: flesh to flesh, soul to soul, the nadir of separateness, the shuttering still point of union and creation, the gasping inception of separation and death.

September then, the time when the spirits camp upon and contend for the earth itself. In the summer's last heat, in winter's chilling first cold, in the sun's golden listing rays I rode to her.

Woman-child in her father's lodge she ignored me.

Time and the journey of over a day had cut apart the quiet cordiality of the early summer's camp.

Three years had passed since my stay upon the mountain. I was no longer a boy, but a man, and, perhaps, if upon returning from the ritual and rite of manhood, I had proclaimed a vision, had stood in council and told of the visitation of some animal spirit who was to be my guardian Wyakin, had taken simplistic interpretation from the appearance of any number of animals, events, or even objects which appeared in strange, distorted context to an exhausted but still cautious—or hesitant—boy of sixteen, perhaps then my acceptance as man and warrior would have been immediate. But I could do no such thing. The storm, the turbulence of that last thunder-filled day on the mountain had increased my anxiety and frustration. And so, to the obvious discomfort of some of my father's own elders and warriors, I came to be, from the moment of my return, something of an enigma. They could not yet place and categorize me, anticipate my actions and reactions, and thus, while they could not easily ignore me and in truth did not dislike me, they were not at ease with me and began to turn even then to my younger brother, Ollokot.

But with the father of Toma Alwawonmi, called Hemene Ilppolp, or Red Wolf, and with her people of the Alpowa Creek region it had been different. Courtesy bade my acceptance as man and as the son of Tuekakas. And so for hours I sat with ritual decorum with the still young headsman and his elders, while Toma went about her business, chattered, and laughed with the young girls of the camp and paid, I soon realized, particular attention to the nearby Asotin leader, Allalimya Takanin, the young Looking Glass, son of the man called Meiway, "great chief." Looking Glass was five years my senior, a bold man, fond of fancy horses, a man who had been several times to the vast buffalo plains to the east. Those about him said he was one of the greatest warriors now living among the Nez Perce.

Cold and white obscure present. Through the fading gold of autumn I ride. Alone. In the growing cold my horse snorts, twists, leaps and lands on pole-stiff legs before turning finally to the trail where horse and rider are becalmed, rendered motionless, while in slow stages the tableau, the living curtain, is itself rent, repainted and reshaped: September with its cherished heat, October in gold and brown, November and December, brown, grey, and white.

Into the winter's cold I ride for now the attention of Toma has returned somewhat to me. She watches now and waits. The early detachment mellows and again we are alone. What we speak is frozen in memory: time-sweetened recollection of momentousness, gaiety and quietude reft with seriousness, and questions about my mystery-cloaked journey to the mountain.

Twenty days now I have sought the vision, have run, and walked, and crawled into the very heart of these mountains seeking a sign, seeking comprehension, seeking acceptance. For, if a man is receptive, the spirits which see all and are all will detach a guardian to watch, inspire, and protect. This is the belief and counsel of the elders, who, each in his turn, has come to the mountain, has sought inspiration and a guiding, guarding spirit, a Wyakin, and has been stronger for it, was received and heard in council for it.

The Spirit, the old men share, may appear in the form of an animal whose virtues and strengths then become the strengths and virtues of him to whom revelation occurs. A simple heart may revel in the visitation of the bear or the wolf for those of equal simplicity will see only courage and greatness of heart—qualities which sway councils, though these are the very qualities whose visitations have constantly sheared man's life.

Even so, a man must have a vision, must create from it what he can. Thus, I sought the vision of my forefathers: a sign, an unusual sight, some indication or source for external strength, some manifestation that I might hold out to my peers—for to the elders I would always be Tuekakas, Young Joseph—as a sign of my spirit and nature so that they might understand and weigh my counsel.

For twenty days I sought communion with spirit or force external to my being—though in the beginning I had doubt: doubt which grew and became more and more intractable as the slow days and cold nights passed. It seemed to me a man should in humility open his spirit, should keep receptive his mind to the Spirits, in whatever form They may exist, that in humility a man could do no less. But, at the same time, I knew that to passively await visitation was weakness. A man must, in and of himself, redeem his time and his place—to do less is abnegation of self.

Did I echoed even then the white man's tongue, the sing-song voice of the emaciated, frantic-eyed preacher, Spalding, who always spoke blindly against our shamans and even our Wyakin? Or perhaps the words and sounds which haunted the recesses of my mind were, even then, those of the Whitman woman.

The beautiful Narcissa Whitman whose light, glowing hair framed the fair molded head, crowned the statuesque body, tall as a man—at least as tall as the fourteen-year-old who stood before her and momentarily gazed straight into eyes as blue as the mountain stone from the South, eyes which seemed momentarily to open body and soul to any who could stand and look into them, but almost instantaneously struck back to any who met the gaze the knowledge that the translucence, the iridescent and penetrating blue reflected no image of the viewer but instead opened him who stared as if this woman goddess could discern his every thought, leaving the viewer the option of forcing the steady, penetrating gaze and, moving against her, gently ripping cloth from the cream sun-touched body—or dropping his eyes and looking away to the mountains to be visited again and again in wringing hot sleep or isolated woodland by the vision of Narcissa Whitman.

So I drift in the blur of present to recall sharply the past, shuttering as the rabbit under the shadow of the eagle above.

Present and past. Reality and dream.

It was with great uncertainty of heart that I went up to the mountain. In the exuberance of youth perhaps I anticipated a vision of grandeur, some indication of impending greatness. Few are without the vestiges of such a vision. The Nez Perce had had great individual chiefs in the past, and among the living Nez Perce no name stood higher than that of Tuekakas, my father. At any moment of crisis I might leap to the head of a unified people as had the great Nez Perce war chiefs of the past, thus attaining name, reputation, and power which some men pretend to shun, but which few ever refuse.

It is equally possible that I went to the mountain simply in search of a sign, some indication, or recognition of individuality, some acknowledgment of individual existence, a vain-glorious drama wherein man sits the passive recipient and opens himself to the gods, condescends to view, and possibly adopts whatever manifestation is presented to him. In reality, however, a man may not know the causes, may not know himself, for truly in the cross currents of self, in the constantly shifting currents of motivation, of dream, and desire, no man can select from the multi-fibrous essence of self the threads to identify the fibre of being, or weave the cord representing soul and identify the individual, saying: this then is the story of young Tuekakas, called "Joseph." This is what he did. This is why he acted.

Say then that I went to the mountain because it was expected of me. My forefathers had gone, and so had my father, Tuekakas. If the Nez Perce were to follow me as the Wallowans had followed Tuekakas, they would look to my vision for understanding and comfort.

So I went out from my father's summer tent in the early fall of my sixteenth year—later than the others of my village, but then my father was Tuekakas, Chief.

As was befitting and traditional, I went quietly and without attention. In the still chill of the darkness, the shuffling movements outside told me morning approached; Natokolas, grandmother, was up stirring the coals of the fire, dropping on twigs and leaves to rekindle the blaze for the day's use. I rose and, pausing only to pick up my heavy overshirt and moccasins, stepped from the tepee into the flickering light of the new day's fire. As I paused to pull on the warm leather shirt and moccasins, the Grandmother came to me to press into my hands camas cake and dried salmon. I took the food from her and quickly turned my eyes from hers to the mountains which stood above us to the west.

No one asked, directly, what I had seen, what I had found in the mountains. Ollokot, brother, and already kindred spirit, met me as I returned. He sat watching on a knoll overlooking the plateau, a day's ride from my father's camp. With him he had food and clothing; how long he had waited he did not say. Silently, we ate in the warm noon's sun. After I had slept, we swam in the cold, clear stream at the base of the knoll, my brother's strength and skill even then nearly equal to my own—a fact he neither acknowledged nor accepted. We talked then, cautiously, evasively. Ollokot told some of the incidents of hunting and root-gathering activities underway now as was common each fall. I estimated the distance I had traveled and the game I had seen.

When we returned to the village the next day, the reserved politeness was much the same. All watched and spoke in their friendliest manner, but no reference was made to my nearly month-long absence.

Toma, shy bride, quiet, feminine spirit, was the only one who ever asked what I had learned upon the mountain. She asked in the evening on a snow-bound day not yet a month after we came together, taking a lodge for the winter with her father's people until spring when it was expected that we would return to my village. She asked in innocence and awe, unaware, untainted by the polite courtesy of our people that would reserve this single element, above all else, to the individual until that individual chose to reveal it. She asked, and though I had always opened my heart to her and would answer, I could not. The shape and form and meaning was not yet clear in my mind. No answer came and she, sensitive woman spirit, passed from the question and opened herself to me.

Beneath the great buffalo hide in mid-winter's cold tent we are one. Her smooth, supple warmth is next to me, now in raillery, now in fleeing, damp, time-bled consummation, now in fitful quietude, until in exhausted life-drain I find sleep in the early morning's rain—rain as that which came to me that last thunder-filled dawn on the mountain, rain drenching body and spirit, thunder rolling with such force from the heights above that the earth herself shook and the trees vibrated in resonance and the rocks boomed amplification.

The rain comes now with stinging sleet, wetting the exposed, upturned face, breaking cold, semi-delirious sleep. Nearby the heavy supply wagons groan and jolt by as the trailing elements of Miles's forces, the 2nd, 5th, and 7th U. S. Cavalry, rejoin the advance units now camped in siege of the Nez Perce trapped in the grassless ravines of the Bear Paw foothills.

On a small knoll, in view but apart from the rain-softening slush of the camp's center stands a new, army-issue tent. Within is the man called Miles—a man I have seen but once, and this when he chose to ignore his own code, chose to violate the white flag of truce under which I came, and ordered me seized and bound. Within is the man who has ordered me held for a morning interview while he prepares his dispatches, announces to the press and to his superiors his capture of Joseph, the Nez Perce, the "war-chief" who has for six months "terrorized" the Northwest Territories.

Now in measured cadence come the sergeant and the guards to take me unfed, unrelieved, still bound, to the tent of Miles to hear the fate of the Nez Perce.

Quickly we are come to the tent itself, the order and unthinking discipline of the soldiers quietly force my pace as they ignore the cold, wet feet, the pain, the stiffness and the hesitation which hold me from Miles and the demands he will make, the position I know he will assume.

Once at the tent the bearded sergeant who walks at my side steps forward and announces in his loud military manner, "Prisoner, General," an announcement somewhat superfluous for as he makes it he sweeps back the dripping cold-weather flap of the tent, revealing the flickering, lamp-lit interior.

There is now left to me only the instant between the announcement and the order, the prod, which will drive me in to Miles. But an instant, that tiny fragment of time that Fate allows all men, is in reality all a man needs. For in that instant a man may drive from him all things, all pain and discomfort, all that distract his mind, and become what he must. He may grow in the instant before he can initiate a step, and become not the hesitant and indecisive individual who dreams in his discomfort and exhaustion of the lost visions and moments of his youth, but in the time fragment which is his own, the instant that is always left to him, he will become what history and circumstance and Fate ordain. He may in this instant become man and chief, husband and father—the spokesman and the protector of his people.

Even a hesitant man, even this man called Joseph, becomes Hin-mah-too-yah-lat-kekht, the Nez Perce. It is demanded of him. He is Hin-mah-too-yah-lat-kekht who bears the blood of the wise and mysterious Tuekakas, his father. He becomes the agent and the spokesman of the legendary Asotin warrior, Apash Wyakaikt, called Meiway, great chief. He becomes briefly, instantaneously, the great warrior, Wahchumyus, called Rainbow, who stood invincible on the plateau above the Clearwater holding his ground, driving back the orderly charge, disrupting and breaking the professional soldiers who came against him, using as his only weapon the great two-bladed axe that shone blood-wet in the afternoon sun. He assumes the voice and cunning of the imperturbable Pahkatos Owyeen, Five Wounds, whose efforts always seemed lackadaisical, whose accomplishments were always devastating.

In that second, the time fragment, left privately to all men, a man may and must become the living vehicle of his brother, the fearless Ollokot, who guarded the camp and people of the Nez Perce, the honor and reputation of the brother he called in intimate moments "Tuekakas," bestowing the greatest honor: the name and love of their common father.

A man will protect the wife of his youth, the honored companion of age. He will do whatever is necessary on this earth to protect the child, the fragile extension of himself, to protect the children of his brother now dead, of his tribesmen now wounded or lost.

So an instant is all a man needs. It is more than enough. Miles sits in his warm tent—clean, shaven, hair and mustache combed, fed and confident. But he has only comfort and food and the strength of his inexhaustible numbers to buttress his position. He has no desperation.

Miles may begin his negotiation: "They tell me you speak English." In his simplicity and arrogance he may even expect an answer. "They also tell me you refuse to speak it," the officer adds. He is a positive man, a forceful man, the dark hair, the dark eyes and the full mustache serve to mask somehow whatever personal qualities he might have—to create a form that is agent only.

The game he plays proceeds, the monologue he has probably rehearsed is mechanical, the names, the dates, the treaties, mere formality as he studies and attempts to analyze so that he may negotiate and add to his career, as he attempts to comprehend with his soulless intellect a man cast and formed by the suffering of his people.

The process can be seen and followed as Miles coldly studies the tattered coat, the army-issue trousers, examines arrogantly the face—seeking the eyes which he believes will resolve the perplexity created for him by moves and battles he knows imperfectly through newspaper accounts, army reports, and unofficial army gossip.

Already I sense a shadow of contempt, a dismissal of the seventeen hundred mile flight and the constant pitched battles. The man before me, this colonel who dreams of being a general, whose eyes and brash confidence betray the lieutenant he was not long ago, sees the tattered clothes, senses the fatigue, and exults in the eyes which yet evade his own. The battles were somehow misrepresented he believes, the escapes the result of ineptness on the part of the older, softer officers who were ordered against the Nez Perce.

I hear the word, "Dreamer," muttered, half-aloud, answer to one of his own questions. Incredulously, I stand and listen, hear again the speech, the lecture, the moralizing: the white's words always given as though there were an audience, a speech which erupts, displacing inquiry and proposition.

"Dreamer. . . . Fool. Agent of Simplicity. Prophet of the Ridiculous and the Illogical." He speaks proudly, pleased with the cadence of his own voice. "Waster of men: exploiter of women and children. Disciple and tool of a madman whose people cast him out, disclaimed him, disclaimed his vision—the vision of a lame slave filled with mescal in the broiling heat of a faraway desert. A vision sired by destitution, nursed by desperation, a vision which has cost the lives of hundreds of men and has wrung into motion this vast, lumbering army—trained only, proficient only, finally, in the execution of mass movements against a defined, entrenched foe—now flung ineffectively against a phantom foe of old men, women, and a few crazed warriors led by men such as this mute-struck Joseph before me, Joseph who believes the moment is at hand when all Indians from time past will return to this earthly life and join in one glorious war to cleanse the earth of white men.

"We have come a long way, and you will listen," Miles continues, overloud, pounding with the palm of his hand the heavy table before him, as the missionary Spalding had done so often years before.

"You may not speak, but you will listen. You will listen because you have no choice—and because we have your best interests at heart. You will listen now to see what we have to offer after you have broken every treaty agreement signed by the Nez Perce in the last fifty years. You will listen to hear what we have to say to a man who broke, deliberately, a treaty not yet two years old—a treaty negotiated in a conference which you yourself attended and to which you acquiesced by selecting a tract of land on which to resettle your people.

"Can you now stand before me with honor?" Miles continues, his eyes lulled complacent by his own words. "Can you expect justice when you have given none? Did you really believe, as your Dreamer prophets foretold, that the great warriors and chiefs from your past would rise immortal from the earth and join you in a holy war to drive the white man from the face of the earth?

"Perhaps you think the journalists who write glowingly of your restraint and praise your humanity in war will convince their eastern readers that you are the last noble savage."

"Perhaps," the abstract words and phrases are gradually refocused now, "perhaps the public will overlook and forgive what even the journalist must know—that your every action is the abnegation and violation of honor, that this war, a war ostensibly against the U. S. Army, is a war in which civilians have been killed, a war in which women and children have been murdered."

"You are a man who has misled and abused his people."

"Where are the warriors who rode with you from the Wallowa? Where are the young women and happy children who camped in your village in the meadows of the Grande Ronde? Are they camped with you now on this frozen, smokeless plain in these barren foothills of the Bear Paws? Are your children happy now? Do they run and play and praise the name of Joseph? Where are the children?" Miles continues, his voice strained, almost violent, his entire intellect focused once again on me. "Where are the children; where are the Nez Perce?"

"The Nez Perce," a man must, may, finally answer, phrasing the words carefully, fearing not the language but the rage within his heart, "the Nez Perce is there, to your north, in camp, entrenched and fortified with the guns we took from you at Whitebird Canyon, at the Clearwater River fight, and at the battle of the Big Hole. The Nez Perce is in camp fed better than in weeks, sustained by the supplies we took at Cow Island less than a week ago."

"The Nez Perce," the words are calmer now, "the Nez Perce is riding on our fastest and strongest horses to the camp of the Sioux and Sitting Bull who is restless and only miles away across the border in Canada. The Nez Perce is waiting behind our earthen mounds for your next charge. You have captured with treachery and in violation of your own flag of truce only this man you call Joseph—a man whose single message will be to fight until death, or until your man, your President, says the Nez Perce can return with dignity to his home.

"Will you charge again, General? Where are the men who made the first wild raid into the heart of our unprepared camp? Will your men charge in the light of mid-day? Will they stand when Sitting Bull comes from the north? How brave will you be when you are not four hundred against a few, but are four hundred against Sitting Bull's two thousand? Will the name of Miles be written beside that of Custer?

"Let us return in peace to our homeland."

Story Teller:

In the days long ago the Earth our Mother rolled and turned in her slumber as a human worried with thought. For the Earth was young and unsettled.

There was lush and plenty for the life to come. There was light and water and soil from which all to come would be, but there was no beauty. The elements of being were, alone, not enough. Within the Mother herself there was heat and unrest.

From the heat and turmoil within there was action, for the Mother does not rest and think, She responds.

And so day and night came to be. The sunrise, stunning deliverance from the night, the sunset glorious farewell to honor each day, each day. The night for reward to the creatures of the night and rest for the creatures of the day. The moon sentinel over the night.

Still not enough. The Mother tossed and turned and created the features of the earth as from garments of sleep piled in symmetrical disarray.

Thus came to be the great mountains from featureless ground. Thus came the great valleys to form and enhance the mountains. Though there was abundance of water the Mother took from some places and gave to others so that there were the high, dry plains for beauty, and there were lush river bottoms for beauty. And the Mother moved this water about as tears from her eyes and where the tears fell there was sound and where the water flowed, there was color and finally there was abundant beauty for the creatures of her body. For the Mother knew beauty was the essence of being.

Beauty. Each type precious. Each type vital.

II. The Wallowa
May, 1862

Bound, tethered like an animal, ignored or abused when not lied to by Miles and those close to him, there is little in the cold and desolation and humiliation of the Bear Paws which beckons my consciousness to the destitute camp of the Nez Perce.

It is the Wallowa I remember, the Wallowa and the warm sunlit days when the Nimpau, the Nez Perce, lived free and at peace with all things. Even then, it is true, the shadow of the white pressed around us and called for council. But Tuekakas stood firm and now only the memory of our joy and strength remains. Toma, the beautiful bride of spring, I remember then as a form and spirit, fathomless, aloof, and yet submissive, ready to blend her being to my own. The passage of time may dim and obscure the memory, may fade and dissolve the sharpness of the particular, but time allows the mind to distill and intensify so that what is left from a man's past, his youth, are the echoes of his joys: the panorama of his highland home, the sound of laughter past, the intimacy of touch, flesh to flesh.

She was—some things remain distinct—tall and capable of surprising grace and strength. Her face, studied objectively, was not strikingly attractive. Her nose, a person might finally conclude, was too large and her teeth, though strong and white, were uneven. But the physical form itself was so shaded by the personality that actual imperfections were meaningless.

A person could, in truth, focus on little more than her eyes, eyes that were dark, and in happiness or mischief grew almost completely black and mirror-like, yet which became, in momentary flashes, plaintive, almost anguished, as Toma sought attention, a type of acceptance and affirmation I would learn in time crucial to her being. With the eyes was the hair, long, soft, dark hair that Toma usually wore bound in some way but which constantly came loose, down into her face to be brushed temporarily back into place. Beyond the eyes and hair was the almost flawless complexion —softer and lighter than any member of my family. Finally, framed in a person's subconsciousness, was the lithe, supple body that somehow conveyed an impression of impishness and boyishness despite the full figure, the high, firm breasts, and the perfectly formed legs.

From the first time I knew her, saw her as a woman, emerging finally from my adolescent disdain, Toma had about her a quality completely maddening. Oblivious to taboo, custom, whatever, she, soon after deciding to accept my existence, revealed her habit of touching. Sometimes she would reach out, touching, pressing gently at first, with the tips of her fingernails the arm, the knee, whatever was convenient. Sometimes she would, in jest, push against me in an unexpected moment—perhaps backing against me, her arms folded, laughing, bumping with the warm, soft flesh of her body my aching, unbraced body into, or nearly so, the fire, or creek, or other convenient peril. Somehow she could do this, unnoticed, at the very campfire of her father, pushing me off balance or against someone —her semi-mad brother was a favorite object—so that I appeared little more than a clumsy fool.

Our first meeting, at least the first meeting when I was aware of Toma as an individual—apart from the band of girls who played, worked, and giggled together and frightened beyond composure all but the oldest and most desperate boys—was at the great fish hole camp on the Clearwater where the bands gathered for the season's camas diggings. She flirted. I tried to respond in my embarrassed and awkward way. She allowed me to follow her about in idle moments of the day or evening and on the fourth day allowed me, encouraged me to come to her. Afterwards she was untouchable, always evading, laughing, knowing perhaps, long before it occurred to me, that after the summer's camp was broken I would make the commitment of visiting her father's village, there joining her to me.

So, to my father's camp was I, finally, to bring my bride, Toma Alwawomi, called Springtime.

Her first success was with the grandmother, Natokolas, already then a small, withered woman, but a person and spirit near my own—a person who seemed to be a part of me, to understand and accept as no other before Toma had done. It was the grandmother who believed in me, who watched calmly, never impatient for the stature and burden others knew was mine.

And so it was somehow that the grandmother and Toma had an instant and permanent bond. The grandmother still scolded me as if I were a child of five; Toma, to the ill-concealed delight of the grandmother, took up, as she teased and badgered in private, the tone and words of the grandmother. While it was not something they did before the village, nothing pleased either of them more than to catch me in some foolish position or attitude and between the two of them to ridicule and badger me, to take the liberties that no one dared or at least dared benevolently before, to embarrass and frustrate me in love and joviality.

The very first exchange between the two of them set the tone and made the alliance. Natokolas, grandmother, with none of the shyness or reserve that ruled the other members of my family, wasted no time in suggesting the possibility of a great-grandchild, expressing in her nodding and merry way that it would be good again to have small children about her lodge. Toma, with boldness and merriment of her own, responded that she too looked forward to the event and wondered if there was anyone about who could sell her a good supply of buffalo horn—the remedy, so our folklore went, for a laggard husband. This was the beginning of a firm alliance that both wife and grandmother reacted to and controlled with small gleeful laughs, that provoked a smile from Tuekakas, a surprised short-lived protest from my mother and sent Ollokot howling away to share my embarrassment with his young friends.

Even though Toma drew from me some of the inner turmoil, the awkwardness, and the intolerance which had made my position within the village of Tuekakas uneasy, it was her acceptance and love for my homeland which perhaps beyond all else formed the permanent bond within my heart. She, of course, knew of the Wallowa valley; her father and other members of her village had visited and camped in our land, but it was with the pleasure of discovery and love and pride that we roamed the hills and ravines and meadows of the Wallowa that spring when Toma first came home with me.

In adventure and love we rode out from the early summer camp of Tuekakas to see and explore those things sacred to me since childhood. From the village formed now on the banks of the beautiful Wallowa lake, whose deep, pure water provided unlimited water and fish, we rode north across the meadow land of the Wallowa where the deep, fertile ground stood horseman-deep in grass and bush-like trees, where rock-strewn streams dissected, in frequent and seemingly arbitrary patterns, the meadow land with the ice-cold water from the snow of the peaks which surrounded us.

We rode north through the cold crystalline air and bright sunlight that flooded warmth into the valley to camp the first night where the great evergreen forests began to intersect and break the open meadow land forming now closed patches of grass, a haven for the deer and the elk who cautiously watched our progress. In the second and third day we worked north to the dry, desolate brown hills, temporarily covered green with fragile spring grass, the domain of the antelope,the goat, and the eagle. In silence and awe we camped by artesian springs that bubbled forth water so cold and pure there was no sensation of taste. Here we made our temporary camp where there was little evidence that any walked this land before. The sensation grew as we sat in the growing cold and watched the sun radiate its setting hue of red and pink and gold that no other humans did in fact exist—that, as we looked in silence across the darkening hills and ravines in the haze and still of sunset, a sunset disturbed only by our small cook fire, we were indeed the only people of the world, that with us alone rested the potentiality and joy of human existence.

Northward we continued to the banks of the Grande Ronde itself, the traditional and natural boundary of the Wallowa. Until mid-day we followed aimlessly the river bank, watching with fascination the hundreds and thousands of salmon fry carrying still their yolk sacs as they fed and played in the shallows of the Grande Ronde. With the noonday sun we stopped, tethered the horses, and entered the water ourselves, floating together in the chest-deep water, our bodies stung rigid and insensitive in the cold, holding ourselves together for warmth and love, stopping finally when hunger drove us to the bank to walk with wrinkled and tender feet along the rock-strewn river bed back to our horses and temporary camp. Here Toma built a small fire and I, without basket or net or lance, managed finally with my bare hands to throw a trout onto the bank where with glee we seized him, feasting later in a silence dominated, overwhelmed, by the pleasant roar of the Grande Ronde, already touched and swollen by the spring thaws.

From this the northern border of the Wallowa valley we turned south and west to follow the Grande Ronde through our northern meadows southward to its junction with the smaller Wallowa river and hence up the Wallowa through the fertile heartland of our valley to return to the lake and camp of Tuekakas. As we rode Toma talked, relating further the incidents and tales from her childhood, increasing and expanding the experiences we shared. With joviality and without self-consciousness she told of the time she fought her older brother, holding him down in the wash-hole of the Orofino Creek, nearly drowning him over a doll he tossed maliciously into the creek. A short time later, in response to a casual question about a mutual acquaintance, Toma allowed me to see—more in the unspoken words in her eyes than in even the tone of the words she did speak—that she had controlled the entire order and sequence of our courtship. Yet, now she formed herself, entirely submissive, to my own existence, rendered herself a dependent part of my own being.

We reached the camp of Tuekakas, suffered the friendly taunts a new couple might expect, and, before a week passed, left camp again to visit the great eastern segment of the Wallowa.

Inexplicably, it was the Imnaha and the desolate land to the east of our main summer camp on the lake that somehow meant more to me than the fertile and less arid great meadowland which provided the core of our sustenance.

We rode then in the spring and the beauty of love through the narrow valley of the Imnaha. We left one day early in May. There was no hurry because time was then ours, time a glorious element in which we basked without worry, without tension, content, immersed in that we had, oblivious to any trial the future might hold.

Across the spring-green meadowland we traveled in serenity almost beyond direction. By the banks of the Little Sheep, the small and swift tributary of the Imnaha, we camped and ate from the food we carried with us. Alone, away from the company of others for the first time in days, we talked of the time when I was a boy in this land, when Ollokot and I would ride the same trail we were now on seeking adventure and excitement, saying to the villagers that we were going hunting, yet moving at the same time we said this away from the meadow-timber land to the north where the deer and elk could be found to some more remote, even more beautiful segment of the great Wallowa—camping as we went, sustaining ourselves usually by berries and roots and an occasional fish, forgetting the bitter boy quarrels we sometimes had in the village to achieve an unspoken union of spirit in the wilds of our homeland. The Wallowa held then for us all that a man or child could ask. There was the scope and expanse of the meadowland valley where our stock found nourishment, the great ravines where we wintered, the north and south woodlands where there was an abundance of game, and even the great expanses of fragile, brown bluff-land with its transient thin spring grass that dominated and surrounded the deeper, more fertile and less arid bottom meadowlands. Cutting through and around the Wallowa in all directions were the never ending streams which almost every year teemed with the firm, sweet-tasting salmon and steelhead.

Here with Toma, along the banks of the Imnaha, in the land where the fertile meadows and desolate brown bluff-land came together, my thoughts turned back to the first near solitary journey I made through this region of our land, the journey I made with Tuekakas to the new mission at Lapwai. There, upon the banks of the same creek where I had camped with Tuekakas years earlier, I began to recount to Toma my first visit to the mission of the Whitmans and the events which were to add yet another dimension of ambiguity to my heart.

It was in the early spring of my fourteenth year, I began, that we rode to the small beautiful valley formed where the tranquil Lapwai creek joined the swift-flowing Clearwater. We departed our winter village quickly and quietly, going with but a day's notice after Tuekakas sent to me the message that he would go and the invitation to go with him. From the sheltered cove north of the Wallowa valley and lake we rode down into the level valley with its earth-saturated wetness and late winter's snow and then outward where the sun's more constant presence had begun to bake away the earth's wetness drawing forth the sprouts and grass of spring.

We rode steadily and usually in silence—not in haste, but in the consistent, determined pace of men with a long journey to travel. Even now, years later, the memory and images stand before me clear, distinct. When Tuekakas spoke, it was usually to recall incidents from his past, casual incidents or events connected with the land we moved through and the adventures of his life as a boy or young man. For the first time, I heard him speak in detail of the land about us: about the location of the great Little Sheep cave, a remote and secret place I thought only Ollokot and I knew. Casually, later, Tuekakas would ask of the table rock at the very peak of the man-thunder mountain which stood guard over the Wallowa lake and overlooked the entire valley—a rock where a man could stand with the wind and the eagles and look to all directions, shaded by no thing of this earth. By the time we reached the junction of the Little Sheep and the Imnaha, Tuekakas had grown silent again, brooding mysteriously about something he did not choose to mention. Instead the secretive and silent journey continued until we reached the first great salmon pool of the Imnaha where we made our camp. In silent amity we went about the making of camp. In the very activity Tuekakas seemed to soften somewhat and come back to the camp and the present. Breaking the repose, Tuekakas suddenly asked if I had done much swimming lately, alluding with restrained humor to an incident from the summer just past, an incident I thought no one, with the exception of those immediately involved, knew.

What had happened, I related to Toma, flushing a bit as I started, was more embarrassing and frustrating than heroic. Ollokot and I, wandering away from the camp as was frequent, discovered far down the Imnaha Canyon, the camp of some people related, though distantly, to our people. With boyhood adventure Ollokot and I decided to scout and spy upon the camp, exercising our cunning and stealth which we naturally considered to be substantial. It came to be that during the second day we watched, still undiscovered, one of the people from camp—a girl of perhaps twelve or thirteen came to the river not fifty feet from the cottonwood thicket where we lay hidden and to our dismay—and, no doubt to her own surprise—fell into the river, which, always swift, was especially deep in the pool before us. Ollokot and I were both in motion, and I was in the water, before either of us remembered our purpose of stealth.

Ironically, the girl was a strong swimmer.

In short the affair was a fiasco. The older people of the camp arrived in time to see us as we struggled to the bank—the girl and I together in the water while Ollokot stood on the bank above us, watching, fully aware the girl was in no trouble. We were of course recognized and taken into the camp for dry clothes and food. As we talked, it gradually became evident that our presence was no great surprise and, with a sinking heart, I came to suspect—though it was never mentioned—that as we observed, we were in turn observed. The most humiliating part of the episode came later. Okhlas Kotneka, the headman, insisted that we camp with them as we all moved to the village of Tuekakas. During the first night with the travelers the girl herself came to me where Ollokot and I slept in our blankets apart from the travel tepees of her family. With awkwardness I sent her away, watching as I did so the motionless blanket-form of Ollokot.

"This was before you became a lover?" Toma interrupted, glee thinly cloaked, digging me in the ribs as she spoke.

"Yes, those were the days when I was building the great reserve and strength I have for you now, my love," I teased back, aware even as I spoke of the greater secret which still lay unspoken, unacknowledged between us.

And so it was as Toma Alwawonmi and I traveled through the full, desolate, untouched wilderness, I saw again with new emphasis the splendid beauty I had last seen in its entirety the spring I rode with Tuekakas to Lapwai. The benevolence of time fosters now in the Bear Paws the euphoria which is time past, fuses now emotions and events to create memory.

Memory is all that remains of the journey Toma and I made down the Imnaha valley. Memory distills, purifies and makes perfect the trail we follow through lush river bottom, makes silent the roar of the river as we push through the cottonwood growth and brush to enter here and there the tiny flood plains where time has deposited layer after layer of fertile soil on the rock-strewn ravine of the river so that the horses sank and struggled in the fecund soil where hooves did not strike, in grinding patterns, the bedrock itself. Memory makes effortless the strain and exhaustion as we climb from the foaming speed and excitement of the canyon bottom to the heights which constantly grow more imposing around us.

From the heights which temporally govern and direct the Imnaha, we are as the goat and the eagle. Above us stands only the soaring hunter and the haze, translucent blue, of the dome of the world. There is not a cloud, nor a sound, nor the sight of any other living being. Below, in the narrow ravine, funnels the Imnaha, already a full day's climb away, seen now as a blue-white ribbon bordered irregularly by incandescents of green, separate, distinct from our elevated vantage point by the abrupt dry rock which channels, evanescently, the haste and force of the water itself.

Over the bluff-land we ride on the dry volcanic crust which breaks inaudibly under the weight of the horses' hooves, puffs tiny clouds of dust which hang momentarily, and dissipate abruptly in the irregular but forceful wind of this high land. Above us there is nothing. Far to the east, there are the Bitterroots, perhaps more imagined than seen. To the west and north and south we are equal to all things, except the peaks which stand guard over the Wallowa lake itself. About us as we ride are the remote and delicate flowers of spring: the fragile cactus whites, the cornflower blues and the downflower yellows which Toma stops and dismounts to see, which we share without picking, knowing the infinitesimal moisture and beauty will hardly last the time it takes to remount. Dispersed with the flowers is the more frequent, but hardly more permanent, bluff grass of the highlands which, for all its thinness, the horses seek—the same hair-like grass the heat of summer will turn brown to break and die, to cling to the legs, to crawl into the crevices of moccasin and trouser.

Once more in peace and in solitude we stand where it seems no man has stood before. The horizon holds shield above us; below, so far away that the roaring turmoil of its current, still faintly visible, loses irrevocably its sound and dimension of force, the Imnaha cuts its way to the Snake's great canyon still invisible before us. Between river and sky stands the sheer rock of the canyon wall—silent, massive, impenetrable, save for the tiny flaws, slightly less severe gradients here and there linked by time and chance to form the narrow crumbling trail of the goat and, with fear and care, the hand-led horse. It is a land where the gods walk and talk; it is a land where man must always come in silence and humility.

We camped that night upon the bluffs ferreted out by the winds that swept that high and unprotected place. Here I would tell Toma, whose receptiveness seemed to demand it, the story of my first journey through this land. Even as I spoke, my mind was haunted with the words of the missionary preacher called Spalding and the memory of the Whitman woman called Narcissa.

Story Teller Recalls:

Into the unnatural camp of the whites at Lapwai on the bank of the Clearwater, rides Tuekakas.

Tuekakas, comes as headman of the Wallowa Valley Nez Perce. He comes because he has been invited and he comes out of curiosity to see these new whites who bring women, cut trees, and build cabins as though they have come to stay.

He comes to see the magic of the medicine it is said these whites bring with them. He comes to hear words from the black book that some of his kinsman already accept as magic.

Tuekakas brings with him his son, a youth in his early teens—soon to be called Joseph by the whites. Tuekakas knows, with the instinct of age, that he will determine his own response to the whites and that many will accept his judgement as their own, but Tuekakas knows that those now young and the Nimpau to come must determine their own paths, and that the response of the boy, to be known as Joseph, is more important than his own.

As they approach and enter the camp, only a few miles from where the Nez Perce found and befriended the whites' "Mission of Discovery," a small crowd of whites has gathered to sit and listen to a speaker. One man, holding a black book, speaks, while all others sit and sway passively.

III. Blessed Are the Meek
May, 1850

Her name was Narcissa. She was twenty-six and I was fourteen. She was the first white I was to see. She stepped from the half-complete shanty the missionaries had begun on the Lapwai Creek into the evening sunlight as we stopped the horses to end the four-day ride from the Wallowa. She stood before me, her body full, supple, statuesque, her hair a radiant blonde-red, her skin smooth sun-touched cream, her eyes a translucent blue, receptive, penetrating, fathomless.

She came with a man called Whitman. With them were the man and woman called Spalding, thin intense people, the first of the Protestant missionaries to the Nez Perce. The first of the whites who come to stay, build cabins and churches, divide our land, and correct our religious beliefs.

Story Teller was there with Joseph when the first of the Protestant missionaries came. Story teller remembers that, in a strange way, these whites who would disrupt and change our lives came by invitation.

To the north the Jesuits had come to move among the Spokan and the Palouse. The first of our people to visit the east, the cousins Tipyahlanah and Hiyutstohenin and their friends Kaoupu and Tawis Geejumnin, reached the place called St. Louis. Here their pleasing features and conduct attracted attention and they chanced to say to a newspaper man that the Nez Perce had heard of the white man's god and awaited those who would come to the plateaus of the Clearwater, the Salmon, and the Snake to teach the powers of this god.

The newspaper story which resulted found its way even farther east to begin the work which was to end forever the freedom of the Nez Perce.

In the fall, two years after the comment of Tipyahlanah, they came. Remembering the honest captains, the Nimpau welcomed the missionaries into the isolation of our high plateau homeland. Late, only days before the snows would close the mountain passes, they entered our homeland. There were seven whites in all: the medicine man, Whitman, who poked with his stiff red hands and gave out foul-tasting medicine with the large metal spoon he carried tied to his belt loop, a man who spoke but little about the great black book and the white's god. With him was his wife of four months, called by the whites, Narcissa. Her carriage and beauty were profound, her beautiful trained voice delightful—as from a spirit.

The second couple was named Spalding. The man, who insisted on the title "Reverend" as though he had no other name, was thin and of medium height. When he spoke his voice was high and emphatic and nasal. When he was not speaking, he stood, his hands close together near his chest, clutching the small Bible he always had with him. As he stood, he nervously rubbed the thumb of his left hand against the back of the Bible, wearing there a distinct spot in the leather binding. Periodically he sniffed, loudly drawing air in through his clogged nose as though he would clear it.

Often beside him as he moved through the mission site was his woman, called Eliza. Her thinness, even more distinct than Spalding's made her seem tall until she stood near Whitman or even Narcissa. Her features were unpleasant; her eyes, nose, and small tight mouth came together at once on her face. The pointed features of her face were emphasized by the way she pulled her sparse, dark hair into a knot on the back of her head, thus exposing her rather large ears. Beyond her physical features was a high and piercing voice that she used freely to direct those around her. However unpleasant, she nevertheless had a tenderness for our children, and she was the only one of the early missionaries to master our language.

With the Whitmans and the Spaldings came an arrogant young Italian named Gray who was to break away before long to form his own trading post farther west. With them also came the man called Goodyear and the youth called Dublin. Goodyear, who handled the horses, was to leave soon for the south and the land of the Utes. The youth, a simple-minded boy of seventeen or eighteen when he came, was watched carefully by the whites who set him at simple tasks and provided for him until years later when he was to die in the flames of the mission building in what would be called the Whitman Massacre.

The strange relationships and subtle hostility within the missionary party became apparent only gradually to the bands of our people who came to camp and then settle, more or less permanently, around the mission site at Lapwai Creek, and it would be years before any understood the cause for the great bitterness Spalding held for Narcissa Whitman.

Whatever the relationships among the whites in that first spring visit to the Lapwai Creek camp of the headman Hallalhotsoot, called Lawyer, I had no real interest or understanding, for here in astonishing and emasculating beauty is Narcissa Whitman whose flesh and spirit overwhelm me.

Before me she stands in the afternoon sun. Her hair is a thing glowing, alive, of incredible color like no other thing in nature except perhaps the fragile and fleeing color of the aspen struck quickly by the frost and cold of fall. Yet, more than the color of fall, this before me changes, constantly shading, glowing and reflecting both gold and auburn as the sun touches and recedes from the luxuriant, heaped knot of hair carelessly drawn together behind her and partially covered with a faded, spotted headband. And yet the hair is only a part of the vision which stands motionless, looking back into my anguished eyes which see the firm, cream, almost golden skin, visited, touched around the nose and eyes with a trace of sun-burnished freckles which frame and set the prominent cheek bones—all of which, the sun-lit hair and cream-tanned skin, even the statuesque astonishing body, supple and fertile: bosom deep-chested, uplifted, covered lithe legs—have to be remembered in retrospect, studied in hurried moments, for when Narcissa sweeps into view it is her eyes, her penetrating and reflection-less eyes, which overshadow the rest of her being, turning her physical impression into a vague, supple image of indistinct, illusive gold flesh, at once unapproachable and, yet, demanding approach with gentleness and strength as the eyes deepen and the unreal statuesque perfection of the body relaxes, softens, into the greatest receptivity a man can experience.

The journey which brought us to Lapwai and the inconceivable beauty of the Whitman woman came to me suddenly without anticipation or preparation. Tuekakas sent word to me that he wanted to see me. When I came, I found him before our lodge examining the hooves of his great black-grey dappled horse, called Kijojo for the meadow where we found him and his dam only hours after his birth. Before the lodge were blankets and a sack of dried salmon.

Tuekakas was to the point, for this was his manner.

"I will ride to Lapwai to see the whites who have come into our land."

Tuekakas stopped. He did not pause as some men do in hesitation or reflection; he simply stopped between sentences and sometimes between words. Those who were often around him grew accustomed to this cadence and worried little with it. As I stood waiting for him to continue, I noticed for the first time in my life the age of the man before me who carefully examined and groomed his horse. It was as if suddenly, instantly, the father who had been around and above me in strength and health for as long as I could remember was aged and enfeebled. There was no decrepitude, but the hands, patterned with the splotches of age trembled a little as he worked the horse, sensitive to this tremor and a little agitated by it.

The face had changed little that I could tell. The skin might be looser, the eyes squinted a little tighter in the glare of the early spring sun, but the hair was still black, untouched with grey, though I did notice for the first time how thin it was. It was the stomach which surprised me most—the stomach and the shoulders. In the shoulders and back the muscles which tighten and hold erect a man had loosened, perhaps only the tiniest degree, but that degree showed in the stoop beginning to appear in the shoulders. In the stomach there had long been something of a battle between the muscles which created tone and tension and the belly which comfort and relative inactivity produce in a man beyond the middle of his life. Now, even through the leather over-shirt, it was evident that the hard roundness of the stomach was wasting away. Both the extra weight and the muscles which struggled to control it had begun to dissolve away in the man, father, before me who was even then over sixty.

"I want you to come with me to Lapwai," Tuekakas spoke again. Though he continued to work with his horse, the words and invitation were evidently for me and only with difficulty did I control my surprise and excitement.

"Go catch your horse." The old man concluded, conveying by the order itself that he was finished on this subject.

Less than a day later we rode slowly through the village toward Lapwai. With swelling boy-pride and yet anguish, I saw the dispassionate face of Ollokot whose resolute heart controlled already at ten his external emotions, foreshadowed even then the steeling discipline which was to place his name foremost among the Nez Perce warriors in fewer years than any would choose to believe.

The journey itself, undertaken in the controlled pace necessary to conserve horse and man for a long distance, allowed me to see a part of the nature of Tuekakas previously hidden from me. For the first time I heard Tuekakas himself speak of the days when he was a young man in the Wallowa. In sentences that were often disjointed, apart from the polished tales the old ones delivered about the evening campfires, Tuekakas told of the time when as a young man he made the two-year hunting journey to the plains to the east. With pride, not for himself or even for his young warriors, he spoke of the vast buffalo herds, and of the plains where a man could ride for the cycle of a moon without seeing another man, where whole bands of Nez Perce moved, often with their Flathead friends, at will, watchful only for the buffalo, cautious only of the Blackfoot and the Lakota.

The pride evident in the halting and piecemeal story Tuekakas struggled with was for the land he visited and the rapport that existed in the Nimpau, the word meaning 'we people,' which we used to refer to ourselves long before the white's term, 'Nez Perce'—for the people and the open skies of the plains. There was pride for the respect and the friendship of the Flathead, whose language was near our own, whose hearts and beliefs were near our own. There was pride for the courage the fierce Blackfoot and the rare Lakota party demanded. There was pride above all for the untouched land and sky where the buffalo and antelope lived, a pride embossed, underscored by the words not spoken as Tuekakas looked silently about him in the valley of the Wallowa, in the canyons of the Snake. There was pride and anguish and joy on the cliffs where the narrow trail to the east followed the rock ledges above the rushing Imnaha, where Tuekakas paused to study a solitary cedar somehow transposed to an unlikely crevice among the rocks where it lived green and healthy though no taller than a man.

Later, with more ease and contentment, Tuekakas spoke of the great councils of our people, describing the places and the headmen who spoke, swelling audibly in voice as he rephrased the issue, described in more detail the speeches of the great Nez Perce orators. In quiet benediction Tuekakas related the concord of the councils, spoke quietly of the tribal structure which allowed every man his voice and freedom of action, which bound no man to his headman, which bound no headman to a wealthier or more powerful headman, and, yet, for all this, produced a singularity of action governed solely by the well-being of the Nimpau.

Tuekakas spoke eventually of the first whites to enter our land, recalling with obvious pride the white captains Lewis and Clark, reflecting with a trace of humor how he had stood shyly as a boy in the rear while the tribal elders spoke with these strong men at their camp on the banks of the Snake River after they had returned from the great sea to the west. The tone of his voice hardened, uncloaking a type of agitation or embarrassment as he continued, relating the moment in council when the young warrior called Tepahlewam, for his winter camp, approached the man Lewis with a puppy and, with some ceremony and ridicule for the whites, who we had learned ate dogs as did their Shoshoni guides, presented the dog to the white leader. Not a man moved when Lewis rose to face the warrior and hurled the puppy into his face, seizing as he did so the man's own tomahawk and, holding it back in a position to strike, called out for his interpreter to say that the whites brought gifts in friendship—not in fear.

So, without regard for the weakness of his men, the man Lewis created the relationship of respect. The headmen would not have allowed Tepahlewam his insult, nor could they have accepted a failure by Lewis to react. After this, one by one the headmen rose to speak favorably of the whites. With reverence and fondness Tuekakas recalled the names of the older headsmen who spoke. There was Walammottinin, called the 'Twisted Hair' by the whites for the braid he wove on his forehead, the first Nez Perce to encounter the whites as they struggled down out of the Lolo pass. Second to speak, Tuekakas continued, his voice barely audible now, was the old man, Tuekakas, grandfather to me, though I hardly remember. Next came the powerful young Asotin, Apash Wyakaikt, a man only a few years older than father Tuekakas, a man who was to become the greatest Nez Perce war-chief of our time. Then came the Clearwater River headmen, Neeshneparkkeook and Yoomparkkartim. Finally rose the war-chiefs, Tunnachemootoolt, called the Broken Arm, and Hohots Illpilp, Red Grizzly Bear, who wore a tippet of human scalps decorated with the thumbs of men he had slain in battle and whose Wyakin, a bleeding Grizzly bear, was to become a legend among our people.

All were to speak of peace and friendship. Not a single man excused himself from the feast celebrating the new white friends.

And yet, for all the time-calmed memories the journey and the land produced, there was about Tuekakas as he spoke of the first meeting and the old councils a shadow, a flicker of something I had not seen before. The women, he recalled, were discontented at even the first great council. Some stood with the boys after the food had been prepared and served and wrung their hands and tore their hair in distress. And so, as Tuekakas spoke, there was both ease and a form of tension, a tension beyond the spoken words which reveal all, or nothing, according to the speaker's will and skill.

Perhaps it was the pauses themselves, the periods of silence and their relationship to the nearly random topics, which reft silently, as we rode, the harmony of this spring-touched land. Perhaps this was the tension that touched, tainted, spoiled at a level almost below the consciousness the splendor of the Imnaha and the Snake and the Lapwai creek, that cried loudly through the spring-pregnant valleys disrupting with silence the lands and waters and skies of the Wallowa range, disrupting, combating the spirit of the Nez Perce, shadowing the belief that since the great god spirit set down the Nimpau upon this earth that there was never to be a time when this land, this spirit, my spirit, was without the image and form of Tuekakas who was, in the extended image of his son before him, the Nez

Perce, the manifestation and affirmation of the earth itself.

In the afternoon of the fourth day after we left the winter camp in the Wallowa, we reached the junction of the Lapwai and the Clearwater and moved slowly up the banks of the Lapwai until we came to the camp of the whites. Tuekakas rode quietly into the mission compound itself, nodding, speaking silently with half-lifted hand to those who recognized him and spoke his name. It filled me with a calm pride to see again that many knew Tuekakas and that all knew of him, for when his name was spoken all stopped and watched with the subdued courtesy of the Nez Perce, gesturing welcoming acknowledgment whenever their glances happened to meet the eyes of Tuekakas.

Tuekakas continued through the beaten, almost grassless yard of the mission with what seemed a deliberate design, for he neither paused nor stopped; instead he rode slowly through the camp as though he searched for something or someone. Past the great square tents of the whites we rode toward the center of the camp where there stood already a building of logs, its imposing mass of bark-shredding exterior overlaid with a roof of sticks and mud and sod. As we moved slowly forward studying the new building and the wheeled cart which stood before it, the first of either I was to see, the horse of Tuekakas shied, jumping, prancing sideways, as was his spirited nature, into a flock of chickens, white man's birds, which were scavenging nearby. For a moment then Tuekakas hesitated, pulling his horse to an uneasy stop as he looked at the squawking, fluttering scene before him.

"Hallalhotsoot?" Tuekakas suddenly said, louder than was his custom, turning as he spoke to a man I did not know, a man of perhaps thirty who stood a few yards away.

"There," the man responded, standing passively, dumbly, as he had from the moment we rode into the compound, not loosening, even as he gestured awkwardly, the two-handed grip he had on the halter rope of the cow behind him. "Lawyer is there in the evening-sun camp of the Lapwai."

Hardly had the young man finished his motion when the man I knew as Hallalhotsoot appeared. Gone was the servile smile he wore in the great summer camps of the Nez Perce. Replacing the smile was straight-faced seriousness that somehow made me want to laugh. On his head, a large head that had always seemed disproportionate to his tiny body, he wore a tall felt hat. In the band that circled the crown were six or seven eagle feathers. He came to us on foot, his large black eyes glowing with excitement, his narrow chin and small, perfectly formed mouth set with official seriousness.

"Tuekakas is welcome to my camp." Hallalhotsoot clasped together his hands in front of his chest as he spoke.

"The son of Tuekakas is welcome, also." He glanced in my direction for an instant as Tuekakas dismounted slowly.

"Come." A trace of self-importance came with the excitement his voice had registered from the first word.

"Come, and let me show you the church Rev. Spalding and I will build by the banks of the creek."

Tuekakas handed the reins of his horse to me and, still without a word, turned to follow, calmly, almost casually, Hallalhotsoot who was already several paces in front, hurrying toward a second pile of logs. With nothing more to do I slid from my horse and, leading both horses, moved to examine the wheeled travois before the door of the partially finished building.

It was as I stood there, examining the strange mechanical contrivance of the whites, that I saw Narcissa for the first time. There was a sound or movement; exactly what attracted my attention I could not with certainty reconstruct, though the almost imperceptible sound of cloth against cloth, cloth against flesh has recurred in memory again and again. Whatever first attracted my attention, she was suddenly there before me in the light of the afternoon's sun, motionless though the still moving fabric of her light blue dress revealed her interrupted movement and her momentary blankness revealed her preoccupation. At her side she carried, I would reconstruct in time, a small wooden bucket.

What amazed me, rendered me dumb and motionless, was both her incredible beauty, and, almost equally, her complete lack of hesitation or withdrawal as she realized she had stepped through the door almost against me. There was no fear or shyness. She simply stood and looked into my face and eyes for a length of time my mind cannot even in retrospect judge. Then, as freely as she came, she reached out her hand to me, touching—not patting—ever so slightly my cheek with the tips of her fingers, searing, with the coolness of her touch, the flushed flesh of my body.

She turned and was gone before I could think or speak or move. Around the corner of the building and away from me she went, disappearing long before it would occur to me that I might have responded in some way.

In bewilderment, I moved away. In the days to come we would hear, in labored detail, Lawyer's concept of the mission. Tuekakas sat patiently, quietly, the guest in the lodge of our kinsman, waiting the return of Whitman and Spalding who left their women in the care of the man Grey—who was himself now away hunting—so that they might travel to the north and west and establish supply contacts with the company of traders who lived in the land of the Spokan.

As we waited, even as Tuekakas tired of the banter of Lawyer and rode to the south to visit the village of Toohoolhoolzote, the Dreamer prophet and headman, I haunted, alone, the mission grounds. In time I came to stand or squat in the rear as each morning the Whitman and Spalding women would call together the children, taking them to the bank of the creek where trees had been felled and the trunks moved into lines to form rough seats. Here I heard the beautiful Whitman woman repeat, again and again, the translators at her side, the Beatitudes of her faith.

I remember her words. My people live the manifestation.

MY LORD JESUS SAID:

"BLESSED ARE THE PEACEMAKERS."

We have striven, sought peace,
attended the councils, heard the whites,
and touched their papers. In the camp
of the Nez Perce the women wail,
mourn Ollokot.

"FOR THEY SHALL BE CALLED CHILDREN OF GOD."

There is hunger and cold in the camp of
the Nez Perce. The children cry no
more but only sit and watch, their eyes
following me everywhere.

"BLESSED ARE THE MEEK."

A man must conduct himself without
arrogance, must achieve harmony, must
maintain perspective: God-Nature-Man.

"FOR THEY SHALL INHERIT THE EARTH."

For they shall inherit the earth. For they
shall inherit the earth.

"BLESSED ARE THE MERCIFUL."

A man must honor frailty, must respect
weakness for here only is his strength.
We have set free the women and
children, have spared those who
showed no arms against us.

"FOR THEY SHALL OBTAIN MERCY."

The flesh pales, weakens, dies. In the
valley and the shadows stand the black
tents and here are the bayonets of
Gibbon. On the hillside above the
camp the Gatling guns wait the light.

"BLESSED ARE THEY WHO MOURN
FOR THEY SHALL BE COMFORTED."

Hear my people.
Comfort my people.

"BLESSED ARE THEY WHO SHALL
BE PERSECUTED."

The soldiers of Howard and Gibbon
march. The man called Miles screams
with his men into our camp.

"FOR THEIRS WILL BE THE
KINGDOM OF HEAVEN."

Two, by two, by two, the
lines are drawn.
The columns form.

Twelve abreast, twenty
deep the horse of Miles wait.

When Tuekakas returned from the village of Toohoolhoolzote I was sitting upon the fence of the crude log and post and rope corral watching the gelding of the mission's horse colts. On the preceding day the man, Gray, had returned, galloping confidently into the camp ahead of his two guides who followed with the pack horse heavily laden with deer meat. Early this morning he was up and about the camp moving bareheaded, his sand-colored hair requiring constant attention in the gusts of spring wind, calling out instructions. Around his neck was wrapped, dashingly a red scarf. Beside him moved Lawyer, repeating the orders in our tongue, ordering and directing the men of his village to do as the white man desired, mimicking already Gray's habit of standing, one hand on his hip, as he waited impatiently for the men to cut out the four colts from the small herd Lawyer's village had given the whites for their use.

One by one, as I watched, fascinated and nauseous, the young stallions were singled out and brought down. First, Gray would decide on the colt. Then, Lawyer would relay his version of the instructions Gray constantly gave. The men, who were skilled horsemen, proceeded, paying, as far as I could see, little heed to the instructions and orders of either Gray or Lawyer. Four men worked. The selected stallion colt would be walked into the strongest corner of the corral, his rump facing back out into the corral. One man on each side, two in the rear, linking arms to crowd him into the corner, the process would begin. Talking calmly, chanting, cajoling, the two lead men would work up toward the colt's head, avoiding his already dangerous strength with skill and luck fostered by the colt's confusion and fear that took the direction and some of the force out of his kicking, rearing, thrashing.

With little ceremony one man, the one who had the first chance, would grab the horse's head, pulling down with his entire weight, turning and holding the head both with his grip on the ear and with the other hand that twisted, forced closed the nostrils and wind passages of the cartilage section of the nose. The other man would quickly wrap and tie around the horse's head the soft deer-hide blinders he carried clinched between his teeth.

The combined effect of the loss of wind and sight usually slowed, calmed, or bewildered the horse colt enough that the almost human screams were silenced and the thrashing and jumping were lessened enough that the ropes the second pair of men carried were positioned and the colt was tripped and thrown while at the same time the flailing legs and hooves were drawn together and lashed and the wild, brute strength was constricted to itself, muscle against muscle, movement against movement.

As I sat and watched irresolutely, Tuekakas came into sight on the trail up to the mission from the south. With him rode the old Dreamer, the long time friend of my father, Toohoolhoolzote, a man recognizable even at some distance for his famous black-spotted horse and the twisted slope of his right shoulder, the result of a fall from a running horse decades earlier on the plains to the east. Even as I chanced to look to the south to see Tuekakas I became aware of two men, white men, close behind me now, moving their horses at a walk toward the corral.

Neither Gray nor Lawyer saw either of the approaching parties and I sat in place and said nothing. The two white men, almost upon me when I became aware of them, arrived first. Neither man dismounted or spoke. The large one, Whitman, his long red hair and beard wind-blown, sat his horse indifferently and observed with a detached air the castration scene before him. The smaller man, Spalding, who managed well the large grey he rode, seemed to have little interest in the struggle within the corral. Instead he studied intensely the figures of Tuekakas and Toohoolhoolzote as they approached. As he watched he looked up at me from time to time, rubbing the bony projectile of his throat as he did so, wheezing in irregular gulps of air through his congested nose.

Calmly, deliberately, Tuekakas and Toohoolhoolzote approached. In the corral Gray became aware of the men behind him, turned, and started to the fence to welcome their return, but said nothing as he too stopped to watch the approach of Tuekakas who soon pulled his horse to a halt some fifteen or twenty paces away from Spalding and Whitman.

No one spoke. Spalding dismounted, dropped his reins, and started toward Tuekakas who, in turn, dismounted and started forward, leading his horse. No one else moved.

Ten feet away Tuekakas stopped. Spalding continued toward him, spoke his name, "Tue-ka-kas" quickly, strongly—learning the name, recognizing him I don't know how—continuing, "Mei-way," our word for "great chief," adding as though he had rehearsed it.

"I will call you Joseph," he said in English, reaching out with both arms to embrace Tuekakas.

As Spalding made the move to Tuekakas, raising both arms quickly as he stepped forward, the horse Tuekakas led shied and pulled Tuekakas back away from Spalding. Tuekakas spoke a moment or so later when he controlled the horse, pulling him around with both hands, speaking as he watched and calmed the horse.

"I have brought the boy to see your ways."

Whitman, Gray, and the men with Lawyer turned, momentarily, their attention to me. Tuekakas and Spalding still faced each other. Behind them the old chief Toohoolhoolzote sat mounted studying Tuekakas and Spalding.

Two days later in the beauty and serenity of spring now come to the Clearwater River country, Tuekakas stood in the rear of the assembly where Spalding preached the first of the alien sermons we were to hear. Against Spalding is raised in the time-distillment of memory the beautiful cadence of Toohoolhoolzote, who will chant once again the verities of our forbears, who will deny the word of Spalding as the preacher presents his instructions to us:

"Hear ye this Word which I take up against you, even a lamentation, O house of Israel."

The women-led singing is over. Spalding stops his pacing and holds open the Book before him. He has a composure I have not seen before; his voice is stronger, more rhythmic. Beside him stand the interpreters.

"For thus saith the Lord unto the house of Israel, Seek ye me, and ye shall live. Seek ye the word of God, Nez Perce. Receive and hear the Word for here I hold out the Word to you; here I hold out the law of the Lord God from whom no man may turn without eternal damnation.

"Woe to them that are at ease in Zion and trust in the mountain of Samaria, which are named chief of the nations to whom the house of Israel came. Beware Nez Perce. Beware the pride of thy heart and the error of thy ways. *The pride of thine heart hath deceived thee, thou that dwellest in the clefts of the rock, whose habitation is high, that saith in his heart, Who shall bring me down to the ground?* He that saith this is in great jeopardy, for

the hand and the power of the Lord, Jehovah, moves even now among you, touches and binds even now."

Slowly, as Spalding speaks, the interpreters move out from him to act their pantomime and chants face to face with those who stand and sit in assembly.

Beyond the assembled people Toohoolhoolzote sits mounted.

"Though thou exalt THYSELF as the eagle, and though thou set thy nest among the stars, thence will I bring thee down, saith the LORD. Set aside, Nez Perce, the false gods of your land. Abandon the apparition of your wyakins, the evil spirits of your shamans, for the Lord thy God is a jealous god and will have no other gods before him, will tolerate no other fidelity once he hath sent his Word to a people."

Toohoolhoolzote frees his nervous horse for a moment to dance into the edge of those standing in the back and begins now his chant:

"IN THE BEGINNING THERE WAS PEACE AND SOLITUDE AND MAN WALKED THE EARTH HAND IN HAND WITH THE SPIRITS WHO CREATED HIM."

Spalding, intense, holds his black book high above his head with one hand. With the other he gestures and points, one listener to another:

"For, lo, he that formeth the mountains, and createth the wind and declareth unto man what is his thought, that maketh the morning darkness, and treadeth upon

the high places of the earth, the Lord, The God of Hosts, is his name. The mountains and valleys and rivers were formed by Him for all men. Now you must put aside the wildness in your heart; you must leave the highland meadows and river canyons and come to the villages and hear with the white man the will of God."

Toohoolhoolzote sings his response:

"THE EARTH IS MY MOTHER. THIS AGED TOOHOOLHOOLZOTE WHO STANDS BEFORE YOU IS BUT A SPRING'S BLADE OF GRASS TIME-TWISTED, A SPROUT DERIVED FROM, RETURNING TO THE EARTH WHICH IS THE ORIGIN OF ALL THINGS. A MAN MUST NOT DENY THE LAND WHICH IS HIS SPIRIT, MUST NOT ABANDON THE SWIFT RIVERS AND THE FIRM-FLESHED SALMON, NOR THE WIDE HIGHLAND MEADOWS WHICH NOURISH OUR HORSES AND PROVIDE THE CAMAS PLANT WHERE OUR PEOPLE GATHER TO SHARE THE HARVEST AND RENEW OUR ALLEGIANCE TO ONE ANOTHER."

Tuekakas stands mute, passive, looks straight ahead, his face drawn to a mask. Toohoolhoolzote, dark-faced, tense, holds his horse to a tight-reined, pranced, pawed circle.

Spalding continues as though he has not been interrupted.

"Hear the Word of the Lord God, Jehovah, so that your hearts may be changed, *For as ye have drunk upon my holy mountain, so shall all heathen drink continually, yea, they shall drink and they shall swallow down, and they shall be as though they had not been.*

"They shall be changed. You, Nez Perce, shall be changed if you hear the Word and obey. But woe to the people who deny the Word for they will be destroyed. *But, behold, I will raise up against you a nation, O house of Israel, saith the Lord the God of hosts; and they shall afflict you from entering in of Hemath unto the river of the wilderness."*

Lather forms now on the restrained horse as Toohoolhoolzote spins him in a tight circle.

"THE SPIRITS HAVE TOUCHED THIS LAND AND FORMED UPON IT THE MOUNTAINS AND THE CANYONS, HAVE FORMED HERE THE RIVERS AND THE VALLEYS. THE SPIRITS HAVE BROUGHT FROM THE LAND THE NIMPAU AND WE HAVE IN TURN REVERED AND RESPECTED THE LAND. WE HAVE TAKEN FROM THE LAND ONLY WHAT WE NEEDED. THE LAND HAS PROVIDED ALL THAT WE NEEDED."

Spalding himself now begins to move. Slowly through the assembled people he comes gradually to Tuekakas. To his right and left the interpreters, who watch Toohoolhoolzote, carefully, began to work back to Spalding's side.

"Therefore the Lord, the God of Hosts, the Lord, saith thus: Wailing SHALL BE in all streets; and they shall say in all the highways, Alas! alas! and they shall call the husbandmen to mourning, and such as are skillful of lamentation to wailing. Such will be the fate of the Nez Perce if they do not come to me, do not cease their wanderings and come in to hear the Word of God."

Spalding's words are interrupted by the scream of Toohoolhoolzote.

"THE EARTH IS PART OF MY BODY. THE NEZ PERCE WILL HONOR THE EARTH. WE WILL NOT RIP THE FACE OF THE EARTH WITH THE GREAT HORSE-DRAWN KNIVES: WE WILL NOT ENCUMBER THE EARTH WITH THE SHARP WIRE ROPES-DIVIDING AND SECTIONING THE CONTOUR AND FACE OF THE EARTH ITSELF, VAINGLORIOUS AND TEMPORARY EFFORT TO STAMP POSSESSION ON THAT WHICH NO MAN MAY TRULY POSSESS."

Spalding stands now before Tuekakas, his book held high, his finger pointed.

"He who once resists the Word will be forever destroyed. His people will be destroyed utterly. And they shall wander from sea to sea, and from the north even to the east, they shall run to and fro to seek the word of the Lord, and shall not find it; and I will slay the last of them with the sword: he that fleeth of them shall not flee away, and he that escapeth of them shall not be delivered. Though they dig into hell, thence shall mine hand take them; though they climb up to heaven, thence will I bring them down. And though they go into captivity before their enemies, thence will I command the sword, and it shall slay them: and I will set mine eyes upon them for evil, and not for good."

Spalding stops, stands now before Tuekakas. He gasps, open-mouthed, for air. The ghastly pantomime of signs and wails is silenced now as the interpreters stand behind Spalding and watch Tuekakas. Watch briefly. Toohoolhoolzote has let his horse go to dance through scattering people until wrenched to a halt at the side of Tuekakas.

Toohoolhoolzote quieter now, sombre, speaks to his people.

"THE NEZ PERCE HAVE RECEIVED THIS LAND IN TRUST: WE BELONG NOW TO THE LAND. WE HAVE CARED FOR IT, WE HAVE LOVED IT, WE HAVE RESPECTED IT. WE HAVE EVEN BEEN WILLING TO SHARE IT, IN PEACE, WITH THOSE WHO NEED RESPITE. BUT WE WILL NOT BE DRIVEN FROM THIS LAND OUR HOME. THE NEZ PERCE IS NOT HE WHO RAISES HIS HAND IN VIOLENCE. IF WE COULD RETREAT, I, TOOHOOLHOOLZOTE, WOULD LEAD THE RETREAT. OTHERS HAVE RETREATED AND FAILED: THE WHITE RIVER FLOWS WHERE THERE IS LEAST RESISTANCE. LET US THEN, IF WE MUST, STAND AND FIGHT, TURNING FROM OUR HIGHLAND HOME THESE WHITES WHO DENY OUR SPIRITS. OR, LET US DIE, RETURNING IRREVOCABLY TO THE EARTH OUR MOTHER."

Spalding stands red-faced, flushed in excitement, both hands grasping firmly the Book he extends to Tuekakas.

"Seek the Lord and ye shall live—lest He break out like fire in the house of Joseph, the Israelite, and devour it."

The words ended. Toohoolhoolzote spun his horse around and galloped away. Spalding stood looking into the mask of Tuekakas before him.

"I will leave the boy for a time."

There was no more. Spalding stood until the people began to cough and shuffle on the log benches. At the front Narcissa Whitman rose and broke the hush as she began alone with her beautiful voice, "Jesus Loves Me," one of the songs she taught the children. To her side came Eliza Spalding, then Whitman. Gradually some of the children and the people joined her. As they sang Spalding turned quickly and walked back up to the front.

A week later Tuekakas left me at the mission in the care of a close kinsman and returned to the Wallowa.

Six years later in the great summer camp at the junction of the Clearwater and the Snake, Spalding held out to Tuekakas yet again the Book of his god and Tuekakas took it, held it open with both hands before the assembly of our people, and ripped it apart, placing as he did so the two halves at right angles to each other, returning with care the book to Spalding who could not utter a word or sound until after Tuekakas had turned and departed the council.

Story Teller: A People Divided

So for the children and the young who listen, the Story Teller speaks of the winds which blew our people. The missionaries promised gifts of goods, and medicine, and another world for eternal life.

To have goods, medicines, and the promise of eternal life, all the Nez Perce had to do was to say "Yes."

"Yes, I believe in the truth of the great black book"–and touch the pen to signify relinquishment of our homelands to the whites who wanted all lands for themselves.

Some of the Nimpau believed the three promises. They forgot that the Earth belongs to no man, that all men belong to the Earth.

And so these of our families, said the word "Yes," and touched the pen. It was not important to the whites that all of our people touch the pen. They did not even seem to care which of our people touched the pen. If a headsman of a particular band in a specific region would not touch the pen, the whites would select another man, even another man from another band and write a name and made-up title under his "X."

So the Nimpau were split into two: one segment the whites called "the Christian Nez Perce." All others, the whites called the "hostiles" for these accepted neither treaty nor the black book

As time passed more missionaries came. More white settlers came. Those who tore the Earth to dig for the yellow rocks came. And the soldiers came to protect the whites from each other.

One by one, the bands were coerced to council where they were delivered agreements promising material goods and support—conditioned upon one of more "touching the pen" agreeing, we were told, to abandon our home valleys and plateaus and come crouch by the missions.

The mission settlements grew. Specified areas where one would live and be Nez Perce were designated. As the numbers assigned to these "reservations" increased, the size of the reserved areas decreased.

All the while, the whites grew in number. As numbers grew attitudes changed. Whites believed the land was now theirs and the Nez Perce were unwelcome guests, even trespassers. Among the newcomers attitudes changed. Some of the newcomers came to prey on both white homesteads and the Nimpau who refused to leave their homelands.

More and more conflict and trouble came. To ensure appropriate outcome, laws were written by the whites. Any conflict between whites and natives could only be addressed by a white court. Even small incidents led white opportunists to insist on more and more military presence.

Pressure increased on the individual bands bands of free Nez Perce. Where once the Nez Perce had functioned as a people united, the Nez Perce became a people divided. The bands of free Nez Perce were few now: the followers of Tuekakas occupied the Wallowa valley, the band led by White Bird remained in the Whitebird Canyon area, and the followers of the prophet, Toohoolhoolzote, moved about in the Snake River area. Each of these areas was somewhat isolated and protected by difficult access.

Sill the whites demanded removal of these remaining free people. The response of the US Army's Department of Oregon was to present the remaining free bands with an order to vacate their lands and report, within a period of two months, to a designated reservation area over a 100 miles away, across the spring flooded Snake River.

The followers of Tuekakas, White Bird and Toohoolhoolzote were to vacate their homes. Chance or politics excluded from the edict those from the Asotin valley who followed Looking Glass, son of one of the most respected chiefs and feared warriors in Nez Perce history.

As the followers of Joseph were trapped beside the swollen waters of the Snake River, an incident, seemingly random, but perhaps unavoidable brought war to the Nez Perce.

Joseph and others sent messengers asking for help to Looking Glass, who had the largest band of free Nez Perce remaining.

Looking Glass believed that the whites were afraid of him and would not dare intrude or instruct him—and so refused.

Now were three. The army edict split the remaining free Nez Perce into two factions.

Ironically, ten days after armed resistance began, the whites struck Looking Glass in his own village, forcing him to flee to the combined camp of the non-treaty Nez Perce

IV. Whitebird Canyon
June 17, 1877

Into the grey, chilling mist of morning one by one the armed warriors ride. Joseph stands and watches, mute, impervious. In the camp about us indistinct silhouettes move, rekindle from the coals of evening the cook fires of morning, stir and poke, set upon already heated stones the camas meal patties, cut from over dog-high perches strips of dried meat for the old men, the children, the women, and for Joseph—Joseph who stands powerless while the young, fasting warriors fade into the mist to join White Bird and Ollokot.

Joseph is to be camp guardian—a position appropriate for the man who opposed war, who argued in council through most of this night that there was no alternative in war, that what the chiefs had, first of all, was the responsibility to protect their people and that in war there is no possibility of protecting the Nez Perce—for if blood flows, the whites will rise in their great numbers against us. The cavalry and troops, slow moving, ponderous, but deadly, will be dispatched and the Nez Perce will become fugitives from this land which is our home.

He who argues dignity and honor in resistance—White Bird and Toohoolhoolzote and those who stand with them—think only of self. A man may ride out, it is true, and oppose those who trouble him, may take arms against the man or the idea which is the source of his trouble, and, in so doing, may die and stain the earth of his beloved home, may return again to the soil which is his origin and is his end, may in fact rejoice in this life-

stain for it ends his dilemma. But this man acts in fear and seeks escape. What will become of this man's wife; who will protect and rear his children? What enemy dare spare the child of a famous adversary? What can a man do but disregard his own dignity and live so that in life he may be of service, may be yet some shield of protection for the wife who nurses in the dim-light and privacy of his lodge the woman child who is his first born.

Joseph will guard the camp, will direct the preparations to flee, will be ready with the women and children and with the old men who sit now in idleness telling how it was, how the battles went in their day. When the first tattered and frightened warrior flees back into camp to warn us, we will be ready to go ourselves, to scurry and hide, to evade, because we must, the soldiers who will pursue and will now never leave us in solitude and peace.

The Nimpau, our forbears, sought peace. Story Teller remembers. Our people chose the path, followed the arguments we believed would produce peace. We stood in place and held our discontented while the diseases and the increasingly evident greed of the whites cut piecemeal the Cayuse, the Yakima, the Blackfoot, the Shoshoni, the Bannock, and the Flathead from their lands around us. We stood in place while Kamiakin, the great Yakima warrior and chief, rallied his people and his allies to drive away the whites. We sat and listened to the messengers—and finally to Kamiakin, the man himself, at night, late, and in desperation—as the Yakima urged the intervention of the Nez

Perce who might have, on that day, put a thousand men into the field.

We listened, we waited, and we did nothing. The Nez Perce sat immobile retelling the old tales of the days when the two captains were among us. And, as the old men talked, the whites who now surround our land pressed inward quietly, often only a few hundred yards at a time, sometimes more boldly when we were away in sumner camp following the fish and camas seasons. The whites hoped, bet the tribe would not rise in its own defense—as they schemed to have an established claim when the government resettled the Nez Perce, drove us from our land to a reservation, boxed us, shipped us, somewhere, anywhere, out of the way.

Once there might have been peace. In 1842, when the churchman called White first came among us, we still had in our hearts nothing but the finest thoughts for the whites. We came to Lapwai and heard with amazement and disbelief the tract White had his clerk read to us, a tract which created laws governing the relationships between Nez Perce and white, a tract which would punish by hanging any Indian who burned a building, a tract which set any white above our tribal laws—whatever his offense.

Our headmen stood in silence and watched the expressionless face, watched the long, white flowing beard fluffing irregularly in the wind, below the hand-held black felt hat, watched and waited for the moment when the old man would stand and contradict the words we heard, contradict and reaffirm our relationship of friendship. We waited and heard the old man say nothing, saw him rise from his seat on the platform of Spalding's open meeting house and walk arrogantly away.

There might have been peace as late as the spring of the year the whites call 1855 when the man named Stevens summoned the Nez Perce to council at Walla Walla. Incredibly we heard the words. We stood, not silent now, as the little man with the large protruding eyes and sunburnt face paced before us, attempted to mask with words the ambition and greed his always moving, nervous hands betrayed. We allowed him to speak; we heard superficially his titles, oblivious to the implied power, indifferent to the paradox of roles in the man who came to us as both Superintendent of Indian Affairs and as Governor of the Washington-Oregon Territories. We heard his speech, heard the condescension, "We did not come here to scare you or to drive you away, but to talk to you as men." We heard the words intended to deceive, "If we enter into a treaty now, we can select a good country for you, but if we wait until the country is filled with whites, where will we find such a place?"

Stevens, the vain-glorious pop-eyed man who would not scare us or drive us away, but who would talk to the Nez Perce *as though we were men,* would select from the land the gods had given us some part, some segment that we might keep, would select for us, would divide where he stood a guest. This man, this white called Stevens was shouted down.

The decorum, the passive hospitality of the Nez Perce was broken. Each headman rose in his turn to denounce the words of Stevens. Tuekakas himself spoke. He spoke slowly, with emotion, with guarded rage, directing as he finished two of his own kinsmen to the east to find and inform Apash Wyakaikt so that he might return from the buffalo lands and add his great influence against Stevens in protection of the Nez Perce homeland.

But none of this meant anything to Stevens, for Stevens was to find the flaw, was to discover the means to achieve his goal. Instead of lamenting the fact that the Nez Perce had no single chief or spokesman, instead of becoming distressed over a system which allowed each man authority and responsibility in his own sphere—to the extent that the headmen rose one after another to condemn his proposal—Stevens used our tribal system to his advantage. He cast about him for those who might be sympathetic or ambitious and found Hallalhotsoot, now called "Lawyer," by his own kinsmen—a man receptive to any proposal which would increase his own importance. For the promise of a frame house, forty plowed acres, and an unspecified number of cows, Lawyer signed the treaty delineating the boundaries of the Nez Perce. To complete his work, to embellish his document, and to resolve his technical dilemma, Stevens affixed to Lawyer's "X" the title, "Head Chief of the Nez Perce."

And so the whites came to claim the first segment of the highland plateau where the gods had set the Nez Perce. Upon the touch of a finger to a pen above a preconceived document and a pre-formed "X," the white was to rest his claim that the face of the earth itself was altered. Upon the consent of a man too cowardly or too clever to argue, the white's tenuous title was to rest—as though Joseph had a fine horse coveted by another man, and when he would not sell this horse, this stranger went to his neighbor, Lawyer, and said, "Joseph has a fine horse I want; how much will you take for him?" and Lawyer, who was too astute not to acquiesce to the whim of this stranger, said, "Offer me a fair price and I will sign the papers, the bill of sale for this horse." And later, "Good, I have enjoyed doing business with you. Come again. And incidentally you can arrange with Joseph the time you come to pick up the horse."

Thus, Lawyer was to acknowledge the first of the documents designed to demean and dispossess the Nez Perce. In response Toohoolhoolzote, the old Dreamer chief, rose and in the trembling, balanced cadence of age declared the nation divided: "From this day forth the Nez Perce will be two peoples. We will part as friends. We will remain friends. But let no man give away my home, the land which is mine in trust."

Behind him, beyond Toohoolhoolzote, sat Smohalla the lame prophet whose vision created the growing Dreamer religion. Around him circled his disciples who echoed the dirge Smohalla chanted:

Those who cut up the lands or sign
papers for lands will be defrauded of
their rights and will be punished
by God's anger.

You ask me to plough the ground! Shall
I take a knife and tear my mother's
bosom? Then when I die, she will not
take me to her bosom to rest.

You ask me to dig for stone! Shall I dig
under skin for bones? Then when I die I
cannot enter her body to be born again.

You ask me to cut grass and make hay
and sell it and be rich like the white
men! But how dare I cut off my
mother's hair?

Still there had been peace in the years that followed. The settlers pressed into the Wallowa, into the valley bequeathed to Joseph in trust by Tuekakas as he lay blind upon his deathbed. They pressed past the old stone markers Tuekakas himself had erected to warn them. Yet, there was still peace even when finally in this winter past, the negotiator who insisted Joseph must speak with him was not a civilian, not a paid government agent, but was an army general in uniform who said only, "The government orders Joseph and his people to leave the Wallowa and come to the new land set aside at

Lapwai. My men and I will wait here while you gather your people."

Thus the time had come. This man, this one-armed general who had achieved fame and self-opinion in the great war between the whites would not hear our protests. The man called Howard stood without reflection or consideration of the spring floods, and set a date for our arrival at Lapwai, a date unrealistic and harsh, not even allowing us the time it would take to gather our winter-foraging stock, a date he would not modify, only repeat as if the date itself answered the objections we raised.

So in the council of our elders Joseph stated that the Nez Perce must go to Lapwai. There were those who rose to oppose the idea. Toohoolhoolzote and White Bird, whose nearby people from the Snake River canyons and the Salmon-Snake junction were also affected, argued with strength against leaving our land. Perhaps their argument would have carried—Toohoolhoolzote was easily the most forceful, and White Bird was one of the most influential in the days when the Nez Perce met together as a nation—had not Ollokot, risen to support Joseph's decision: "Hin-mah-too-yah-lat-kekht, brother, has stated the paths we may take. We can go with Howard, or we can resist. I do not wish to fight the troops of Howard."

There was peace when the Nez Perce assembled in silent grief for the long journey to Lapwai, an area many had not seen since before the arrival of the whites and the beginning of strained tribal relations. There was peace, a passive, sullen acceptance permeated with sadness, as the Nez Perce began to move—in make-shift order the long diverse column of dispossession, struggling to carry the old and the young, to keep together whatever livestock time and Howard had permitted collected. There was peace, the peace of exhaustion and frustration, until the Nez Perce reached the spring-swollen, impassable Snake River. Once again messengers were sent to Howard, who followed our move with a parallel march two or three days behind, to explain the delay. The stock and especially the children and old people could not cross the Snake in its present, raging flood stage.

Howard, who had not yet even seen the river sent his answer: the Nez Perce were to move on. The date for arrival had been set; all must be on the reservation by this predetermined day.

Again angry men rose to speak for action, adding their voices once more to the constant demand of Toohoolhoolzote. With patience, Joseph persuaded them against violence: the Nez Perce had agreed to go to Lapwai; we had come this far. In our homeland there was little chance of resistance; here, camped in dismay with our people tired and our stock scattered, with our retreat cut off by a raging river there was no hope for anything. We must with care and courage cross the Snake and continue to Lapwai.

And so with considerable anxiety we entered the flooded swift river, sending some of the young men with the strongest horses across to test the current. Then we made small hide-covered boats and rafts and sent them into the water drawn by three or four struggling horses which were guided by the young warriors. On the rafts, in the hide boats, precariously clung the old and the young. For two days we worked. Horses tired and went down; the weaker stock, some of the herd mares, many of the young colts, and most of the few cows we had were lost. Even some of the stronger animals were swept away. With them went clothing, tents, and supplies. But no human life was lost. The Nez Perce emerged on the north bank of the Snake exhausted, but intact.

Yet, here, on the north bank of the Snake in the spring of 1877, war came for the Nez Perce.

War came almost as if by chance quietly and unexpectedly in the first hours of our camp after crossing the Snake. Joseph left the camp soon after all the people were safely across the river and, taking with him several of the headmen, went to the banks of the river to see what could be salvaged. There the group split into two segments. One group recrossed the Snake so that we could work both banks downstream of our crossing to pick up salvageable items, to recapture stray stock, and to dress out the recoverable carcasses of beef.

While the headsmen were gone a young man, his name was Wahlitits, rode mounted double with his cousin Sarpsis Illpilp, through the exhausted camp. The horse shied—or was made to shy by the cousin who rode behind, in the way boys will seek pranks even when near exhaustion—and trampled some kouse roots spread out to dry by the tepee of the old and bitter man called Heyoom Moxmox, Yellow Grizzly Bear.

Tired from the strenuous day and bitter by nature the old man cried out to Wahlitits: "See what you do! Playing brave you ride over my woman's hard-worked food! If you are so brave, why don't you go kill the white man who killed your father?"

Embarrassed, Wahlitits whirled his horse in silent response and rode away. The insult reopened the wound in his heart, rekindled the hatred simmering for years since his father had bled to death on the ground before him, shot down by an outcast white who was trying to fence off a section of Nez Perce land containing the garden of Wahlitits's family. The father, even with his mortal wound, had been able to exact from the boy the promise that the son would not attempt to avenge the act. The son was all that was left of life to him; revenge would compound the act and eventually take that life too from the earth and this was what the father feared in his dying moments. The promise the son made to him had restrained Wahlitits for almost five years. But the chance insult before the open camp and in front of his peers intensified the boy's brooding.

For a large part of the night the cousin, Sarpsis Illpilp, and two friends, Wetyetmas Wayakaikt and Lahpeealoot, sat with Wahlitits around a small fire outside the main camp. At dawn Wahlitits and the three young Nez Perce rode from the camp to seek the man who had killed the father of Wahlitits. Less than twenty hours later four white men known for their hatred and abuse of the Indian were dead and a fifth was mortally wounded. No woman or child had been touched.

Ironically, the man they sought, the man known as the killer of Wahlitits's father, escaped.

Seventy-five years of peace had ended. The young men carefully avoided returning to our camp after their raid. Instead of coming back to their families and homes they turned up river toward the desolate canyon country of the Snake into the area the whites would come to call Hell's Canyon. Once away from our base camp, Wahlitits sent a single messenger in a wide, curving ride into the camp to warn of possible reprisal.

The camp was preparing for siege when Joseph returned.

Children, the small ones at least, were not to be seen. Here and there groups of young men huddled together, sometimes talking with bold gestures, sometimes sitting—they were almost always mounted—in near silence. Toward Joseph, from the direction of White Bird's camp, came a young woman who cried loudly, over and over with no change of volume or intonation, the name of her child. To Joseph's left, from his own camp, two young warriors, Hiyuts Tohenin and Sarpsis Illpilp, kicked their horses to a reckless gallop to move through the village and rein to a stop at the lodge of White Bird. Here they turned their horses to watch Joseph's movement as he came to White Bird, Toohoolhoolzote, Red Owl, and the other older men seated, smoking before White Bird's lodge.

Within the group there was an attitude near relief. The insults and frustrations of recent years had been drawn to focus. War was no longer an issue of debate. The Nez Perce were once again free and unified. Every effort to maintain peace had failed. The day of White Bird and the war chiefs had come.

In the beginning Joseph tried to argue for reconcilement. He urged that the emissaries to Allalimya Takanin, the younger Looking Glass, be held, that the Nez Perce hold as well the messengers to the Palouse and Yakima. He argued that we draw together our people and defend our position while delegates were sent to Howard and the officials at Lapwai to weigh their intentions. But this was to no avail. The hearts of the people belonged now to White Bird, the plain-spoken Salmon River headman, and to the eloquent old Dreamer, Toohoolhoolzote, who had no trust whatsoever for the whites.

"Joseph advises that we negotiate. We will negotiate." The words were White Bird's, but the sentiment was that of the entire camp.

"We will send Joseph to Howard. We will leave the great camp tepees here, building in front of each a fire of green hardwood, and, while Joseph seeks the intentions of Howard, the Nez Perce will go with White Bird to the south to our homelands where we will prepare to meet Howard after Joseph has found this man has no place in his heart for the Nez Perce."

It was as White Bird said, as White Bird and Toohoolhoolzote had planned. The Nez Perce fled south and now Howard marched to us, his strength increasing slowly, the total troops in our area increasing rapidly, as day by day by rail and steamer the reinforcements came and were ordered into position against us.

Why those who came in advance of Howard chose to test our strength at Whitebird Canyon we were never to know. Perhaps they knew of our disorganization, knew through Chapman, the loud-talking, self-styled expert who left his Umatilla wife to join Howard as scout, that at this time we could put no more than sixty or seventy poorly armed warriors out to protect our camp—a camp pitched precariously at the end of the shallow, treeless canyon formed by Whitebird Creek where it joined the Salmon. Perhaps they sought to strike a telling blow before our runners could reach neighboring bands to recruit help.

Whatever the motivation of Howard's cavalry that bright, hot morning in June, the Nez Perce were hardly prepared for war. In the intervening days, the rebelliousness created by the Snake River incident had cooled. Our scouts told of the size of the columns which approached us and spoke in clipped sentences about the forces gathering for Howard at Lapwai. Some were ready to hear again Joseph's words for reconciliation and peace.

From this lack of readiness and confusion a course of action slowly evolved. Joseph would go out of camp and await the troops under a flag of truce, would determine what choices remained for the Nez Perce. With Joseph, almost as a reprimand, were to come the Dreamers, Toohoolhoolzote and Husishusis Kute—the first headman to join us after the raid of Wahlitits. At the same time, the warriors would go in two groups, under White Bird and Ollokot, from the camp and rest in readiness out of sight behind the bluffs of the canyon slopes in case the soldiers disregarded us and moved against the village.

And so Joseph, too, rode from the camp that morning. He took with him the headmen who were to accompany him and rode from the camp some time after the warriors left, still, in the hazy light of early morning, far too early to do more than wait. Even as he sat astride the nervous, smoking, surface-wet back of his horse, waiting for the column of soldiers now moving against the Nez Perce, his thoughts were on Tuekakas and the council at Lapwai where Tuekakas first stood in opposition to the papers the whites brought to the Nimpau.

In the beginning, before the Nimpau, was the great benevolent spirit the Sahaptins called Coyote for his wit and cunning. With Coyote were the animal spirits who walked the bountiful meadows and mountains and plains of this land with peace and contentment. Then there came from the east a ravenous monster who destroyed and consumed the quiet, peaceful spirits who inhabited this plateau, a monster which grew stronger and bolder with each motion, feeding and fortifying itself on that which it wasted. And all the spirits feared this monster and fled its presence until it had come to ravage and dominate this entire land.

In the cool, dry morning air the sound of moving horses becomes more distinct. Joseph sits, mounted, with the elders beside him, hushed, and trembling, as the soldiers and volunteers of Perry become visible.

Unopposed the monster ravaged the land, destroying one by one the creatures who had inhabited the land. And then it came to pass that the monster cornered Coyote who, seeing that resistance would avail little against the creature's still growing strength, Coyote gave himself quickly to the monster, diving, when at last he must, into the creature's horrid and deadly mouth, where, once past the deadly teeth, Coyote could make his way without resistance to the internals of the beast itself there working his will, tearing asunder, ripping and shredding the soft interior of the beast until the life passed from this alien creature and Coyote reemerged bloody, wet, but victorious.

Into view now come the troops of Howard. Slowly, but continuously they emerge from the hidden reaches of the upper canyon. At a ground-consuming tireless trot they come—a column almost fragile with its precarious breath, but, even in the distance, alarming in its great length.

And from this body, torn and reft, Coyote sought to rekindle the life, the spirits of our homeland. With gravity and reverence and love he distributed the parts of the body over the ravaged land. And from this act of reverence and love there sprang a new life as it had been before. From the great heart itself, put down in this splendid plateau, sprang the Nimpau, the Nez Perce. And so this land is the Nez Perce. It is we who are rekindled from the spirits who have always resided here. We are of the land, an extension of it, a temporal breathing spirit projected from the passive fertility of the soil itself and cannot thus sell or negotiate away the earth which is our body no more than the shadow can deny or cut away that to which it owes its origin. The Nez Perce have no choice. We will share where we can; we will resist where we must, but we will not negotiate and deny our spirit upon a sheaf of papers however fragile: instead we will strike back against the soft internals of those who oppress us.

As the column steadily draws nearer we can identify the forms and carriage of some who compose it. The man Perry, who rides at the column's head, has for two years now been in our area. The Nez Perce know him to be an outspoken man, an honest man of limited views, and a man whose courage is unquestioned—though tainted with a head-strong disregard for possible consequences. By his side is an officer not known, a man who is probably one of Howard's staff officers. Grouped around the officers is a contingent of civilians. Here, even in the distance, the large white hat of the man Chapman is recognizable. And it is this which troubles me most, for in the decreasing distance we can see the antics of Chapman, a man who might be respected for the force of his personality, but a man, ultimately, who could not be trusted, a man who would take gifts in friendship: the daughter of a chief, the use of a tract of land, but a man who looked constantly with greed and ambition around him. We watch him as he spurs up beside Perry, talking and gesturing with animation, for a few minutes before he falls back, still continuing his argument, to the side of the man known as Shearer, a man who served bravely, we have heard, those who lost the great white war in the east, a man who would not create trouble, but a man whose primary commitment is to the ever-growing ranch he has established on the plateau between the junction of the Salmon and the Snake.

Before the troops we sit, mounted, motionless—the white flag, limp, inert, on the spear shaft above us. Three hundred yards away the column is drawn to a halt by the uplifted hand of Perry. I can now hear the words of the whites, though the nature of their argument is indiscernible because of the distance and the snorting, blowing noises as more than one hundred horses and the supporting pack animals come to a serpentine rest.

What was discernible—if memory can be trusted in those anxiety-filled minutes when I, almost alone, stood between that column of trained and professional soldiers and the defenseless camp of women and children—was that Perry, motioning for Shearer to accompany him, started forward at a slow canter. He came no more than twenty yards, Shearer now at his side, when behind them Chapman raised his rifle and fired. Husishusis Kute, my impetuous companion, fired quickly in return. The shot, quite by chance over a great distance and from the back of a horse, brought down one of the troop's two trumpeters.

Almost instantaneously Ollokot, who had abandoned the slopes, was past Joseph, racing his horse straight down the canyon floor toward the troops. Behind him were a dozen horsemen, each cloaked in an identical, new flame red blanket.

With unbelievable slowness, yet irreversible sureness, without a sound in the death-still canyon, Ollokot, brother, gentle spirit, floated away from Joseph and against the head of the thin, long column which recoiled temporarily, regained its presence and launched its strike against the handful of warriors already turned and racing back down the canyon which resonated now a shrill, ringing wail punctuated with staccato, courage-sustaining yelps, and the dimensionless, sporadic dry clapping of rifles.

Incomprehensibly I turn my frantic horse from the field to the village and the flight that must come.

Story Teller: Tecumseh

Joseph, still bound and guarded, waits the order of Miles. Joseph remembers the days of youth in the Wallowa as Ollokot lies mortally wounded in the destitute camp of the Nez Perce.

Story Teller recalls the Battle of WhiteBird Canyon, the Nez Perce's first armed confrontation and the most strategically executed victory by Native American warriors over white troops.

Story Teller chants the warrior reflections of Tecumseh, the Shawnee.

My forefathers were warriors.
Their son is a warrior.
From them I take my existence.
From my tribe I take nothing.
I am the maker of my own fortune.

I will come to no man to ask him to
honor the treaty.

I will say, as the Spirit who rules the
Universe would say:

'Sir, you have the liberty to return to
Your own country.'

V. The Day of the Warrior: The Battle of Whitebird Canyon

June 17, 1877

Story Teller recalls the snow-covered, desolate camp of the Nimpau at the foot of the Bear Paws. He sees the armed, heavily provisioned camp of Miles just visible on the plains beyond, feels again Joseph's cold and exhaustion.

Story Teller remembers, for those who gather and listen, Joseph and Ollokot as young men in the Wallowa Valley.

Ollokot was fourteen and Joseph was eighteen when they raced that last time on the foot trail leading north and south through the Wallowa. It was not a planned race, not the matching of fine horses—which would continue from time to time throughout their lives—or at least until Howard fell against the Nimpau at the Clearwater. This was a contest unplanned and unannounced, perhaps even avoided until the moment it began.

The boys—already young men—were returning from their rabbit snares set along the tiny arm of Cold Creek a mile or so south of its junction with the Wallowa River. In the pleasant coolness of mid-morning they had begun to trot. Around them the late summer's aspens had just begun to change colors.

The pace was altered and suddenly, without a word or a challenge, the runners were at full speed. By the nature of his position on the trail Joseph was ahead a pace or so as he bent himself to the exhilaration of speed, leaning forward, straining and pumping with perfect rhythm, cupping and pulling to himself the handfuls of air as do the great sprinters of our tribe in the summer camps along the Clearwater. For a mind-frame now blank there is no dimension of time or space, for the sprint obliterates—as no emotion or activity, save the desperate, precarious union of man and race horse in the flat, asymmetric rhythm of final speed—the consciousness of self. Temporarily, but completely, there is only the total dedication and subservience to motion and speed as each muscle reacts to the forward lean which speed demands, and the brain functions only to control, to balance, to harmonize the physical flailing that total physical effort produces.

For seconds there is only the consideration of speed and then, as the mind allowed the first impressions of exhaustion and fatigue to register, Joseph realized Ollokot was still with him, matching stride for stride his sprint—more than matching now as Ollokot pressures forward, pressing, in the second or so and the ten yards that time represents, up to Joseph's left elbow, forcing him to the right of the narrow trail, asserting for the first time a tiny lead at the instant when Joseph's right foot jabs down onto the sharp rock which cuts up into the leather of his moccasin, forcing him to pull up to a limping halt.

Four years later Ollokot was to defeat, in the foot races of the great summer camp at the Clearwater, all of the young men of the Nez Perce—before being defeated himself in a sprint by the great eastern warrior Wahchumyus, called Rainbow by the whites, a man no challenger had ever defeated in physical confrontation.

The Story Teller remembers with pride the strength of Ollokot, who, twelve years later led the warriors of the Wallowa and the Whitebird Canyon Nez Perce against the cavalry of Howard in the battle of Whitebird Canyon.

The Teller recalls with shame the refusal of Young Looking Glass to lead his warriors to help defend the Nimpau camp in Whitebird Canyon.

Story Teller is with the free Nez Perce when, two weeks after Howard's man, Perry, ordered his charge against the Nez Perce village in Whitebird Canyon, Allalimya Takanin, called Young Looking Glass, rides with hauteur into the camp of the Nez Perce. His fiery, smooth-gaited, pony prances in response to the sawing bit, while Looking Glass leers from beneath the black felt hat pulled forward and down upon his prominent nose, looks for the headsmen and the people he expects to welcome him.

Pole-straight and arrogant sits the Asotin—who, less than a month ago, condescended to lecture and instruct the man called "Young Tuekakas" by the people.

Here is the man who turned away our messenger, saying to this youth, the agent and representative of Tuekakas: "My hands are clean of white men's blood. They will remain so."

Before our people, in the swirl of the dust kicked up by his dancing horse and the din of welcome raised by the camp dogs, is the headman who would not stop with a simple "no," choosing instead to harass the young Wallowan before him.

"You have acted like fools. I will have no part of such things. If you are determined to fight, do so. Do so without Looking Glass. Call your warriors away. Camp in your own home valleys. Looking Glass and his people will live in peace upon the Asotin Creek."

Passing before the Nimpau, too proud to stop or acknowledge a single man is Allalimya Takanin, the son of Apash Wayakaikt, recognized by even old Tuekakas as "Meiway," "great chief," a title bestowed on only a handful of men in the history of our people. It was Apash Wayakaikt, Flint Necklace, called Looking Glass because of the trade mirror he wore, who ordered seized and whipped Pambrum, the arrogant, foolhardy Hudson Bay Company agent, in the days when most Nez Perce thought the strange new ways and medicines of the whites made them invincible. It was Apash Wayakaikt who led his men on the two-year hunts across the Bitterroots to the buffalo land where he achieve reputation as the greatest Nez Perce war chief.

Apash Wyakaikt fought with courage the Blackfoot, the Bannock, and the Lakota in the turbulent chance battles on the hunting grounds of the plains when no white men dared challenge the Nez Perce. With equal confidence he opposed the white when Stevens and White first came to the Nez Perce with the papers and codes most came to fear and detest. But for his complete indifference and arrogance Apash Wyakaikt might have slowed, or halted, the continued encroachment by the whites, but Apash Wyakaikt gave the white man not even the consideration necessary to disrupt his own migration pattern. Every third or fourth year Looking Glass would strike his lodge from the banks of the Asotin and, taking with him whatever followers who wished to come, make the traditional journey to the buffalo lands.

Those whites who came with papers learned to wait until the old war chief was too far away to intimidate Lawyer, trusting that Tuekakas could not, or would not, prevent Lawyer's paid "X' s."

And so Apash Wayakaikt, Flint Necklace, the elder Looking Glass, came to hold a position within tribal order so unique that even the government agents were aware. Years before age humped the back and tamed, almost gentled, the face, Apash Wayakaikt achieved fame in the pitched battles and raids on the plains to the east. Later, at fifty, he led a giant retaliatory raid against the Snakes to the south, achieving thus a responsibility and position accorded to only a few earlier chiefs in the legends of our tribe. From this raid the Nez Perce brought back over four hundred horses and a former Snake slave. Out of this raid grew the final name and reputation of Apash Wayakaikt. Out of this raid grew as well the Dreamer religion, for the Snake slave captured and returned to the Nez Perce homeland was Smohalla, the Dreamer prophet.

Now to the camp of Joseph comes the war-like Asotins. At their head rides Allalimya Takanin, called Young Looking Glass for the great chief who was his father.

Later in council, after Looking Glass and his principal men have come into camp and his women are setting up their lodges, Joseph and the elders will call on Ollokot to tell, in welcome to Looking Glass and the Asotins, of the battle of Whitebird Canyon. In pride for the Nez Perce warrior and because Joseph, in innocent flattery, requests it, Ollokot will stand before the council. With him, beside and behind him, are the warriors who fought for the village in the ravines leading to Whitebird Canyon.

The Story Teller can see, through the slits of light in the time-frame of being, the gaunt, but powerful form of Ollokot as he stands before the night fire and addresses the Nimpau council, speaks to the people clustered to the side and behind the elders, addresses Looking Glass himself with little effort to hide his disgust.

Ollokot speaks,

"Hear me Nez Perce. Ollokot is asked to speak for the warriors who stand here beside him.

"Ollokot stands to welcome to our camp Looking Glass and his people from the Asotin valley. How happy we would have been to welcome our brothers when we stood fearful in Whitebird Canyon and faced the charge of the soldiers who outnumbered us two to one, whose guns outnumbered our own four to one.

Ollokot speaks:

"How sorry we were to hear that the white friends of Looking Glass, who assured him of peace and extended the bounds of the reservation to include the Asotin Creek, chose to enforce peace by bringing a company of soldiers with Gatling guns to arrest Looking Glass. How unfortunate that Looking Glass, son of Meiway, whom we all revere, could not see that from the moment the first Nez Perce raised his hand against the White that no Nez Perce, at least no non-treaty Nez Perce, had a choice.

Across the campfire from Ollokot, Joseph sits, his eyes squinted and his face drawn tight, as he stares away to the west and the Blue mountains which stand watch over the Wallowa. Ollokot moves closer to stand directly in front of Looking Glass, who studies, mechanically, the fire. His man, Peopeo Tholekt, glares about, his eyes meeting, but not holding Ollokots's, his animosity shifting from Ollokot to White Bird who is embarrassed, and finally to Joseph who is unaware of his anger, who is unaware, perhaps, of the words Ollokot speaks.

Ollokot continues.

"Looking Glass might have foreseen the panic and hostile reaction of the white. After seventy years of peace the whites no longer had anything to gain by peace and openly sought to drive us to fight. There is no need to recount the details for Looking Glass knows the treaties and the abuses that Nez Perce history holds, that perhaps even the whites will some day acknowledge. Looking Glass knows that even the incident which finally brought war was an act of justice —delayed five years because of our restraint and hope to avoid war.

"And so why did Looking Glass sit in camp and turn away our pleas for help?" Ollokot glares down on Looking Glass, close enough now to touch him.

"While Ollokot lay upon the cold, wet ground on the slopes at Whitebird Canyon, Looking Glass slept in his tepee. While Ollokot fought and the dry heat and thirst hardened his mouth and throat into a speechless, dry cavity that could only suck air, Looking Glass sat in camp upon the cool, clear Asotin and drank the white man's whiskey.

The Asotins call out now. Across the fire Peopeo Tholekt is on his feet moving toward Ollokot, but he chooses to stop and shout his anger as he moves. Yellow Wolf and Bighorn Bow rise to stop him. White Bird calls out a reprimand from his seated position, reminding Ollokot that Looking Glass has come to our camp as a guest. Further across the fire even Joseph watches and listens now.

"What Ollokot says is true. Who will dispute Ollokot? The words are wrong, but the anger and fear of Whitebird Canyon boils within.

Listen then as the Teller paces in step with Ollokot to share for those gathered the Battle of Whitebird Canyon where the warriors of the Nez Perce destroyed the cavalry of Howard.

Listen and remember what it is like when the troops of Howard march each day nearer. Feel again the anguish as our scouts stand before the village and tell the headmen that Howard has detached his cavalry, that the long column of blue-coated soldiers with their steel-shod horses is already a day away from Howard's walking soldiers and now less than two days away from our camp.

Where on this earth is there such dread for a warrior. What can a man do. Each day the white general marches by the relentless schedule which brings him ever nearer. The size and force of Howard's camp make attack impossible, the steadfast, passionless routine of the soldier brings fear to the bravest warrior. Each man in his turn serves to watch and report the position of Howard and each man is in turn dismayed for Howard does not hurry. His camp is awake at daylight and one hour later marches. Riders go to Lewiston and Lapwai with messages and directions. Already the first of new supply wagons starts for the slow moving column that marches for two hours, halts for thirty minutes and then marches again in a never varying routine that alarms and frightens by its very consistency and determination.

What choice had the Nez Perce when the column of horsemen was detached? There were many among us who had laughed at Howard and his slowness, for the Nez Perce had his horses. Our herd of over two thousand was still largely intact even after the Snake river crossing. But these smirks came no more when the horse soldiers, a fragment of Howard's strength, but still greater than our own, was detached and began its ride straight for our camp. The horses remained to us, but, finally, as the troops themselves rode against our position the realization came that free and easy flight was an illusion. A man, a warrior might choose from the herd which represented his entire wealth a string of the fine, spirited horses the Nez Perce bred and loved and flee beyond any man or body of men. The stamina and speed of our horse created the illusion of safety.

Yet, there was not safety. The cavalry of Howard, led by the man known as Perry and Howard's officer called Trimble, had nothing to hamper or slow it. Ammunition and supplies were loaded and packed on mules and each man had only his weapons and his bedroll. Man for man the Nez Perce could move at ease until the fine, but single, horses of the cavalry were exhausted and could go no more. But there was little chance of loading the old and young, the sick, the lodges, herding together the stock that remained, and outriding the column of men who could make fifty miles a day, were trained and supplied to make fifty miles a day almost indefinitely.

And so the Nez Perce sat in council to determine what to do while hour by hour our scouts came in to report the progress of the cavalry.

The headmen faced no simple decision. There was no proof, as White Bird repeatedly pointed out that the horse soldiers came to fight. The provisions and arms were to be expected. Should the headmen send Wahlitits and his fiery cousin, Sarpis Illpilp to the troops with the explanation that they were the men who raided the white cabins? Perhaps, then, the troops would go away. Against White Bird, rose the angry young warriors of his own band—Tipyahlanah Kapskaps, Strong Eagle and Wetyetmas Wayakaikt, Swan Necklace. With them stood the brave warrior Chuslum Moxmox, Yellow Buffalo Bull, the father of Sarpis Illpilp. Others rose to denounce the suggestion of White Bird, who, rebuked by his own band, sat nervously rubbing against his face and nose the eagle's wing he wears, symbol of his role as shaman, medicine man.

Joseph argued for reconcilement, insisting that even victory in battle would last no more than a day or a week or a month before the troops of the whites came again to our home lodges. Joseph asked the question, "What people have successfully stood against the whites?" It was Joseph who finally calmed Husishusis Kute, who believed that the Nez Perce might recreate Crazy Horse's victories at the Rose Bud and the Greasy Grass only a year ago.

The compromise came. The warriors would be held until the soldiers' intent was known. To determine intent, Joseph would be sent out of the village to await the arrival of the troops. Under this flag of truce would go Joseph, Husishusis Kute, and, since Toohoolhoolzote refused, Hahtalekin, the Palouse cousin of Husishusis Kute.

So the warriors must protect the village, but must show no hostility while Joseph and the other headsmen waited under the white's own "flag on truce."

The danger of this decision was that no defensive position behind the lower hills could be taken by the warriors while the soldiers descended from the plateau above—for the warriors would be plainly visible from the higher elevation. Our problem, thus, was to position the warriors after the soldiers descended to something near our own level, but before they entered the valley where they could observe our movements.

Story Teller recreates for his listeners the slow process of decision in council.

White Bird spoke from his seat of buffalo hides to say that the warriors should wait until the soldiers reached the jutting rock on the left where the trail was washed and was nearly impassable. Yellow Bull still enraged at White Bird's suggestion that the Nez Perce turn over his son, Sarpis Illpilp, jumped to his feet to say that the spot White Bird suggested was so far down in the valley that even if the white soldier were blind and could not see, he would be so close when the warriors moved to their positions that he would certainly hear their balls bumping together as they ran.

Yellow Grizzly Bear, who is from the Wallowa and has traveled the trail fewer times but thus with greater attention, rose to point out with the snarl we have come to expect from him, that there were two big rocks and washes. "The one Yellow Bull is thinking of has the rock on the left leading out of the valley toward the north and is far too low; the one White Bird refers to has the rock on the left coming south into the valley and is far too high. Neither of which matters," the old man continued, surprising us with his perception, "for as we wait on the ravine floor we cannot see when the whites reach either point."

"We must send out a man to study the trail to choose a position from which he can signal the warriors into motion. We must trust that a single man does not alarm the troops, who might be, after all, suspicious if they saw no activity."

And so in council the decisions were made which determined our reaction to the cavalry of Howard sent against us in Whitebird Canyon. Joseph, Husishusis Kute, and Hahtalekin would ride out to await the troops and their terms. White Bird, with his men and those of the Palouse, Hahtalekin, would position themselves, when the signal came, on the slope of the east hill. Ollokot with the Wallowans and the men of Toohoolhoolzote would wait out of sight on the west hill. Seeyakoon Ilppilp, Red Spy, the nephew of both Looking Glass and Toohoolhoolzote, was the man chosen to stand watch above the trail, to signal the warriors into position simply by turning his horse from the north and the direction of the troops to a position which faced us when, in his judgement, our chances were best for moving without detection.

Until the signal came there was only to wait, restlessly, knowing the weakness of our plan was that the women and children had to remain in the village, with the lodges standing and no visible sign of preparation for flight

The Story Teller continues.

In the assembly gathered before Ollokot to welcome the Asotins, Zya Temoni, No Heart, an old man with irregular habits rose from his seat near the front and shuffled off in the increasing darkness to relieve himself, thus breaking momentarily the general hush of the nearly three hundred who had gathered to hear the story of Whitebird Canyon, to participate in the welcome of the Asotins and Looking Glass.

Ollokot stands in silence as the men shift, passing the tobacco pouches and making themselves more comfortable as they wait to be reassured by the story of this battle. Ollokot waits, his thoughts on the time and emotions left private to a man, the moments and hours when he sits in the shelter of his own lodge and family and waits the false dawn, the signal that he must go out to lead the warriors of the Nez Perce against the white troops.

Ollokot speaks, more reflective, the listeners attentive.

"It was still dark when Joseph spoke my name that morning at Whitebird Canyon.

"Ollokot rose, grabbing boots and top shirt. Outside, Joseph stood, his back to the lodge, watching the quiet preparations of the warriors. 'Wahlitits, Sarpis Illpilp, and Wetyetmas Wyakaikt are in our camp. Take care, my brother.' With these words he moved away and I started toward the horse herd, feeling once again the tension and anxiety that sleep had momentarily resolved.

"The horses were caught, each man selecting his best and hobbling before his lodge two others so that his woman, or son if he had one old enough to manage them, could bring them up to him later should he need a fresh one. No man touched food, for all here have seen the corruption food adds to a gut wound. Instead, the warriors rode out individually or in small groups when their horses and weapons were ready. There was still dark on this moonless early morning, but there was no reason for a man to wait in camp until the camp itself and the children were awake.

"To my own lodge Ollokot returned, leading my horses. There, without ease, they were given over to my woman, already heavy with our child. Quickly mounted, I fought the horse, the roan you know which is Ollokot's favorite, and, temporarily calming him, took up the weapons she passed to me. There are no words for neither of us spoke. The horse reared again and I let him go but turned him toward the east and the gathering warriors. He moved abruptly and stiffly, muscle against muscle, tearing the rocky ground as he jumped and landed. Beyond my lodge I saw Joseph standing, holding the bridle of his horse, the grey one, the speckled one, the pride of our herd, controlling the horse which danced from side to side behind him, watching, though his features were still indistinct in the coming light, my preparation for battle.

"And then it was as if we were boys again in the Wallowa. The shouts, the images were there when we raced the horses on the plain of the valley floor, when we fought together with the intensity of youth our cousin, Black Feather, already a warrior, twice our size and three times our strength, fought him for his slight to Joseph. At the same time we were two old men whose lives and emotions had been long and joyous if troubled. In this moment the great joy and the great burden that was our heritage from Tuekakas passed as well to Ollokot as I understand for the first time the weight Joseph carried from that moment when, near death, Tuekakas turned to the two sons he had always treated as equals and said the words, very near his last, 'protect this land and protect these people as I have tried to do for my father and the generations of Nez Perce who have lived in this valley since man walked upon the earth.' And as I looked to Joseph that dawn in Whitebird Canyon, with the ache of blood for blood, I made the pledge that my young friend Yellow Wolf overheard and spread quietly among our men and even now, there, across the campfire shouts out for me to acknowledge: *this I pledged to Joseph before me, to the wife and sleeping children then before me, to the Nez Perce now before me, 'as long as Ollokot lives no soldier will walk among the lodges of the Nimpau.'*

Suddenly Ollokot's face was wet before the council of the Nez Perce. Those who might have seen, did not, for they chose to study the fire before them, each man inseparably a part of the story and words he heard, each man completely isolated by the resolution he must find to the dilemma which the battle at Whitebird Canyon permanently imposed upon our people. Without embarrassment Ollokot stands before the council of the Nez Perce to speak again the events of battle.

"They rode to their deaths. The soldiers who came with Perry against the camp of the Nez Perce rode to their deaths. The councils and the treaties are over. The elders, our headmen, Toohoolhoolzote, White Bird, Hinmahtooyahlatkekht, and Husishusis Kute have sat in anguish. We have all sat in anguish. We have all sought to survive with the white. The councils have failed. The ambiguities and complexities which consume my brother, Hin-mah-too-yah-lat-kekht, fade and resolve for Ollokot who need be only a warrior.

The Story Teller continues.

In the morning's darkness and chill the Nimpau gather. In the ravine at the head of the canyon where the old trail from the north reaches down from the plateau above to the nearly level, if narrow, arm of Whitebird Creek two miles from its junction with the great Salmon, Ollokot sits mounted with the warriors of the Nez Perce and awaits Joseph and the headmen.

Milling, speaking in hushed tones about the camp are the young men of Toohoolhoolzote who will follow Ollokot into battle. Here are the original fighters, Wahlitits, Shore Crossing,

Sarpis Illpilp, Red Moccasin Tops, and, Wetyetmas Wayakaikt, Swan Necklace. Some here would question the temper of Sarpis Ilpilp who is known for his hostile and angry moods, or the age of Swan Necklace who is only turned seventeen, but no one can question the courage of these who will be our principal warriors in the years to come. With Ollokot as well are the best of our Wallowans: Tipyahlanah Kapskaps, Strong Eagle—who fought with the whites against the Yakima receiving the great cut which now disfigures his ear and cheek; Yellow Wolf—the young nephew of Joseph, respected for his seriousness, who will become, many think, a wise headman; Laphpeealoot, Geese Lighting Three Times On Water—courageous and loyal, the opposite of his father who now sits in Lawyer's council at Lapwai; and Otstatpoos, Firebody—the young Dreamer whose visions are known throughout the land of the Nimpau.

With White Bird stand calmly Haltaletin and the Palouse who came to show their courage by tying their horses and sitting in quiet conversation. With White Bird as well is Koolkool Snehee, Red Owl—whom the women consider the most handsome warrior among us; Two Moons, plain, unpretentious, a strong fighter; Seeyakoon Illpilp, Red Spy—respected for his great accuracy with the rifle; and Chuslum Moxmox, Yellow Buffalo Bull—the father of the raider Sarpis Illpilp, experienced in the plains battles with the Blackfoot.

Many more stood bravely in Whitebird Canyon that day when the soldiers of Howard came to attack our village. The deeds of our kinsmen are remembered.

The sun stood more than two hours above the horizon the day of battle before we saw in the great distance of the clear morning air the first movement of the cavalry of Howard on the high trail above us. Impatiently we waited and watched the distant outline of Red Spy who stood guard on a ridge above and apart from the trail itself. For hours we waited seeing only occasionally the troops as they wound down into the valley. Here for the first time the young men were restless and would not stand in place. The constant march of the armed troops moving ever nearer on the trail above was too much. Angrily, Sarpis Illpilp called out for men who would follow him to attack before the troops reached the valley floor and the camp of the Nez Perce. Disregarding the plans of council, Swan Necklace turned his horse and galloped back along the banks of the creek to the camp where he gathered up a dozen fire red, new blankets taken in the recent raid and passed them out to his friends to wear as a taunt as the young men rushed the troops.

Joseph moves between the young warriors and the troops—still out of sight on the trail above. Calling to his side from the village Toohoolhoolzote, and, from the warriors, Ollokot, Joseph entreats the anxious young men.

"Will you charge the troops now and ruin our chance for either peace, or, if we must fight, victory? Will you stand apart from

Toohoolhoolzote who is our wisdom and Ollokot who is our strength?"

"Will you," Joseph asked, turning his horse now to face squarely Wahlitits, "will you now, after avenging finally your father, attack the troops of the whites and bring more danger to your people?"

Wahlitits, his eyes upon the ground turned, finally, his horse back to the thicket where our men waited. Here he dismounted and, picking up his weapons, walked forward where he could see the signal of Red Spy. As Sarpis Illpilp remained defiant, facing Joseph and watching Wahlitits, the cry of White Bird came. On the ridge, far above, the solitary horseman had swung himself to the south to face, motionless and soundless, our camp.

As the soldiers rode down into a series of gullies that dropped their elevation and obscured their vision, the warriors of our people ran, sprinted silently to our positions on the treeless hills. Here, crouched or prone, covered with the maddening tickle grass, in the shadeless, scorching heat of mid-day, the young men waited.

The irritating discomforts emphasized and exaggerated the passiveness of our position. Here the warriors crouched, apart from their horses, apart from their lodges, and apart from the headsmen, awaiting two full troops of trained cavalry which might at any time alter its march, choose a side trail, and by-pass us by hundreds of yards and leave us crouched uselessly in the sun and heat guarding an empty pass.

But the troops did come. Their coming was welcome. Their countenance and speed displaced at once the trivial concerns of waiting. Two by two at a forced trot the lathered horses and sweating men poured through the funnel-like slope from the trail above us to the relatively level, narrow bottom-land of our ravine. The funneling effect of the trail, first restricting, then freeing their descent, seemed to pour them upon us, horses spilling into sight and onto the haunches of those ahead of them before the riders could—or chose—to react.

Instantly Ollokot saw a new flaw of our plan. The first lines of troops drew to a halt as they achieved an unobstructed view and saw ahead Joseph and his small party who waited to speak of peace several hundred yards ahead on the banks of Whitebird Creek. If the troops did not come further and fall into the crevice between the warriors' positions, not only might they escape the defense we had set up, but, with only a little imagination and leadership might turn, and, racing around the base of our hills, flank our position and put themselves between both our village and our horses.

Speaking quietly, moving feet first, then back and haunches, carefully angling, sliding down the slope of the incline, Ollokot moved to where Wahlitits, Sarpis Illpilp, and Swan Necklace had positioned themselves. Leaving Yellow Wolf and the more seasoned men to hold position, Ollokot took the young warriors with him down the slope to more level ground there to race toward the creek and the horses. Their speed—young Swan Necklace, who each day grows stronger, leading the way nearly matching, stride for stride, Ollokot—brought them quickly to the unprotected area where the hill breaks away, would expose the young warriors to the upper canyon and the troops. Here, there was no choice. Weapons were dropped and the young men began to walk across the open area calmly as if in amiable discussion—trusting that four men, unarmed and on foot moving to Joseph casually, would not alarm over a hundred armed troops.

The movement to Joseph was successful. As the four walked in first view of the troops Ollokot thought to make a joke to create the impression of conversation, and so chided Swan Necklace, a likable if impetuous young man, for his speed—asking if all Whitebird Nez Perce could run in the opposite direction from the enemy as fast as he. Swan Necklace who has, even in youth, poise beyond most of us, turned the joke on Ollokot, saying that, next to the Wallowans, the White Birds were the fastest of all people. In the tension all felt in Whitebird Canyon, the joke was sufficient to send the rest of the small party into laughter which coupled with the exhaustion of the half-mile sprint generated the appearance of idle loafers.

As the warriors moved toward Joseph, whose distress was obvious and increasing, a small group under Perry began to move up the draw toward the Indians visible to them. Joseph responding to Ollokot's Wallowan idiom moved ahead, coming between the warriors and the troops, motioning and shouting them away to the rear as though he would not have idlers standing about as he spoke with the soldiers. Fortunately the failing senses of old Tipyahlanah Oikelaziken, called James Rueben by the whites with whom he rode, prevented him from either detecting our identities or guessing our motives.

The warriors with Ollokot turned away to the stream bank where the horses were hidden. From the older boys who guarded the horses, eight were chosen to join the warriors with Ollokot. To each was given one of the new red trade blankets Swan Necklace had brought from the camp so that they might make a loose, poncho covering that would partially conceal their size and youth. Each warrior also took a blanket. Before there was time to mount, a single shot ricocheted into the rocks to the right of the group. Chapman, a loud talking rancher, whose job was to help guide the troops, fired.

"Mount." The single word from Ollokot was punctuated with a responding shot from the area where Joseph awaited Perry.

More shots came quickly now. In a time-frozen moment of absolute clarity, Joseph and those who have waited with him see the war horse of Ollokot explode from the cover of the creek bank. Behind Ollokot, at full gallop, emerge the young warriors and the herd boys—all cloaked with the bright red trade blankets—who stream at top speed past Joseph and down the canyon floor against the troop of Perry.

Listen with Story Teller to Ollokot.

"My horse reached his great top speed quickly and cut away the distance which separated us from the soldiers. As we closed, we wove abruptly to the right and then the left—giving more credit to the foolish and inaccurate fire of the white troops than necessary. At two hundred yards I began to bring down my horse. At one hundred yards I had him fully restrained, and at seventy yards I cut him sharply to the left, turning, firing as I did so the rusty trade rifle I took from one of the boys who stood guard with the horses. Behind Ollokot, simultaneously, Wahlitits and Sarpis Illpilp, almost stopping as they did so, arched arrows toward the troops. Close behind them was Swan Necklace and the boys with their slower horses. Hesitating a moment by holding my horse tight to his turn to complete a full circle so that I might be sure the boys would break off to follow me, I turned loose again my spirited horse to stream back down the canyon floor between the hills which hid our warriors. As I rode, I called out, screamed repeatedly I am told, 'no fire, no fire' in Wallowan dialect, so that only later did those with Perry who spoke our language realize I was pleading with our warriors on the hills instead of chanting a mystic song of self-preservation.

"Our men did hold their fire. From childhood we are taught neither arrow nor bullet will strike unless carefully aimed. And it was our good fortune to face that day in Whitebird Canyon troops who, in an ironic reversal of roles, seemed to think that it was the very noise and fire and smoke which protected them and brought damage to the other side. So no Nez Perce fired while we came down the canyon to the startled Perry and then turned and fled, already setting into motion the body of troops behind Perry and the small party he had detached to approach Joseph.

"They rode to their deaths. Neither compassion nor pity nor human sympathy touched the Nez Perce warriors in Whitebird Canyon. We were men of peace, strong warriors who chose friendship and allowed the white into our land. But each white man turned into ten and then twenty and now a hundred. The white no longer hid his greed but moved without regard farther into our land, taking the winter campsites and filling the summer pastures with his cattle. To us he came year after year with his papers and demands. To the Wallowa the white came first as welcomed guests and then as intruders and fugitives who moved in the dark and lurked along the outer boundaries avoiding the warriors. Past the great stone piles, artificial and meaningless signs of "possession," Tuekakas had erected to dissuade them, the whites pressed into the Wallowa where since time began the Nez Perce had walked alone with the spirits who made us, land made sacred by the life-joy and agony and bones of our fathers.

"And so now the troops came: Perry and Trimble and Shearer and those under them who rode to capture, to chastise, to punish a foolish chief and a silly group of warriors who thought to pretend they could fight—could stand against the discipline of trained troops, could stand against the ordered fire of the Sharps carbine, could stand against the weight and speed and bottom of grain-fed, steel-shod horses.

"They rode to their deaths.

"For a warrior's life is simple. The ambiguity created by the white's spirit god is no more. The councils for peace where we receive only anguish and insult are over. The beautiful cadence of Joseph's language no more tangles a man's heart and holds him to his tepee and family. The whites are too many. Their guns are too many. And above all else there is their army, men who live alone without women, who ride in long columns, whose sole reason in living is to fight and kill. But the fighting has come and a warrior may at least fight and in the sweat and dust and hot sun devote his entire being to destroying any who come against him.

"Down the narrow canyon the soldiers rode. Closer and closer they came at a weary trot until we could see the fatigue in their faces and smell the lathered horses they rode. We fired the first shots from concealment. Almost casually the aimed shots came from White Bird's hill. With a sort of dull astonishment some of the lead horses went down and two of the soldiers did not get up. The fallen and stumbling horses now blocked the narrow trail and, from the hill on our left, Yellow Wolf and our Wallowans began their fire.

"In the dust and confusion of screaming horses and shouting men it is difficult to relate exactly what happened in the moments which followed. Having now regained the weapons we threw down to cross the open canyon floor and reach the horses, the "Red Blankets" with Ollokot took what scant cover we could find at the end of the two hills which formed the sides of our trap. Before us the troops began to dismount to form a line. The settlers with them frantically turned their horses to gallop as best they could through the milling cavalry horses back up the canyon floor in the direction they had come. One settler, plainly visible before us, went down with his horse but managed to hold onto the mane after the girth broke and the saddle came off. Grimly, the settler clung to the mane as his horse clambered up and now, headed somehow toward the rear, galloped in fear and panic with the horses running ahead of him, interrupting his weary pace only to shy, kicking out sideways at the man he dragged with him for almost a hundred yards before the man fell motionless from his side.

"To our left, one of the officers started his men up the hill the Wallowans held. Later we were to count eighteen soldiers who fell on the slope of the hill as they exposed themselves both to the fire from above them and to sheltered men of White Bird on the ridge which faced them.

"Soon the soldiers began trying to withdraw. As they attempted to control their retreat, we started our move up the canyon floor from one horse carcass to the next over the otherwise shelterless ground. Behind me Wahlitits, Sarpis Illpilp, and Swan Necklace came. Taking up the soldier's own strong rifles, we now held the advantage. Toward the rear one squad of soldiers mounted to flee. From the ridge top above us, Two Moons and a dozen warriors, now mounted on the horses the boys and women had brought them, drove down the steep slope of the hill they held into the flank of the troops which fled. Tired horses and panicked troopers went down in the increasing dust of Whitebird Canyon.

"Unit by unit those soldiers who would fight were driven back by our and their own abandoned rifles. Soon the soldiers fired only to protect their flight which we harassed now from horseback. Finally, at the place where the trail into the canyon makes its first cut against the plateau walls to begin the winding ascent out of Whitebird, the soldiers drew themselves together in desperation. Here Ollokot called back the warriors, so causing the frowns some before me still hold.

"Ollokot called back the warriors and let the survivors of Howard's cavalry escape. Ollokot did so before any of the young warriors sought to test their courage by charging an entrenched and desperate foe. He did so while we had but two wounded and none killed, while our greatest injury was the brave Two Moons who lost his horse in the charge against the mounted troops and fell, bruising and cutting his side on a rock. Ollokot called back the warriors though White Bird and Husishusis Kute would chide me now for doing so. And it was right, for we took all of our men from Whitebird Canyon; we took our families and all our possessions and we took the supplies of the troops. We took sixty-three rifles, over a dozen pistols, bayonets, hatchets, and two mules loaded with ammunition. We beat the troops, we drove them back, and we have brought Looking Glass and the Asotins into our camp."

The moon stood well above the hills when Ollokot finished his account of the battle at Whitebird Canyon.

For some time after Ollokot finished speaking there was no sound anywhere—a hush, a mood, created in reverence for those who fought, a quiet, permeating the people assembled who could but anticipate the consequences.

The silence slowly became awkward. Looking Glass rose to compliment the warriors who fought at Whitebird Canyon and to explain that the Asotins came late to the free camp because the lies of the whites had ensnarled them and because he, Looking Glass, did not want to frighten the whites by camping with the Nimpau who had struck back at the whites.

As polite phrases of welcome arose, Looking Glass stood proudly, looking over those who sat around the council fire before him. Occasionally he nodded, bending slightly his proud carriage, acknowledging a compliment... flashing as he did so in the glimmering light of the fire, reflections of light from the small trade-mirror he wore on a leather thong around his neck.

Story Teller: Victory and Flight.

From Whitebird Canyon we flee, expecting reprisal, imagining safety. Skirmishes with local militia distract our scouts.

Then, from the banks above the Clear Water camp, Howard is upon us and we fight for our existence.

When the last man has perished
And the memory of my people shall
Have become myth,
These lands will swarm with the
Invisible dead of my people.

When your children's children think
Themselves alone,
In the field, the store, the shop,
Upon the highway,
Or in the silence of the woods,
They will not be alone.

When the streets of your villages and
Cities are silent and
You think them deserted,
They will throng with the returning
Hosts that once filled them,
Spirits who love this beautiful land.

The white man will never be alone.

Seattle, our brother

VI. The Bear Paws
October 4, 1877

The rain, having fallen through the night and into morning of this second day in the camp of Miles, turns now with the dropping temperature to snow and sleet. Once again the men who stand with me as guards have returned me to the picket line for the camp horses and mules. Before, the act seemed random; now it is understandable, for the supply people—some of them still arriving—have stopped the grain wagons near the horses and have stretched great canvases to protect both feed and workers.

Joseph sits now upon the heaped sacks of grain, under the great flapping canvas, drier and warmer than I have been in days, and stare across the whitening plain to the abrupt terrain of the Bear Paws. Yet, while my eyes would examine the pure, white peaks of the Bear Paws, my thoughts come involuntarily to the dimly visible ravines at their base and the camp of the Nez Perce. As I sit staring into the encompassing wall of sleet and snow now grown impenetrable, severing, and detaching me from the camp of my people, the words and gestures of Miles shadow my consciousness.

Strength, deceit, and cunning form the character of Miles. Adopting a stance of compassion, he listens to my story and hears my wish to return to the Wallowa. With lowered, serious voice he speaks his support for our position. With boldness he demands our surrender. In quieter tones he injects the names of Howard and

Sturgis and calculates their rage and animosity after four months of pursuit and frustration. In confidentiality he speaks of the Sioux, moving from behind his desk, stepping closer in his new and unblemished uniform, speaking slowly, addressing me: "Hin-mah-too-yah-lat-kekht, chief of the Nez Perce," pronouncing with care and surprising accuracy the syllables of my name. "The Sioux, Joseph, are not allies of the Nez Perce and never have been. Crazy Horse himself offered to lead his Oglala warriors out of Fort Keogh against the Nez Perce. Crazy Horse pledged to me that the Oglala would fight until no Nez Perce was left alive. Neither will Sitting Bull risk his sanctuary and harmony with the foolish, misguided Canadian officials to help Joseph and a handful of Nez Perce—especially when among the Nez Perce is the man called Looking Glass, a man I understand to owe a part of his influence to his success in killing Sioux."

I had stood mute, emotionless then and stared into the eyes of Miles. Now, equally passive, equally emotionless, I must sit between armed guards and survey the obscured ravines at the base of the Bear Paws, knowing that there the children and the Wallowans left to me crouch upon the wet and freezing ground, unprotected from the rain and sleet, knowing that here at last the Nez Perce are surrounded, that the warriors are dead, and that at any moment the soldiers may be ordered from their tents and hot food to charge into the wretched and almost defenseless camp.

With time-smoothed abruptness, the spirited horse of Joseph explodes, strains against the distance to the turbulent Whitebird canyon camp of the Nez Perce. Momentarily there is only strain and wind and space, and speed-distorted sound as with violence Perry and the cavalry of Howard fall upon the warriors of White Bird and Ollokot. The grey mist of fear and detachment permeates my being.

It is the camp itself which must be saved. Joseph has sought peace, has stood behind Tuekakas and heard the white man's terms, has later buried the father, creating himself, stone by stone, the memorial grave on the knoll overlooking the pristine Wallowa Lake—since time began the sacred burial ground of the Nimpau. Joseph has stood alone and has heard the terms and has refused to sign the scraps of paper, has refused to touch the pen the whites believe transforms the bounds of the earth. Joseph has stood and heard the anger of the white agents and generals and known the futility of peace and war. Finally, with frustration and moot rage Hinmahtooyahlatkekth, called Joseph by the whites who must alter the surface of all they touch, has stood silent as a stone for there was nothing more to be said.

Perhaps in the end only the warriors speak for a people's struggle and dignity—the warriors and perhaps the Story Tellers, for when the shouting and crying and agony of Whitebird Canyon was over it was Toohoolhoolzote, the Dreamer, who stood in wild-eyed reverence upon the battlefield and spoke his dirge, singing to the spirit of our ancestors: "TASTE THIS BLOOD; FEEL THIS FLESH, FLESH UPON YOUR FLESH; RISE UP WARRIORS AND CHIEFS OF THE NIMPAU; JOIN US AS WE DRIVE FROM OUR HOMELAND THOSE WHO WOULD DIVIDE AND DESECRATE THE EARTH ITSELF."

Later, when the winds of emotion had their course, Toohoolhoolzote made the argument we had heard before, the argument that none could counter, but that few wished to execute. Toohoolhoolzote urged us once again to withdraw with him to the canyons of the Snake and Imnaha where desolation and deprivation would return to our people the virtues of time, and the corruption of the whites would be drained from our bodies and spirits:

Return, my people, return to the wild and desolate lands which have nurtured and formed our spirits in times of trial and maturation since the Nez Perce were first set down upon this earth. Come with Toohoolhoolzote to the land of my heart and there learn with me again the strengths and virtues of our people. Wait with me there for any man the white may send against us; let the white seek us in the canyons of the Snake: let him seek us there and die there, let us gird our souls and cordon our boundaries so that when our fathers who walked with the gods upon this land choose to return they will find the spirit and the heart of the Nez Perce.

Yet it was to be, in the irony that Fate and Circumstance create for man, neither Toohoolhoolzote nor Joseph that the Nez Perce followed from the field at Whitebird Canyon, for two days after the battle, Looking Glass came into our camp and the war-famed name alone was enough to persuade our people to follow.

Looking Glass turned our direction from the northward march in which we intended to recross the Snake, fortify our position and wait in the Wallowa—falling back to the Imnaha and Snake if we must. He turned us to the east and the center of our tribal gathering places. He urged that here we camp and show the strength that had begun to flow to us after the success of the Whitebird Canyon victory. And so, under Looking Glass, the Nez Perce moved to a pleasant summer camp on the Clearwater.

We moved to disaster. For it was in the pleasant summer camp upon the Clearwater, where our people visited and worked and celebrated as in the great tribal gatherings in the past, that Howard blundered, fell almost accidentally against the Nez Perce.

There is no sound on this earth like the stomach-sickening whine of the cannon ball as it arches above, falls down into a village of matchstick tepees and frailer bodies. For seconds which seem like eternity the whine has no dimension of direction or distance. The sound of the first ball hangs with incredible tenacity over a world apprehending only the time-suspended whine, anticipating in all life only completion, unity, the collision and the explosion. And then, when the first ball spends its energy, disrupting, destroying, it is as if a man can do nothing, must do nothing, but crouch in stillness in a noonday dimension gone dark and wait passively, almost as supplicant to the next whistling ball, tuning his spirit, not to the source of the ball or those who fire it, but to the ball itself—as though the ball which is life or death has discretion and character: benevolent, benign, malevolent—as if the ball itself assumes the role of deity and a man must supplicate, placate its wrath and direction, urging, turning, persuading it away from his being, away from his people.

In a time frame gone nearly blank now in the exhaustion of the Bear Paws, there is only the memory of the whine of the cannon accentuated by the cries of the women whose voices rise involuntarily, gradually, to a wailing harmony with the death hymn above us. There are only the wails of the women, and then instantaneously, the guttural chant-scream of Toohoolhoolzote whose walleyed horse leaps and slides in violent surges through the village—its right flank, hacked, gashed, covered blood-red as the old man, steel war hatchet aloft in defiance, slashing downward in desperation, screams, chants, NIMPAU, NIMPAU, NIMPAU, NIMPAU—my people, my people, my people. Then in time without sequence, the beast-strong horse, restrained, wrenched back with violence momentarily from frantic top speed, is turned loose and horse and frail old man plunge into and across the shallow Clearwater, mount, with a great straining, blowing audible even against the wail of the howitzer, with astonishing and desperate speed the hillside plateau opposite our camp, to charge the cannon and oblivion.

On the plateau ridge above our camp the warriors who streamed after Toohoolhoolzote—Ollokot, Rainbow, Five Wounds, and, a little later Looking Glass and most of our able-bodied men, fought the troops of Howard, held his charge, stopped his cannon. Two hundred Nez Perce flung themselves against the six hundred of Howard and for thirty hours held the line while below we prepared to abandon the camp, to flee, taking away the women, the children, the old, and the wounded, to seek a greater and more permanent safety.

The nature and direction of that safety was disputed. In a strangely calm, desperate confrontation, Looking Glass and Joseph faced each other in the breaking camp, while above the warriors struggled, filling the valley ravine with the sporadic spurts of fire and cries of battle. Bringing with him the tacit consent of White Bird, Looking Glass directed that the Nez Perce pull back—not toward the Wallowa or the Snake-but that we begin a semi-circular cast that would take us to the Lolo Trail, the age-old torturous path which connected our homeland with the buffalo lands two hundred miles to the east. Here, Looking Glass boldly stated, the battle sounds sometimes obscuring even his vociferousness, the Nez Perce would find safety and peace. Howard, the Asotin argued, stated, arrogance and pride flashing in his eyes, would not dare follow us into the Bitterroot valleys, would not dare face us in alliance with our friends in this distance valley.

With despair I turned from Looking Glass and walked away. As I moved away toward the camp center I called to me Zya Temoni, No Heart, the aged cousin of my mother, a man known in youth for his foolish obsession for practical jokes, but a man known as well for his overwhelming loyalty to those he trusted. With difficulty we made our way through the confusion of the camp and the constant, sometimes almost hysterical pleas for information and instructions, back to my own, now dismantled, lodge. Before my lodge I paused, reaching out for the shoulder of Zya Temoni, who, respecting my privacy, had not altered his slow gait.

My hand still on the old man's shoulder, feeling there in the protruding bones and atrophied muscles a frailness beyond that I expected, I stood in silence, looking to the west and the Wallowa range. With a calmness beyond my emotions I turned full circle, drawing as I did so the old man to me, to face the unbroken rise of the Bitterroot Mountains and the Lolo Trail. Holding the old man to me by both frail shoulders, leaning slightly over to him, to create with embracement the sentiment I would not trust my eyes to convey, I spoke—the words remote, surprising as from another being—asking him to go to Howard for me, to say to Howard that Joseph would bring his own family and any who choose to come with him in peace to Lapwai in return for Howard's promise of fair treatment.

Zya Temoni, the old one, stood a full moment without a word, then bending, nodding his head once ever so slightly, he turned and moved away, his eyes on the ground before him.

There was with me then the emotion which would follow and haunt my thoughts and being even to this grassless, treeless plain of the Bear Paws: driven from our homeland the Nez Perce would be no more. From this emotion came the overwhelming agony of our journey from the Wallowa under the threat of Howard: it was as if while we moved at our plodding, encumbered pace from the green valley of the Wallowa through the desolate and beautiful Imnaha that the earth closed behind us—for we did no less than turn our backs on the land of our birth and the source of our subsistence, abandoning it for all time to those who would camp and abuse its surface in our absence. It was so even when we went to Lapwai, the land of our brothers, made the journey all had made before for the camas gatherings, the salmon runs, and the great tribal meetings—for we were driven, directed there, by Howard.

Now Looking Glass dictates that we abandon entirely the plateaus and valleys which have been our home. Looking Glass orders that we withdraw, that we move our children and women to the buffalo country to the east where no Nez Perce has been or belongs except on the temporary challenge of a hunt. It must not be done

... for a man is the land from which he comes. The trees of his home, the waters of his streams and lakes, the profile of his mountains, the grass of his meadows, the animals that walk the land with him, are the essence of his being. He can with dignity be no less than the land

he walks; he can with humility be no more. And so it is that to be driven from the land and essence of one's being, to deny and abandon the bones and spirit of one's forbears, is to negate self. To flee like the waves before the wind is to become characterless like the waves. A man may do no worse than fight, for in so doing he denies the sperm of self, the child who follows, inherits; yet, he may do no more than fight, for in so doing he affirms the spirit of self: he affirms and acknowledges the fabric of the earth of which he is the sun's corpulent reflection.

Yet, even then long ago on the banks of the Clearwater as Joseph sought to evade the decision of Looking Glass and White Bird, even as Joseph's messenger sought Howard, the warriors, slipped away from Ollokot, White Bird, Looking Glass, and the old Dreamer and came to the camp to join the flight to the Lolo.

Story Teller: My People

The stories of the past tell the life of a people. More than one family, more than blood-linked family groups, more than the groups of a region. The stories of the past tell the birth, the strength, and the success or the decline of a people who choose to associate with one another.

In these stories lie exposed the heart of a people and the heroism which sustains them. These stories preserve for all time the beauty of a people and the plight of a people.

So it was with our people, at peace with the spirits of the earth. Then come the preachers with word of disquiet and descriptions of the burning fires of hell. Then upon us are unleashed the diseases: diseases of bottle, diseases of blankets, diseases of water.

Entire villages, entire tribes are lost.

Finally we face the weapons of steel. Not a hunting knife, not a hand-loaded musket for hunting, but the roar and thunder of the cannon, and the fire-spitting gatling gun against which nothing of this world can stand.

Against the canon and the gatling gun the Nimpau raise the beautiful bow of our ancestors: laminated strands of horn from the high country sheep of our land, laminated together, held with glue processed from the horn and hoof itself. Bound with sinew from the gut itself.

Magnificent bows that can drive an arrow completely through an elk or a buffalo. Incredible bows, coveted by all who encounter them.

Solitary bows the warriors raise against the cannon and the gatling gun, to defend the women, the children, and the old of our village.

One man, one arrow at a time we confront the gatling gun. This, and the random rifles we find when the white soldiers throw them down and run is all we have to confront Howard and his force of 600 fighting men, soldiers who seek us out, seize the high ground and pour fire into our peaceful village on the Clearwater River.

Yet there is hope.

To the threatened camp of the Nimpau upon the Clearwater have come the great warriors Wahchumysus, called Rainbow, and Pahkatos Owyeen, called Five Wounds. On the plateau above the Clearwater, Ollokot, Rainbow, and Five Wounds lead the warriors of the Nez Perce against the six hundred of Howard. For over thirty-six hours, as the Nez Perce fight from a fixed position longer than any Native American resistance in history. Howard is forced to halt and entrench. Below the families flee, the last protected only by desperate hand-to hand fighting by the warriors on the plateau above.

VII. The Clearwater River
July 12, 1877

Story Teller is of time past, time present, and time future. Story Teller is with Joseph and Ollokot, with the headsmen, the warriors and the families of the Nimpau. For those who listen he recounts again the strength and heroism of the warriors who fought and defeated the troops of Howard. From those who listen now will come the Tellers who will preserve the story for time future, will preserve the truth for those who wait.

There came to be a time on the plateau above our Clearwater River camp when the defense of our village was almost easy. For twenty hours the warriors had stood. The frenzy and apprehension and fear were over. The sickening whine of the howitzers had stopped. The sun burned in full heat upon our backs, blinded and rendered ineffective the six hundred men of Howard who held their positions and waited the order which would send another orderly, determined attack against the position we held.

As we stood and held the ridge for the second day against Howard, pride and man's love grew in the privacy of our hearts. The Nez Perce stood defensively for the first time, held away from the bowels of our village the armed troops of Howard. We rode in haste and fear up the great hill after Toohoolhoolzote, and saw the old Dreamer's solitary charge of Howard's astonished men. We watched in awe and heart-swelling pride where courage squeezes out and purges fear while Toohoolhoolzote charged straight into the lines of troops, scattered from the cannon itself the very men who serviced it. We watched with heartache as the old man circled the cannon before turning to drive his floundering, blowing horse back to us—while the troops, who could not stand against him, responded finally to their red-faced officers and opened a systematic and deadly fire upon his exposed back. With rage we responded, covering as best we could the old man's retreat only to see man and horse go down eighty yards from cover. Amazingly, almost as if the bullets of the whites could not harm him in body or spirit, the old man rolled from his horse and got up to trot toward safety in the stiff-legged gait of age. As the old war-chief came determinedly to us, he banished still the blood-covered hatchet, his only weapon. As he came his eyes were steadily on us, oblivious to his rear—as though he would deny with his lack of recognition the force and power there. Toohoolhoolzote was still sixty yards away when Five Wounds reached him, pulled him up onto the haunches of his spinning horse, and brought Toohoolhoolzote to the safety of the rocks which guarded the rim of the plateau.

With courage instilled by the old man, we positioned ourselves on the verge of the plateau which overlooked the narrow Clearwater Valley to turn back Howard, to bend our bodies and spirits to the hard, clean task of courage at the moment in time when a man has no choice, where a Nez Perce warrior stands between his family, his people and any who would do them harm, simply because this is what a man would do, is privileged to do.

The Nez Perce stood that day against Howard. We stood in strength.

Into the Clearwater River camp of Joseph and White Bird had come Looking Glass and the strength of his village which added a third to our warriors. More important to the spirit and effectiveness of our camp than the name and the numbers Looking Glass brought to us was the arrival, ten days after the battle in Whitebird Canyon, of the great eastern warriors Wahchumyus, called Rainbow, and Pahkatos Owyeen, called Five Wounds.

Side by side they rode into our camp at Horseshoe Bends. Even as they rode a part of the uniqueness of their character and reputation was manifest. Through the river crossing and up to the camp Rainbow and Five Wounds rode, trailing behind them their followers, a half dozen men, a dozen women and a few small children. All were young; all were strong. Into the camp they came, Rainbow a little ahead now, silent, erect upon his fine grey horse which carried in paint upon his shoulder the mark of Rainbow, the three parallel bars, two black slashes enclosing a white slash. Rainbow said not a word. Toward him pressed the boys of the camp, too shy to approach directly, but too curious not to follow the movement of this awesome warrior whose strength and fierceness was known even beyond our country. Among the adults it was not so much the horse and its identifying marks which created the murmur of recognition and acceptance as it was the head and hair of Rainbow where many recognized the birthmark they had heard described, the strange patch of white hair, the streak that started near the temple on the right side of his head and extended diagonally downward past his right ear to mingle with and streak the braid he wore. As the boys pressed forward in awe and curiosity, the adults stepped back a step or so to give horse and man more room.

Behind Rainbow, moving at a more inconstant pace came Five Wounds, a darker, more outgoing man whose progress was slowed as he called out greetings to men he knew or paused to compliment and embarrass individuals within the small group of older girls who worked and gossiped together. As he reached the place where Ollokot stood near the camp's center, Five Wounds called out Ollokot's name in his enthusiastic way and came over to lean down and snatch away the child, Nehemini, daughter, who clung to Ollokot's leg. Five Wounds raised, with his great strength, the child vertically, turning her, startled, to seat her in front of him on the horse, teasing before she could cry out, "Help Pahkatos Owyeen ride this horse, little daughter. And when we are good enough we will go with your Daddy to fight white men."

And so without notice or fanfare our camp received the two greatest warriors of our time, men who would alter the very nature of our spirit. From their carefree lives on the buffalo plains Rainbow and Five Wounds had returned to our highland plateaus. They were astonishing men already warriors of great renown. Rainbow, the silent one, opened, it is said, his heart to no man. The very origin and past of Rainbow belied the mystery he neither sought nor resolved. Rainbow came from the far eastern segments of our lands, from one of the small bands who had come to make their home more or less permanently with the Flatheads and Crows on the plains across the Bitterroots.

Rainbow came to us, into our awareness at least, as a man nearly grown. His people ventured too far to the east one dry summer in search of game. The Blackfoot came west to hunt and raid and Rainbow's small band of Nez Perce and Flatheads simply disappeared.

Six months later Rainbow, a young man then at fourteen, was found, gaunt and exhausted in some bushes which overlooked a large Nez Perce camp in the Bitterroot Valley. He had come over two hundred miles alone, on foot, through country incontestably held by marauding Blackfoot parties. Rainbow survived, and, as the years passed, time and nature added to the already unique physique, to mold, finally, a form that even a carver with the truest eye, the finest grain and infinite skill could not surpass. Only a slightly hawkish, over-sized nose and the patch of colorless hair marred, outwardly,

Rainbow who had come to stand a little over six feet and possessed strength and speed beyond anything within the memory of our people.

With Rainbow came the story of a vision, a voice from within a dryland rainbow. This vision, the people whispered, spoke, saying that as the sun shone upon him, Rainbow could not be harmed by any man.

The flaw, we would learn in time was within. Twice in the first ten years after he alone escaped, the Blackfoot came west in raids. Twice Rainbow went berserk.

The first time no one, in the beginning, noticed Rainbow's conduct. The attack was heavy and there was danger of being overwhelmed. The Nez Perce and Flatheads fought for their lives with desperate intensity. Only at the end of the first attack was the countenance of Rainbow, who ignored the water and buffalo jerky the women brought up, noticed. Quickly he moved among the bodies to pick up those arrows and weapons of use to him when the Blackfoot came again. Once, as he passed, a Blackfoot warrior moved slightly—or those who watched assumed the man moved—for Rainbow spun and seized a huge rock beside the fallen man and, lifting the rock high over his head, brought it down, smashing the skull and face of the wounded man on the ground before him.

In the second part of that same raid the Blackfoot came in fewer numbers and with less conviction. Rainbow stood, exposed, as though he invited them to make him a target, taunted the young Blackfoot warriors to him, those who would count coup on a Nez Perce warrior. The Blackfoot surged to him and Rainbow slaughtered them. One he managed to pull from his horse as he passed. With a single sweep of his knife, aided by the leverage of the fall, Rainbow disemboweled the Blackfoot, ripping upward with the honed blade as the man fell until the rib cage stopped the deadly arch, turned upward and inward the blade into the chest cavity. Even before the death agony had ceased, Rainbow had pulled away to confront another man.

An older warrior, reigning his horse over and beside Rainbow so that he might come down on him from above, fell short—or Rainbow leaped aside—in the dust and confusion it was difficult to tell for Rainbow had always a speed and dexterity that made those who opposed him even in a trivial game seem clumsy and slow. Whatever the cause, both man and horse went down and Rainbow, without a lost motion and in seeming leisure and ease smashed the man's head with his own war club.

Other Nez Perce, spurred by Rainbow's courage and success, came out to join him and the Blackfoot who survived withdrew to speak in their camps the stories that would become the legend of Rainbow, the Nez Perce.

Rainbow's fury continued even after the surviving warriors withdrew. He walked the field with his war club to seek those who might remain alive. One warrior, a headman or chief from his dress, Rainbow stood over even after he was dead, smashing the testicles with heavy, deliberate kicks. Other Nez Perce and Flatheads stood silent in wonder and did not approach him.

The next day Rainbow appeared normal except that he said nothing of the battle and walked away from those who spoke of it.

A second encounter with the Blackfoot came later, after Rainbow and Five Wounds had come to be inseparable companions. Its events were equally grotesque. Rainbow, Five Wounds, and their followers fell by chance against a similar-sized Blackfoot hunting party. Surprised, confronted with the demonic strength of Rainbow and the controlled efforts of Five Wounds, even fierce Blackfoot warriors had little chance. Finally, the men all dead and the women and children scattered and hiding in the ravines of plateau, Five Wounds had to intercede. He stood before Rainbow with outstretched arms to block his pursuit. Rainbow stopped, stood motionless looking Five Wounds full in the face with a focus-less, wild-eyed gaze. Then he turned and walked away from the wasted camp.

The man who led Rainbow away from that senseless slaughter was, in his own way, a man fully as remarkable.

Five Wounds never knew his mother. The aged grandfather who raised him—or at least provided him shelter while the village women by turns cared for him—would not allow the mother's name mentioned. Only in time did the boy learn his mother had abandoned him, had simply put into order the sparse nursery articles she had, and, carrying her own possessions, disappeared from the village to be with the infant's father, a Spokan man from a village to the north on the Columbia River.

The old man, the grandfather of the boy to be called Pahkatos Owyeen, was a man who retained from his youth an enormous and free humorous spirit. Age and disappointment in his daughter, his only living child, little changed his easy-going countenance. In the end he was an indulgent, if never doting, parent.

Only once in his entire life, excluding the day when he discovered that his daughter had abandoned his grandchild, did the events of the world overcome his disposition. That was the day when the father of Five Wounds appeared at the grandfather's tepee to claim his son. While the child, now almost two, played in the brushed area before the lodge, the father rode into the village, sought out the home of the child he had only days before learned was his, and announced his intention to take the child away with him. The grandfather, whom his fellow tribesman had seldom seen either solemn or angry, reacted so quickly and with such uncharacteristic violence that had not two mounted hunters been passing by one of the men, probably the boy's father, would not have survived.

Owhei, for that was the grandfather's name, upon hearing the demand, without a word reached back into his tepee and drew out an old, rusty trade rifle that was probably not loaded, and doubtlessly would not have fired had it been, but served adequately as a club which sent reeling the young man with the first blow, knocked him to the ground with the second, and might easily have ended his life with the third which Owhei was already in position to deliver had not the spinning blows and final assault carried the two men past the bewildered child into the path of the hunters who intervened.

The village headman with the elders—which would have normally included Owhei—assembled and heard the case based solely on the statement of the father—for the grandfather refused to speak. Quickly, summarily, the Spokan was dismissed and ordered to leave the village. The headman added, to the obvious discomfort of Owhei, that the mother was still free to return and visit the child.

And so the child grew to young manhood in the free and easy village of his grandfather developing rapidly a physical prowess and wit that set him apart from youths years older, developing as well a fondness for adventure that would lead him restlessly over the plateaus and plains of our homeland to the inevitable confrontation and later friendship with Rainbow.

With pride for our people the Story Teller sees again the arrival these warriors, the greatest of our history.

Parallel, pace for pace—one in silence, one with jovial shouts of recognition—Rainbow and Five Wounds rode into our camp. With them came their enormous personal reputations and their small but adventuresome band of followers.

The arrival of Rainbow and Five Wounds added only eight fighting men to the Nez Perce camp at Horseshoe Bends, but their arrival brought to us an element we had not had before. The Nez Perce now had a force which could be extended outward, away from the immediate defense of our camp.

Soon after the battle in Whitebird Canyon, Rainbow, along with Five Wounds, the raider Wahlitits, the boy Wetyetmas Wyakaikt or Swan Necklace, the bitter Sarpsis Illpilp, and several others, destroyed the thirteen man force, led by the officer named Rains, who came to spy on us at the prairie plateau we call Aipadass.

Not a man who came with Rains was to escape. The whites blundered against the shield we formed to protect our fleeing camp after Whitebird Canyon. Within minutes after the first shots no whites lived. Six soldiers fell in the first attack. Those who survived reached temporary shelter but fell quickly, silently to Five Wound's scheme of attack. The brave Tipyah Kapskaps, Strong Eagle, charged the whites, working closer and closer under the protective fire of our marksman warriors: Seeakoon Illpilp, Red Spy and Tahwis Tokaittat, Bighorn Bow. While Strong Eagle moved, holding the whites' fire and their attention, Rainbow and Five Wounds began the sprint which carried them behind the soldiers. With them went Sarpsis Illpilp and the burly Two Moons.

One by one the foolishly separated soldiers dropped behind their cover, never to reappear. Rainbow himself took down the first men, allowing the passionate Sarpsis Illpilp to try his stealth only in the end when the outcome was certain.

Yet, despite their fierceness and success in battle, it was Rainbow and Five Wounds who spoke against an attack on the much larger force of cavalry the man Whipple, fresh from his raid on Looking Glass, hurried into place in a vain effort to save Rains. The small defensive force of twenty warriors sent out from the camp with Rainbow and Five Wounds was brought back intact to stand guard again as our people were led by Joseph to a safer camp. While the Nez Perce moved, Whipple crouched behind his Gatling guns and imagined the silent rush of Rainbow and the war-scream of Five Wounds.

Again in the Cottonwood fight the whites were to call Mount Misery, Five Wounds and Rainbow guided the attack. What they faced here was not disciplined regular army troops, but a company of volunteers, rangers, and misfits from various sources led by an old retired regular army officer called McConville. McConville's numbers had reached ninety; his men were heavily armed but poorly provisioned. His men had ridden out on impulse with all the ammunition and available weapons they could carry, but with little more in the way of supplies than a canteen—which might have been empty—and a handful of jerky.

Yet, after McConville had blundered against us he fell back, quite by chance, to an almost invulnerable position on a nearby hill. Here with his men bunched together, their shoulders and backs pressed together in fear, their plentiful weapons aimed outward in anxiety, McConville presented a formidable defensive position.

Rainbow stood dispassionately in place while Five Wounds persuaded the warriors with them against frontal assault. Instead, under the cover of darkness our men harassed the position of McConville and drove away his horses. Meanwhile, the camp, beginning the pattern that was to eventually exhaust our souls and spirits, fled beyond the immediate danger.

So it was that when one, or both—for they were most often together—of our great plains warriors led our young men, our strength was conserved and the whites, except those who formed to show the rifle, were unmolested. At Billy's Creek a band of warriors with Rainbow and Five Wounds at their head watched, unobserved, a fleeing party of twenty settlers. Only once in the high-land plateaus of our home did any white family suffer needlessly—and that was at the hands of outcasts, whiskey-loving young men, who sometimes slipped into our camp to visit relatives, but who were never under our control.

And so our medicine had been good. At White-bird Canyon we brought the brooding frustration of decades and the element of total surprise against the exhausted and indecisive troops of Perry. Later, with Rainbow and Five Wounds in the camp of the Nez Perce we fought only where we chose to fight. We were spared the bloody attacks which rage and foolishness brought to the other tribes who had opposed the whites. Constantly we evaded the army of Howard. Twice we turned forces of over a hundred men from our camp. Often we were harassed by various smaller militia groups. Yet, until the first cannon fired, until the still peace of the Clearwater camp was abruptly shattered, no Nez Perce had lost his life to the white troops. One man, Weesculatat, lay seriously wounded in his lodge, but no man had died and few had been seriously wounded.

This good fortune was a powerful influence on our people. Our belief that the spirits of our land stood with us reassured the Nimpau—until Howard brought the full force of his army against our unprepared village on the Clearwater.

At the Clearwater battle there was, at first, only fear and confusion. The sound of the cannon filled the valley and somewhere above us was the ball itself. Again and again, after the first balls struck, came the hollow roar of the cannon. Brave men dropped their weapons and ran for the shelter of nearby rocks. Women cried in shrill shrieks for their children. One man, Meopkowit, a kind old man, a respected, if minor, headman, walked slowly through the village chanting a death song. He looked at no one, did not appear frightened, but with singular, calm preoccupation sang his lament as he walked through the turmoil and disappeared on the hillside to the west.

Near the center of the camp a ball hit, bounced, where all could see it and folded around itself the scraped buffalo hide of a summer tepee. There was no scream or cry of anguish. There was something more terrible; a stifled, involuntarily grunt and a popping sound. Then the ball, nearly spent, tore through its flapping leather confinement to roll a few yards farther, the fine river sand sticking to, coating its now wet surface.

Then, as Ollokot and the warriors stood transfixed, the horse of Toohoolhoolzote was on them, past them, as they heard over the din of the frightened camp the cajoling chant, the defiant scream that the old Dreamer fused into the single word NIMPAU. Somehow, from somewhere, there was Ollokot's own horse and rifle and he was mid-stream in the summer shallow Clearwater following Toohoolhoolzote when his horse went down, throwing Ollokot headlong into the shallow water and against a boulder. Instantly Ollokot was up again, on the horse trying to force him up the hill before realizing the horse was lame. Without pause or reflection Ollokot continued on foot across river and uphill, wiping impatiently the hot thick blood that ran down his face to blur his vision.

With Ollokot came the strength of the Nez Perce.

Two hundred warriors came up the cliff wall to fight Howard, more fighting men than the Nez Perce had assembled in one place since the councils and treaties on the Lapwai Creek tore apart our tribe. From the Wallowa came fifty men. Joining Ollokot at their head was the dependable "redcoat" Tipyahlanah Kapskaps, Strong Eagle, who was with us at Whitebird Canyon when our band of young warriors charged Perry. With us also was Koolkool Snehee, Red Owl, the handsome young man whose reputation as a lover was soon to be matched by stories of his courage in battle, and the young Yellow Wolf whose age did not lessen his steadiness and dependability.

At the head of the Asotins came Looking Glass himself—one of the few men of our tribe whose heritage and position included both council and war functions. Detached and vain in camp, the courage of Looking Glass on the battlefield was never questioned. With him came the Asotin warriors, men such as the fearless fighter Tahwis Tokaittat, Big Horn Bow; Peopeo Tholekt, a bright man known best for his intense devotion to Looking Glass; and Metat Waptoo, Three Feathers an older man, a lesser headman always cautious of Looking Glass' plans. In all the

Asotins were to bring a little over fifty men out of camp to face Howard—matching in number the men from the Wallowa valley.

With White Bird's men came Wahlitits, and the other raiders—vicious Sarpsis Illpilp and the boy Wetyetmas Wyakaikt, Swan Necklace. Thirty warriors in all.

Further south, on the ridge beyond White Bird, were the men of Toohoolhoolzote. With them was the calm Seeyakoon Illpilp, Red Spy, who stood watch at Whitebird Canyon and who covered Strong Eagle's attack in the battle with Rains. Also with the Snake River Nez Perce was Seeskoomkee, a man whose tribal origin was unknown, who came to us from the great Yakima chief Kamiakin where he was a slave until he lost both feet in the winter cold. Seeskoomkee, "No Feet," was the name given him by the children of the camp. Amazingly he rode as well as most men and was not ineffective with his lance.

To our numbers were added the eight hard men who followed Rainbow and Five Wounds, the twenty Palouse warriors who had brought their families to our camp with our cousin, Hahtaletin, and the eighteen warriors—none yet of any reputation-brought by the great orator Husishusis Kute. Finally there were with us as well a dozen or so men from the small, shifting bands who came into and out of our main camp at will.

Against our strength was matched the troops and cannon of Howard. For the first time the warriors of the Nez Perce had to face the soldiers on grounds the whites chose. Howard forced us to defend our village. With strength and desperation we rode and clawed our way up the steep canyon wall to stop him from charging down the same incline into our very lodges. And because we had strength and courage and the conviction of men who stood between their families and troops who would destroy them, Howard's six hundred, his cannon and his supply trains were not enough.

At least they were not enough for thirty hours. From the protected points, pockets of rocks, and tree-sheltered ravines which enclosed in semicircular fashion the center of Howard's attack, we fought and held the soldiers. Choosing their own time and place of attack, they came against us at a point and on terrain which allowed our warriors cover and some semblance of shade. The soldiers, when their momentum was stopped, were forced to sweat belly down on the level plateau before us. For hours after we drove back from the plateau lip the advance units which had been stationed there to hold it, the troops of Howard huddled anxiously under the mid-summer, noon-day sun on the plain before us. They had no water—certainly no fresh water for the river was behind us and the only spring in the area was immediately before us, under our rifles. They huddled, drew back to maneuver, charged and drew back, all with little conviction. The white troops feared us, seemed astonished to see their comrades fall to our fire, and, as at Whitebird Canyon, fired their fine, rifled weapons without aim as though they depended on the noise to drive us back.

But the whites had the cannons. And the cannon and the repeated, if ineffective, charges and the pressure of the constant fire would eventually wear down the warriors of the Nez Perce who were forced to fight, at the Clearwater River battle, from a fixed position. The cannon was especially terrifying for the southernmost segment of the line we had thrown between our village and the troops of Howard. There the men of Toohoolhoolzote and Husishusis Kute caught the brunt of the sporadic fire which had been turned from the village against our positions. Looking Glass, White Bird—all those to the left and north of the Wallowans and far to the north of Toohoolhoolzote and Husishusis Kute—were spared most of the frightening fire of the cannon.

So, while the headmen met to the rear in a sheltered place on the bluff of the river to argue the proper course of action, the warriors held our position and repelled the soldiers. We watched and waited, saw the effects of the heat and absence of water on the troops and knew at the same time the growing uneasiness and tension the unrelenting sniping and the occasional cannon hits created in each man who stood with the Nez Perce against Howard.

After the first terrifying explosions in the village, the cannon was silenced for a while. Once we gained the plateau against them, the men who serviced the cannon were only interested in protecting themselves. Later, after the first attacks on both sides had failed, after we had fought hand to hand and had to fall back, the cannon was once again turned against us. Fortunately the village below had been forgotten; fortunately the cannon was inaccurate. But, in the end, the cannon was to do psychologically what it could not do physically. Randomly, unselectively, the cannon took its toll. Dediedan, Ground Squirrel, an older man of White Bird's band who was with his nephews in Husishusis Kute's area, was blown apart. The man called Tunnachenostoolt had an arm mangled. The Palouse, Klickitats, had his jaw blown away.

And it continued. The men of Howard lay behind whatever rocks they could find, or in whatever shallow depression they could scoop out with their awkward trowel bayonets and maintained their constant if inaccurate rifle fire at our positions. Despite our concentrated fire, again and again they managed to service and fire the cannon. Most often the ball missed its mark, but even when it missed the ground-shaking explosion affirmed the destruction the next ball might bring to a man or group unable to move or defend themselves.

As the evening and then the darkness of the first day came, the desperateness of our position was apparent. We stopped and held Howard, but it was now evident that we had trapped ourselves as well. By mid-afternoon of the first day the argument of most who came or were invited to the sheltered ledge where the headmen and shamans met to decide our fate was for withdrawal. Only the always arrogant Looking Glass and, surprisingly, White Bird favored attempting to maintain our position. Looking Glass argued, and even seemed to believe, that we might beat the whites. White Bird, revealing a new aspect of his character, was enraged that the whites had attempted to shell our peaceful village and insisted that we stand until the whites gave up their attack and went away.

Late in the afternoon of the first day, while the headmen met under the ledge below, Rainbow and Five Wounds led their immediate followers on a raid that was to convince most that we might attempt to hold our position a bit longer. The information was brought to us by Rainbow who, alone and on foot, had moved unobserved all the way around Howard's men, that a supply wagon with a small number of reinforcements was coming up to Howard from the south.

Even as the information was passed to the headmen in the council below, Rainbow, Five Wounds, and more than twenty others were mounted and moving against the approaching unit. Around and behind Howard they rode. Using what cover was available and a technique of milling that Five Wounds devised so that some warriors rode by an open and exposed position two or three or more times, the raiders were able to throw Howard entirely on the defensive. His riflemen bunched themselves together back to back, his cavalry was dismounted, useless, anticipating an attack now from two sides. And at the very moment the firing came to be most intense, when the troops were most apprehensive, Five Wounds and Rainbow broke off their bluff to race across the plateau to the south to attack in earnest the oncoming supply unit.

They almost succeeded. The detachment of reinforcements quickly abandoned the supplies they guarded and fell back to a sheltered ravine to their left and rear. This lack of courage, ironically, saved them and saved a portion of the supplies they brought, for although the men who came with Five Wounds and Rainbow had come to fight, the temptation of the supplies of food and ammunition was too great. About half of the raiders fell back from the attack and milled in excitement and disorder around the supply wagons. The small number of warriors left fighting could do little but hold the larger unit of reinforcements in place. In the confusion and delay, Howard recovered his perspective and sent his horse soldiers to rescue his men and supplies. With a hundred troopers galloping up on their exposed rear, Five Wounds and Rainbow abandoned their attack and fled, taking what supplies and ammunition they could with them.

The daring raid of Five Wounds and Rainbow brought into our camp precious ammunition, but it brought as well the impression that Howard was weak and disorganized and that we might yet hold our position against him. Looking Glass, his pale grey eyes flashing conviction, now said, "The brave Wahchumyus and

Pahkatos Owyeen have shown us the weakness and fear of Howard. We are strong here. The women and lodges are nearby. If the camp below is broken and the women are gone we cannot hold the men against Howard. Let us stay and break his courage."

Joseph, Ollokot could see when called back to express an opinion, was increasingly withdrawn —more so than even before the Whitebird Canyon fight when it became apparent that we would have to face the troops. Now the reserve, the aloofness—or whatever it might be called— was even more open. As a result the newcomers to our camp turned more and more to Looking Glass whose voice had already begun to dominate our council.

And so the warriors, most of us, held our positions through the dusk and night of that first day at the Clearwater.

On the morning of the second day Joseph, made his decision to withdraw from the besieged Clearwater River camp. Throughout the night warriors had slipped away from their positions to return to the shelter and warmth of their lodges. Some, exercising the autonomy our tribe allowed each man, began preparations to flee. Joseph, Yellow Wolf would recount, came to the smoking lodge where the headmen met. Abruptly, but calmly he made his announcement, facing Looking Glass as he spoke.

"Hold your warriors here if you wish, Allalimya Takanin. Hold them if you can. The responsibility is yours, as the choice of campsites was yours. The Wallowans who wish to do so will go with Joseph.

Looking Glass was on his feet, his face flushed with anger.

"Ollokot," Joseph continued, turning his back to Looking Glass to face White Bird and Toohoolhoolzote, "Ollokot will hold our warriors in place to protect our withdrawal. My nephew here, Yellow Wolf, will carry this message to him. He will carry as well Joseph's suggestion that the warriors of the Wallowa come away from the cliffs of the Clearwater once our people are safe."

Abruptly Looking Glass began to shout his taunt to Joseph demeaning the courage of the Wallowans. The taunt was short-lived, for from above on the plateau came the noise of Howard's huge, final assault—the assault which was to break our lines and bring disaster to our people.

The warriors had seen the troops moving, but had made no defensive move. It appeared the troops had been detached to march to the south to join and escort yet another body of reinforcements. The detachment of the unit caused no anxiety, though it did create further division. Many of the warriors, seeing the adventure and near success of the raid of Rainbow and Five Wounds, urged that we attack again and destroy this second reinforcement unit. This plan Looking Glass managed to deny entirely on his own. His argument was vehement, threatening. We were already outnumbered: he would not allow a division of our strength with Howard's men, still nearly six hundred of them, in position before us. Even in his chest-slapping arguments, he did not condemn the earlier raid of Rainbow and Five Wounds.

Whatever the case, and many of the details are blurred and obscured by the events which exploded abruptly against us, a unit—perhaps a hundred men in all—moved out of Howard's entrenched position to meet the oncoming reinforcements. Harassed only by occasional sniper fire, the foot soldiers marched hurriedly in the military fashion some of our warriors found so amusing. To the right and south the new troops came into sight and in less than an hour the two units met to turn and march back to us. The incoming unit appeared to be about fifty men, though our scouts had reported it as being slightly larger.

We sat in almost tranquil inactivity. The fighting had become no more than a long range contest of marksmanship—a contest which worked greatly to our advantage. Only the infrequent cannon fire unnerved our confidence. As we sat and watched, the troops marched with precision and order back along their original route until they were approximately even with the ravine to our south that was guarded by a few men of Toohoolhoolzote's band. Suddenly they turned to their left and with discipline and determination charged straight against our southernmost men.

There was little way to withstand this attack. Toohoolhoolzote was below in the camp where he had finally gone to rest at the urging of those around him who realized however heroic, however determined, the old Dreamer was exhausted and almost incoherent. Though we had seen plainly the troops marching out and then back before us, the attack was totally a surprise; it was a surprise,we would learn later, even to Howard, for it originated on the spur of the moment in the mind of the captain Howard had detached to provide escort cover. Its surprise produced disaster, for we were unable to adjust to the nature and direction of the attack. The brunt of the attack, the weight of the now passionate and inspired force of nearly one hundred and fifty men came to crush or sweep away individual warriors or small groups of warriors who had chosen their cover and position against a frontal attack and who now faced destruction from the side or behind over terrain that did not allow us any advantage for our usual accurate and careful fire. As individuals fell back or were overrun our confidence vanished and the aggressiveness of the troops became even greater.

For Story Teller, to the Nimpau who sit together and listen, Ollokot speaks:

At the beginning of the attack I stood with my kinsmen from the Wallowa in a secure position near the center of our line. Most of the balance of this dark, frenzied time is unclear. Somehow I made my way to the troops —or perhaps they simply forced their way to me—but the fighting soon raged around me and the soldiers who earned our disdain, who hung back hesitantly in the open, who shot poorly and marched slowly, became something else in the confining ravines above the Clearwater river. The savagery and physical strength of the whites surprised me, shocked and numbed me. It was as though at once, everywhere there were rifle-swinging, cursing soldiers. Always they were together: two, three, four or five moving as one. Quickly, there was no more ammunition. No time for ammunition. The grey mist of anxiety and fear came for the first time since the morning cold of Whitebird Canyon. Against me, on me, was the weight and heat of the soldiers. I could feel their strength through the fiber and steel of my rifle butt, could feel their strength under the coarse cloth on their backs, could feel their heat and passion in the warm blood that spurted across the gap quickly closed to join our bodies.

Sometime later, with no concept of time or space, I recognized the form of Rainbow beside me. Around us were bodies, both warrior and soldier—how many I am unsure. How long I fought I am unsure. In exhaustion that permitted no fatigue I saw the strength of Rainbow whose perfectly coordinated steel-sinewed body glistened with sweat and blood. He had no gun—or had long ago abandoned it as useless and time-consuming, for when I first became aware of Rainbow he held only a huge and finely honed double-bladed axe. It was a massive axe, a prized, and unusual possession that he had brought to our camp. I had never seen Rainbow take it into battle before and still do not know how it came to be on the plateau above our camp, but I will never forget the mask-like face of the athlete who bore it. He held it with a wide-spaced, two-handed grip that I at first did not understand. But quickly, against the first man I saw it used, I saw the simple effectiveness that Rainbow instinctively adopted. From somewhere, nowhere, a soldier was suddenly on us. With him were two other forms, forms that were indistinct, indescribable—seeing, registering somehow only the older man and the open mouth of tobacco-stained and rotted teeth-seeing and recording the basic forms and shapes in the lull during which my senses returned enough to realize that I was no longer isolated and fighting alone. They were there: the grizzly, unshaven heavy trooper with the poor teeth was suddenly upon us, throwing himself from somewhere over the fallen trees around us. Before him,the metal agent, the glistening dirt-polished bayonet was almost to Rainbow's body. I remember being transfixed by the blade itself as it surged through the air toward Rainbow, almost ripped into the flesh of his stomach before I could utter a sound from my mouth long open, seeing, as I lunged across the brief and momentary opening to grapple with the faceless trooper before me, the move Rainbow made. I saw him fade away, melt away from the blade almost before he saw it at his stomach. As he moved the wide-gripped axe handle came up forcing with amazing ease the bayonet away, the rifle up, parallel to the man's body and back into the soldier's face with such force I could hear the thudding pop even in the darkness of my own effort. As the sound completed the upward movement of the right hand, the head of the axe was already down seeking and finding the man's stomach, ripping upward with ease, powered by the forward motion of the two coming together, into the chest cavity in one continuous uniform movement that never stopped, nor slowed, nor seemed impeded in any way. Only as the man fell, his mouth still open, his face and eyes blank in shock, was there as light hitch to Rainbow's incredible form as he twisted and freed the axe.

Eventually, to my left, above and slightly apart from us I could sense, more than see, Five Wounds who fired from cover, calmly achieving without rage the calculated damage which was his strength—covering as he observed and fired both Rainbow and myself. With us came to stand about thirty of our best men. Haltalekin, the Palouse; Wahlitits; Strong Eagle; the handsome Red Owl; Lalpeealot; the emotional Otstatpoo, Fire Body; and the boys Swan Necklace and Yellow Wolf. To my right was Looking Glass himself with a small core of his warriors. The line with which we had entrapped and held Howard was now driven back to our single unit of resistance. As we fought desperately overwhelmed by the increasing numbers of Howard's troops, the families in the camp below abandoned their possessions and fled the Clearwater.

Story Teller:

The warriors have held the soldiers from the village, but the people have no choice but to hurriedly break camp and seek safety. A contentious decision is reached to flee the homeland and attempt to cross the Bitter Roots mountains using the Lolo Trail, the ancient passage from the Columbia drainage of the west to the Missouri drainage to the east.

Words

I have heard talk and talk
And nothing is done.
Words do not pay for my dead people.
Good words do not give me back
My children.
There has been too much talking
By men who had no right to talk.
The earth is the mother of all people and
All people have equal rights.
Allow us to return to our homeland.

You might as well expect the rivers
To run backward
As to expect a man born free
To be contented
When penned up and denied liberty to
Go where he pleases.

Hinmahtooyahlatkekht

VIII. The Lolo Trail
July 14–30, 1877

In the second day of the battle at the Clearwater River the camp of the Nez Perce was broken. There was then no time for reflection, no time to consider what should be, might have been, for suddenly among us were the warriors who had fought bravely on the plateau above. The horses were brought up. The children and women were mounted, two or three together, the young and weak clinging to the strong. The old and sick and wounded were raised up, placed on whatever horses were available or on the few travois we had. Some fled on foot with nothing more than what they had in their hands when the first group of exhausted warriors came back to us. To the north and east the Nimpau fled. To the Lolo Pass, to the buffalo grounds to the east we fled.

Above us, inaudible, nearly forgotten in the turmoil of the camp stood Ollokot, Rainbow, Five Wounds, and Looking Glass. With them stood the best of the Nez Perce warriors. Together they made the stand, formed the island of resistance to stop Howard from charging down the banks of the Clearwater into the chaos of our camp.

So it was to be that from the strong and peaceful camp on the Clearwater River we were driven to the ridges and ravines of the Lolo trail to begin the flight which ends now in the despair of the whitening Bear Paws.

As anxiety for future brings memory of past, Story Teller shares Joseph's memory of Tuekakas's death, fourteen years earlier, and his prayer that Joseph hold, in trust, the Wallowa Valley.

For seven days Tuekakas lay upon the couch of skins and blankets. The late winter's dankness of smoke and herbs and sweat-agony permeated the walls of the lodge. Around the constant fire moved, occasionally, the women who kept the lodge and served the old chief. On the side, creeping always closer to the fire's warmth was Natokolas, the grandmother, who stayed, insisted on staying in her son's lodge, until in the end they lifted and carried her away, child-light, to the lodge of a niece. Tuekakas watched passively, mute, his eyes turning again to stare through the open flap to the west and the Wallowa range, to the triple peaks which stood guard over the lake and the homeland of the Nimpau. Quietly about him, around his hearthfire, gathered the old men of our people. At times their voices would rise in unison to echo the myths of the people in agreement with the story of the Teller. At times there would be total silence. Occasionally, a solitary councilman would whisper to himself, would chant alone the deeds of the days when Tuekakas moved strongly among the Nez Perce, stories to be left to the Tellers to come.

"Tuekakas will recall the great summer camp when the man called Stevens came to the Nez Perce in the days of our strength and begged our aid and friendship

against the Yakima and the Spokan." The reminiscence would begin formally, slowly, the speaker neither expecting nor receiving response and affirmation for the recollection which was all that remained to any of them.

"Tuekakas knows. He was there when we told Stevens he might take scouts to show him the country, but that though we had befriended the whites we would never raise up our warriors against the Yakima, our neighbors.

"Those were the days when the Nez Perce stood in place and the white came to seek him out, to ask his consent, to gauge his reaction, to elicit his permission. Those were the days before the missionaries brought their restraining and deceitful words to disrupt and poison the minds of our people and alter the character of our headmen."

And so they continued, recalling the days of strength and friendship in the Wallowa, beckoning out with their wild gestures the quiet rage which grew within their spirits. Yet, even as they talked, Tuekakas grew weaker, slipped in silence further and further from the world of men, slipped before my eyes to the mountains over us, there to fuse his spirit in timeless harmony with the heights which had stood above and apart from him for over seventy years.

And then one day, after the strength and spirit seemed gone entirely, the old man spoke again, expelled the idlers from his lodge with but a single word. Calmly, though straining with the physical effort even this required, Tuekakas looked about him, looked to me and, shedding the dream-like trance, spoke his instructions:

"Ollokot. Ollokot, your brother."

Again I came, Ollokot with me. The dream and trance were gone now, but the old man sat still and studied the mountains. We took our places beside him in the empty lodge, wondering not after the state of health—which we knew—but after the state of mind which held for me then and now the greatest mystery and wonder: the thoughts, the moods, the memories, the old joys and old pains now sacred and time-venerated.

To us the old man, the flesh-strong force of childhood, began to speak:

"A man must know of his life that it has been good. There must be, in the life experience which each man suffers, the knowledge that he did what he could. That what he did do accomplished a part of what he hoped and that the joy which he had overshadows the pain."

The voice was thin, weak; the tone was firm. Indistinctly, the sounds of death came to me.

"A man must reach peace, must achieve harmony, must know that he is one with his kinsmen, the selfsame flesh he touches about him."

Tuekakas, blind—or very near it—touched by the years and agony life brings, lay upon his death couch and spoke to us as the father, the spirit, each man knows—or seeks, held out to us even then the wisdom and strength beyond our own, offered father, that constant center, that benevolence and authority and love to which a man may bend his own spirit, may carry his own burden.

Tuekakas spoke to us of the land, the Wallowa.

"It is said by those who speak often the old tales that we, the Nimpau, sprang from the earth herself, that from the flesh and blood of the old creature sprang the Nez Perce. Nurtured by the earth, warmed by the sun, watered by the cold mountain rivers, we rose from that which had been always before.

"The old ones—I am old and upon death myself, though this is hard and indifferent to believe—the old ones have their stories for all things, explanations of the mind for those things which are, in fact, about us. Those who follow the Dreamer, Smohalla, hypnotize themselves with the belief that the spirits of all things are immortal, for they are but an extension, as is the very flesh which propels them, of the land which has nurtured them. So it may be. For whatever the frailness of man's body, whatever the larger strengths of his spirit, there is nothing beyond the land which forms him—for he is the land. From the land comes his flesh. To the land turns his spirit. They are one. They are inseparable. The sperm of his father, the flesh of his mother, the life-shadow of his women and children, these are the earth risen, raised to him. We are all life-shadows from the earth our mother.

The old man paused, gasped almost inaudibly, labored to regain his wind for the words he must finally say.

"Beyond the temporary life tension which raises man erect from the beyond the momentary confusion which may come if he loses the awareness of the earth beneath his bare feet, man may suffer no great disharmony. The events and incidents of his life are of little joy or difficulty. Beyond a man's role as son and then husband and father they are of no consequence. A man is but the vehicle, the living shadow, the reflection which passes life: the mirror image of the earth. Thus, no act of man is of great consequence; no act of man is of more than passing significance.

"So a man must revere the earth, his forbears, his descendants."

In the growing darkness the old man, the father, continued his slow and deliberate cadence, pausing, stopping for minutes at a time in total silence, while I sat, Ollokot at my side, not with impatience or fear, nor any emotion other than love, heartache which reached out, demanded union with the old man, sought to extend the arm, to join the hand and the flesh, to create from the sheer power of human affection one flesh where there was one spirit, to instill and transfuse fleshwarmth, to rejoin and return bloodsurge, to foster and preserve and protect this spirit, this frail and dried body.

"There are some who may think my mind has grown old and withered like my body," Tuekakas spoke again, turning his eyes back to the mountains which stood in the last full glow of sunlight above the darkening valley.

"They see me sit and stare away to the mountains and think my consciousness has left me, that my thoughts

have grown narrow and brittle—and so it is true, at least to the extent that I have no great interest in their stories of the past. And this is as it should be. A man within the hour of his death has no time for the past. There is only the future. There are the mountains and this valley which is always my spirit and to which I will soon again fuse my flesh, passing the temporary inconvenience of infirmity and age. Here is before me the future, in flesh stronger than my own. Before me are sons of strength and sensitivity who encompass and extend Tuekakas. Between these sons and our mother the earth I have been but a temporary bridge, that the Nimpau may continue to walk in the sun of the Wallowa, that we may foster and protect this our origin as we must, that the reflection of what the earth herself has raised up will not perish.

"So I return to the earth my origin. I have peace. I leave to you, Joseph, this land, in trust, as I have held it—this land made sacred by the bones and flesh of our fathers, made sacred once again to you and to Ollokot who holds it with you by my flesh, my bones, made sacred for all time by my spirit which remains here, here in this highland valley."

Five days passed before Tuekakas died. On a knoll, at the foot of the Wallowa lake, shaded in the evening sun by the great Wallowa mountains, we buried him. Stone by stone we covered the grave, joining Tuekakas with the generations of Nez Perce interred there before him, doing the work ourselves, allowing no one else to touch the grave or the stones, marking and protecting the wasted remains that was once our father, forming, grasping piecemeal with each stone a knowledge of our own mortality—the weight and realization of mortality that must come to each man as he buries the father who stood seemingly immortal before him.

And so somehow in the mid-afternoon's sun and the distillation of time it is the death and burial of Tuekakas which stands clearer and nearer to my mind as I await Miles than the events which took place there in the huge stationary camp on the Clearwater River, though one happened as yesterday in the time of men and the other, the clearer, was now fourteen years ago.

And perhaps this is as it should be, for one, the memory of Tuekakas, stands paramount to my being, and the other, the withdrawal from the lands of the Nez Perce stands at the beginning of the blackness and despair which has consumed my spirit for the past weeks, has consumed and wasted the Nez Perce, has brought the Nez Perce, my people, to the cold and desolate rifle pits of the Bear Paws.

From the moment the Nez Perce turned to the east most hated the Lolo. We came in disarray; we came as fugitives. The pleasant camps of the Clearwater and before were gone. Before when we had moved there was pattern and direction. Before with first light had come the smells of food: coffee, camas patties frying on heated rocks, and the taste of the dried salmon strips and the wild berries with which our highland river meadows abounded. There were the pleasant and routine duties: the selection of horses for the day's use, the pipes of tobacco while the great hide and canvas tents came down creating the peculiar vacant air of abandoned campsite, the review of our direction of movement with the young warriors who assumed the responsibility of watching our back trail and scouting the trail ahead.

Now furtively we moved, camping when we must, where we must, taking shelter in the caves and rock ledges where we found it, spreading the remaining blankets over the young and the old and the wounded now with us. Indecisively we moved. Those who stood against Howard, who held him from our camp were absent from us—some forever. Ollokot and Rainbow, Five Wounds and most of the young warriors who followed them, watched over and guarded our retreat. In camp were the men whom Howard had beaten, the ones who abandoned the fight above the Clearwater and came below to sit and brood. Looking Glass and White Bird were back as well. They came to move their families with us, to make slighting remarks to those who had quit the fight early, to enrage and insult and further divide our people. In their bitterness, they questioned our speed and direction on the winding Lolo which became each hour steeper, more obscure and difficult to follow.

On the third day after the final attack at the Clearwater, word came to us from the warriors who had remained on the plateau while their families below fled. To our fireless camp in one of the tiny meadows of the lower Lolo came the young man, Wetyetmas Wayakaikt, Swan Necklace. He came for food and ammunition and in the pale moonlight he stood and then crouched before us, streaked and dirty, warrior now and not child, to tell of the survivors and how they fought.

The great ones survived. The Wyakins stood guard and protected them, sheltered them as they fought against Howard in the chaos of our breaking camp. Many were wounded, though few were hurt seriously. Some were missing, but only two were known dead. Husishusis Kute, headman and orator, a man who sometimes spoke in anger and acted rashly, was dead. Lahpeealoot, lighthearted cousin from the Wallowa who joined the raids of Wahlitits against the advice of Ollokot, was also dead. Both died in flurries of fighting after the main charge of the troops and so the bodies of both were recovered and brought away.

Incredibly that was all—or all the exhausted young man knew for certain. The rest remained together, slowing and harassing Howard's advance to allow the people the space and time to move away to safety. The technique was simple once the camp and the families were not at the warriors' backs. The men would fall back from Howard's army to rest and watch its movement. When Howard, who was slow to pursue, to press his advantage, was finally in motion, the warriors would select a protected position and make the appearance of a stand. The sharpshooters would bring the march to a halt; soldier units would be detached to work their way up to attack the twenty or thirty men who remained with Ollokot and Five Wounds and Rainbow. Then without casualties or even great risk, the band of warriors would gradually dissolve before the advancing troops. One or two men, usually Seeyakoon Illpilp, Red Spy, and Five Wounds, the best shots with the best horses, would hold till the last—forcing a squad of soldiers to crawl, usually with casualties, almost to the very rocks which provided our snipers cover. Then silently, with the stealth for which he was famous, Five Wounds would be gone. Even then, the soldiers were not safe. After the first encounter they rose, stood together to curse the elusiveness of the sharpshooters only to learn that Seeyakoon Illpilp was but a hundred yards or so farther away watching with the keen eyes, waiting with the steady hands that made him the best shot among our people.

Four days after Swan Necklace brought the first news, a moon's full quarter after Howard's first cannon shots upon the Clearwater camp, Ollokot and those who had stood with him came by night into the camp of the Nez Perce.

With a man's firm joy Joseph rises to welcome him. Silently Ollokot stands before him, before the make-shift shelter which now served both families.

"You take our families away from our homeland." Ollokot's voice was flat, inflectionless; his eyes were less controlled.

"Our families are safe." My words came louder, harsher than I intended.

And that was all. Ollokot stooped to pick up Nehemini drawing to them Aihits Palojami, sister, who stood with Toma before the patched canvas sheller. Together they entered, ducked beneath the shelter's flap. Toma moved to stand at my side, to walk with me through the sleeping camp along the trail we had already traveled, the path to the west and the Wallowa valley, a path now blocked by the military camp of Howard.

As the days passed a fitful pattern emerged as our people struggled with the Lolo. The camp would break with the sun's first light. Food, such as we had in the game desolate higher altitudes of the Lolo, was taken on the move. Children were given a hand-size piece of camus cake by a still-hungry mother and lifted, sometimes two and three together, onto the gentle lead ponies. Many of the men would drop back to collect and bring up the horse herd. A few warriors—Ollokot always, Five Wounds frequently, occasionally Rainbow and others—would slip back along our trail to watch Howard. No longer did we oppose his advance. Our ammunition did not permit it and many argued, as did Looking Glass, that Howard would find the trail impossible for his men and supplies and so would give up and turn back, satisfied to have displaced us and seized our land.

So we moved higher and higher up the confining Lolo. The narrow, steep ravines, green black with dense foliage and strewn with an infinite variation of obstacles: boulders of every size and shape and trees fallen and woven together in an impossible tangle, made more difficult and impassable the already precipitous foot paths which, winding in the same general direction, came to be called the Lolo Trail. The path, the trail itself led constantly up and down. With care and exertion a man could pick his way carefully down the slopes, but he still had to control the first hesitant and then sliding horses he led which carried the remaining possessions. He had to control the horses and not slide into the family struggling ahead of him. He had to gauge his descent so that he could still reach the very young and the very old who depended on him, who could not manage the steepness of the trail alone.

Once down one slope there was no respite; the tiny ravine bottoms could be spanned in a few steps and then the trail started its ascent. The ascent was ever more tortuous, more trying for the varying strength of individuals caused our lines to string out dangerously. Here, even the strong, who were forced to move back and forth, up and down, were exhausted as they pulled and pushed and sometimes lifted with ropes and travois the weak, the wounded, and the old—now totally dependent on the physical strength of their families.

Driven by Howard from our homeland plateau and the cool, fish-laden waters of the Clearwater, the Salmon, and the Snake, we moved hesitantly up the steep ravines and ridges of the Bitterroots seeking the pass, the passageway to the east and the buffalo grounds, hoping by the difficulty of the terrain and the distance to leave Howard and the war behind us. Surprisingly, as the days passed, as we continued our ever more difficult ascent through the Bitterroot Mountains, much of the animosity within our camp began to dissipate. Movement itself required cooperation and produced exhaustion, and since the presence of Howard behind us and the very terrain which surrounded us permitted no choice but to struggle on, the discord and humiliation of the flight at the Clearwater gradually began to fade.

The vigil of Ollokot was also to have its effect on our camp. Ollokot, Five Wounds would joke, knew Howard's men—their position and their temperament—better than Howard himself. In the days immediately after the battle at the Clearwater Ollokot was certainly with Howard more than he was with us. Ollokot realized, knew instinctively what it took Joseph time and conscious thought to discern. Howard, who had already established his disposition for slow movement, had little chance to overtake us in the confines of the Lolo—even though we were encumbered with our families and our horses, and even though our trial and error route on the indistinct and unmarked Lolo left a plainly marked and even, in the lame and abandoned horses, provisioned route to follow. Howard, if past performance held true, would not be able to move his men and his supplies fast enough to overtake us. So, Howard had clearcut options open to him: he could stop and let us go, follow accomplishing nothing, or he could detach his cavalry and strike. And in the confines of the Lolo any surprise attack could bring final and complete disaster, for there was no room to maneuver, no place to flee.

Yet, even with the delays brought by the warriors who harassed him after the Clearwater, Howard was still only days behind us. He could mount two hundred men, could send them after us, riding where they could, walking, climbing where they couldn't ride; they could be on us in a single night—or ahead of us, circling and trapping us in one afternoon and night.

So Ollokot watched. In the day he shadowed Howard's columns, was amused by Howard's refusal to give up the supply wagons even though he must have known what lay ahead, must have known that no wheeled vehicle, no mounted party the size of Howard's had ever passed the Lolo, was worried because Howard moved on slowly, surely, with no apparent consideration of turning back, was dumbfounded when into Howard's camp came yet a final reinforcement. Howard had somehow secured from the white settlements in our homeland a force of fifty axemen. These men he set about the task of clearing his path. And clear it they did, working tirelessly, skillfully. With axes and horses and windlasses they cleared the path enough to move the wagons. With ropes, windlasses, and foolheartedness they raised and lowered the wagons where the horses could not move them.

As a result, we gained time and space, but Ollokot's watch was no less systematic, the lines around his mouth and eyes no more relaxed. For Howard came on. Slowly, relentlessly, he came. In the mornings, long before the camp stirred, Ollokot was gone to watch the waking of Howard's camp, to determine that no early morning raid was being readied against us. In the afternoons Ollokot would come into camp to rest, to sit nodding as about him the night's camp was made.

The evening meals were sparse but were heated and Ollokot was usually in camp for them. But after the meal, after the subdued sounds of the camp had subsided further, Ollokot could sit calmly no longer. Suddenly he would be gone, taking nothing with him but a single rifle. Even as we came to anticipate his departures, all were still surprised at their abruptness. One minute Ollokot would be seated before the fire; the next minute he would be gone, the place he had been seated seemed still partially occupied.

Somewhere near our back trail, he slept. He slept, listening, becoming, in the fusion of his senses and spirit with the night, a part of the night so that every sound and every segment of silence had its proper sequence and place. I know he slept. It had to be that he slept here, huddled in some dark spot just above our back trail—for it was now the second week after the Clearwater and no one had seen him rest or sleep, at least no one had seen more than the nodding Ollokot permitted himself in the camp as the evening meals were prepared.

Yet, even though I knew he must have slept I never came upon him asleep on those nights when I, too, haunted the back trail—nor did I ever find him before he spoke to reveal his position. Ollokot, the gentle brother of youth, had become a warrior whose spirit and being were attuned to a single purpose: that he would deny any man who came armed against the Nez Perce camp access to that camp, would deny him at whatever cost, at whatever place, at whatever time.

Ollokot, with whom I sat in the cold nights on the backtrail of the Lolo, now stood apart from me—not that he drew away in argument and contradiction as did others, but that he became a man with different interests, with a different focus: Ollokot was then on the Lolo a man of the present. His existence was set against that of Howard's men and it was not the Wallowa of the past nor the Bitterroot valley of the future that formed his conduct; it was the here and the now and the position and speed and number of Howard's men.

Against Howard he had set himself on the plateau above the Clearwater. In bits and pieces I learned of Ollokot, learned what Ollokot himself did not remember—or chose not to recall. Days after the battle I came upon Five Wounds and Rainbow as I made my rounds of the camp. They were alone, and without thinking I was speaking of the last hours above the Clearwater camp, trying, in the egg-fragile realm which men deny to men, to thank them for their help for I knew that at one time all those around Ollokot had fallen back and he was entirely within the lines of the troops. Rainbow said nothing, did not even look up as I spoke. Five Wounds, who rolled the bone dice over and over in the palm of his hand as I spoke the words, said the "Thank you" which was enough and was too much, did speak finally, answered where there was no need for answer, chose to say the words a man may say of another man: "Ollokot is a man to whom another may turn his back in battle."

Still it would be weeks before the phrases and half-formed sentences of the young men made partial sense, before I could understand the awe and even the fear the young warriors held for Ollokot. For in time the stories of the Clearwater fight would be told quietly, discreetly, around our campfires. The stories were of Rainbow and his great, bloodied axe and of Five Wounds who knew no fear. The stories were of Ollokot, the Nez Perce who fought alone, who was surrounded by soldiers and they, in admiration of his courage or in perversion did not fire, but came against him physically with rifle butts and bayonets until they overwhelmed him, forced him, with the weight and strength which can finally overwhelm even spirit, to the earth going down with him in a tangle that now prevented even bayonets, pinning him briefly, momentarily before Rainbow was above them with the axe, cutting and tearing, throwing apart with the strength that only Rainbow could command, until the last soldier was wrenched away in a motion which tore the flesh and sinews of his throat from Ollokot's clinched teeth.

Even then, even after I heard the stories, even though I knew the strength and the will were there and could sense now the obsession, I could not fully comprehend the man with whom I sat nightly to listen in the silence of the Lolo trail for the sounds we prayed would not come, for sounds we could not afford to hear.

I was not fully able to understand or comprehend this man, Brother, now warrior, until weeks later when the troops of Gibbon crept by stealth into our sleeping camp and Ollokot and I stood side by side before the lodge which sheltered our families.

Story Teller: Respite and Shadows

In the peaceful Montana valley of the Bitterroots, our people found quiet and time to rest. The open spaces and highland summer heat were much like our home valleys—far more pleasant than the dark, tree shaded, twisted confinement of the Lolo.

Here lived our old friends, the Salish people—and an ever increasing number of whites. Our supplies were replenished. The children played and laughed again.

These are the memories Joseph attempts to recall as he waits again interview with Miles.

Yet, as he waits Miles's convenience, pleasant memories of the Bitterroots are displaced: Joseph cannot but relive in his mind the account he overhears on the Lolo of the burning of the Whitman Mission and the death of Narcissa.

Even deeper and darker flashes of loss he attempts to control: the death of Rainbow and the death of Five Wounds in the Battle of the Big Hole haunt him. The darkest shadow, which he cannot yet allow himself to acknowledge, is the mortal wound of Ollokot in the Nez Perce camp in the foothills of the Bear Paws, visible at a distance to his north.

IX. The Bitterroot Valley
August, 1877

Story Teller speaks of Joseph in the battle camp of Miles where Joseph sits confined, guarded by a dozen armed men. Gone are the pleasant memories of the Bitterroot Valley where the Nez Perce found temporary rest.

As Joseph crouches, nodding with exhaustion in the snow and desolate cold of the Bear Paws, even the dark and tortuous trail of the Lolo was more palatable, more bearable than the hunger and cold the Nez Perce camp suffers in the gullies and ravines of the Bearpaw foothills. Even the precarious camps of the Lolo held a hope and safety the present lacks, for less than a hundred paces from the corral where he is held Joseph can see in the dulling haze of the late afternoon's sun the form of Miles as he paces, studies the advantage he holds, determines how best to use—or first explain, and then use—this capture effected under a flag of truce, schemes how to force a surrender, so that he may claim the surrender itself and achieve the general's star he seeks.

Weeks, even days ago the Nez Perce did not know the man, Miles, existed. Through the Lolo Pass, down into the valley of the Bitterroots we came. At the end of the trail, in the last funnel-like ravines which guarded the eastern mouth of the trail, we were blocked by the log and earth fort of the man called Rawn. Howard had somehow managed to order into place against us this patchwork collection of soldiers and militia. But Rawn had only a hundred men. All of them knew what we had done against Howard's six hundred on the Clearwater. All of them knew what the warriors of the Nez Perce did at Whitebird Canyon against a force larger than their own.

And so the men with Rawn did not choose to fight. On the afternoon of the first day we sent our spokesmen to find their intentions, to explain that we had no quarrel with the whites of the Bitterroot Valley, to assure them that we came in peace. On the morning of the second day we formed a line with our warriors across the position of Rawn and sent our women and children and old people up the ravine and then back around Rawn by the old game trail that led to the east and the valley floor. Finally, after the families had passed, the warriors withdrew to follow the indirect trail of the families—around and by the soldiers, in deference to their decision to let us go in peace.

As the Nimpau left the desolation and confinement of the Lolo and entered the summer-warm Bitterroot Valley our strength and confidence began to grow again. Howard was far behind. And, Looking Glass argued, the whites of Montana had no reason to bear us ill-will.

We had lost men on the Clearwater, more to desertion and dispersion than to Howard, but our best warriors were still with us. And, into our camp in the Bitterroots, came the last of those to join us. The French-Nez Perce man called Hototo by his people and Poker Joe—for his great love of that game—by the whites. Hototo, true to his nature, was out for a lark, but his name and courage were known to us. More importantly, his knowledge of the Bitter Root Valley, where he had grown to manhood, was unsurpassed.

With Hototo came twelve men and a number of women and children. Among these men was Tomahas, a Cayuse outcast, who was to boast of the massacre at the Whitman mission.

The story came in the first days of our camp in the Bitterroots. As was Joseph's custom, he moved slowly through the camp in the evening, talking to first one family and then another. After reaching the camp's edge, he would continue into the night, along the back trail, to sit in the darkness and listen with Ollokot.

As I moved from the camp that night—long before I had gone far enough to expect Ollokot—I suddenly sensed men on the trail before me. They had no fire; perhaps it was the smell of tobacco or the faint glow from the pipe that first caught my attention. More likely it was the hushed and secretive voice which caught my attention, which commanded the attention of those on the trail ahead of me so that I approached undetected.

The phrase, the name I heard first, was "Whitman." The speaker was the Cayuse loafer, Tomahas.

"Their medicine became bad. The sore disease came and many died. The black robes at Walla Walla told us the whites brought it to the Cayuse. They told us Whitman spread it among us with the bitter medicine he dispensed with the old spoon he carried in his pocket.

"We told them to leave. They would not. They were arrogant. We killed them and burned the mission.

The words rushed at me. I heard the sounds, but the sounds were without sense, without meaning.

Narcissa, dead?

Whitman, dead?

The mind recoils and falls, floating to a place familiar.

The dream comes again. In the dream it was I who stood against Whitman.

I was he who seized the red-bearded Whitman man by the shoulders, by the throat—shaking, pushing apart and away from Narcissa this rough and insensitive intruder. In my dreams, the involuntary ones I learned by the rhetoric of Lapwai to carry with guilt, it was I who came between the burly, bearded man and the woman goddess Narcissa.

On the banks of the Clearwater, in the warmth-bringing morning sun, hand-in-hand we walked. Space-free. Away from the Lapwai Creek we moved. To the fishing hole below the Lapwai junction where the restless, virulent waters of the Clearwater received the Orfino and the Lapwai, whirled, paused to mix and stir the waters of our eastern highlands, we came to stand above the great deep pool where for untold centuries our people had gathered for the camas and the salmon. Here we moved together, at peace with the land and the sky and the water.

Here we walked in time-distilled motion that had neither beginning, nor end. The river and the land itself were uninhabited. The sweet turbulence of the Clearwater, gathering to rush headlong into the mighty junction of the Salmon-Snake, formed the cascades against which no other sound existed. On the strand below the swirl of the fishing hole where the Clearwater had built, deposited, distilled through eons of time layers of the coarse wet river sand I looked again into her eyes, felt again the firmness of her flesh, felt the yielding heaviness of her cream and sun-touched breasts against the skin of my chest and stomach. Here again I looked into the eyes, fathomless blue against the sky, impenetrable, unreflective.

From exhausted sweat-cold sleep, I wake. Stiff, hunched against the cold, drained, exhausted, by the sweat which soaks, the dreams of past and the reality of present interlace. Nearby the guards—now only two—dozed, wrapped in their great army blankets while the children of the Nez Perce huddled fitfully upon the freezing ground in the mud ravines and holes of the Bear Paws.

It is possible that at that moment I might have escaped my captors and returned to my own camp. The ropes which earlier had bound my hands and feet behind my back, had pulled together hands and feet beyond the possibility of movement, were now changed. After my confrontation with Miles my hands were tied in front, almost casually, by the sergeant himself. Gradually the number of guards had been reduced. Both of the guards that remained slept soundly. One, in fact, making little pretense of diligence, had crawled with his blanket into a supply wagon behind me. The other guard, an older man with fewer stripes and a dazed, bewildered look, slept more dutifully by the smoking, hissing fire.

Perhaps I might escape. The ropes, retied less tightly after the interval with Miles, might be, with the determination of one who has but a single goal to which to devote his being, loosened and removed. With stealth and care Joseph, a man who has spoken for the Nez Perce in council with white governors and generals, might free himself and with cunning elude the guards and the sentries in this armed camp and return to his own people. Perhaps he might hold a little longer waiting for the dark, and in the dark carry, as he escaped, food and supplies to his people.

What would Joseph, with stealth and cunning, choose to carry from the camp of Miles? What did the great wheeled wagons contain that would help the Nez Perce? For six months now we fought as best we could —when finally we must. We fought still. Would Joseph take from the wagons the ammunition needed for the defense of his people? Could he select—groping in the darkness, feeling for the appropriate calibers—sufficient ammunition for the rifles of the Nez Perce warriors who survived, who lived and fought, who remained to guard their families, somehow, miraculously, far beyond the valley of the Wallowa, beyond Whitebird Canyon, beyond the Clearwater and the Lolo and even beyond the terror of the Big Hole. Would that ammunition provide reparation for the constant harassing attacks of the Bannock and the Crow—attacks paid for with army money, provisioned from the same wagons that supplied the uniformed troops—attacks which drained our energy and lifeblood even more than the direct, pitched battles of Whitebird and the Clearwater. Would Joseph find in the wagons of the whites, somewhere among their supplies, the lifeblood spilt, lost forever to the Nez Perce? Would Joseph choose to escape and take as trophy and gift to his people the ammunition to draw out further the battle. Would he, could he, take a Gatling gun and turn the battle? With luck and a horse, even with one of the mules tethered within reach, a man might load a Gatling gun and enough ammunition to drive back the troops, to cause confusion and disarray enough so that the families of the Nez Perce might reach Canada and safety. Surely Sitting Bull and the Sioux who sit passive, remembering old animosities, and do not respond to our request for permission to enter their territory would not refuse the families of the Nez Perce warriors who even the Lakota consider, man for man, the most dangerous warriors of the plains.

Will Joseph take the Gatling gun, or will he take blankets and food for the women and children? Probably there are more blankets in the wagons and certainly there is food. Somewhere in the great wagons which allow the soldiers to live as a casual and comfortable camping party there will be both.

How many blankets can a man alone carry? In the dark through the snow? A dozen? Will Joseph escape then and carry to his people a dozen blankets? Maybe two dozen. Or three. A man can carry what he must. How many tins of food could he carry with them? What purpose will hand-held blankets and food serve in the morning when the soldiers move again against our position? What would the ammunition serve without the blankets or the blankets without the ammunition? Would either return our land and our people, our brothers who even now die encircled in the snow-bound camp of the Bear Paws? How profits it a man that he take to his people all they need. Can he then say, "Here are the blankets and the food and the weapons you need: go and drive away the soldiers who circle your camp. You have fought long and bravely for your freedom. Don't let a thousand troops stop you now. Canada, the free country we have heard of, lies almost within sight to the north. Take your women and children and old and wounded through the soldiers and escape."

Who would lead the Nez Perce warriors? Ollokot, brother, flesh of my fathers, kind benevolent spirit of my youth, is dead.

There is a time when a man can do no more than sit and dream of what was and what might have been. This then drives me to the camp of Miles, holds me in the camp, forces me to wait his leisure so that I may negotiate as best I can the surrender of the Nez Perce. The complexities of the whites fall away, can be finally sheared away from the core of what is, for Joseph need not consider the motives of Miles, need not determine if the opportunity of escape is provided so that murder may be covered, justified. Joseph can only sit and wait.

For Ollokot is dead. The mind will not admit it, can tolerate only the words and with the words close out completely the concept. There is yet the memory of what was: the days when the Nez Perce lived free in the Wallowa, when a man sought peace and solitude and communion with the spirits who made him for he was one with his land, lived, enacted the pageant that the aged, travois-carried Toohoolhoolzote chants as his death dirge, sings through the Story Teller his dying curse to the whites:

> *"We, the people, are the spirit-formed images of benevolence. The Nimpau exist as the shadow of the earth our Mother. From her bosom we are raised, from her countenance we take our sustenance, to her bounty we return our flesh, joining irrevocably our spirits to the underlying energy which radiates infinite life throughout our plateau.*
>
> *"Beware he who violates or attempts to stand against this energy. For the Earth itself is sacred and inviolable and will not long tolerate those who dig and cut and fence with greed upon its surface.*

"There will be a time, a time that is at hand, when the earth will raise its energy against those who have lost harmony and will return the spirits of all the creatures who have lived upon and reflected the benevolence of the earth, to cleanse, to cast out, to wipe clean the taint from the earth.

"A host of warriors will ride again upon the bosom of the earth. With them will be Rainbow and Five Wounds and Ollokot. The countless heroes of legend will be raised up and the plateaus and the valleys and the plains will shake with the weight and the number of their horse. The white and any with him who violate the spirit and essence of the earth our mother will be driven irrevocably back into the sea. And there will come again a peace and a harmony to our earth.

This then was the homeland we gave up, fled—denying the spirit of our fathers in the foolish, futile effort to preserve the blood of our fathers. Toohoolhoolzote knew it, loved it, even as it was touched, spoiled by those who came increasingly to it to use it, to abuse it. The trappers touched it, altered it here and there taking away the beaver and the otter. But the trappers were temporary, transient wanderers without women who were content to camp and trap and leave. The missionaries were the first to change our land. The missionaries came, the Spaldings and the Whitmans, the beautiful and kind and sensitive Narcissa Whitman who spoke to the Nez Perce of Jesus and who died speaking to others of Jesus.

We camped a week more in the pleasant Bitterroot Valley. Lodge poles, abandoned in the flight from the Clearwater, were cut and the remaining material was spread to form make-shift lodges. Hope and confidence continued to grow in our camp. Howard, our scouts reported, was far behind us still struggling to get his men through the Lolo Pass.

The dissension which existed concerned our direction. Looking Glass wanted to move south, down the Bitterroot Valley, and then east into the land of the Crows where he had friends, where he believed we would gain allies.

"The whites will never move against us when we are joined with the Crows," Looking Glass spoke. His confidence and persuasiveness, quieted for a time by the near disaster at the Clearwater, had returned.

Five Wounds, with Rainbow and Ollokot behind him, spoke to Joseph urging that we turn north, through the land of the Flatheads, our oldest and most dependable allies, and move quickly to the northern plains where we might retreat to Canada if the soldiers continued to press us.

White Bird, persuaded by the arguments of Look Glass, spoke for the idea of moving down the Bitterroot Valley. Hototo, influential for his knowledge of this country agreed south was best. "Better hunting there," he urged. "Pleasant country with much game."

And so the Nez Perce broke camp to move to the south and the land of the Big Hole Basin. Two days later we camped in the meadow of the famous Medicine Tree. Here stood a giant pine which held, higher than a man could reach standing on a horse's back, the enormous horn of a Bighorn sheep embedded deeply in the living fiber. It was a place of legend, known for good spirits and good luck. Here, between the medicine tree and the rushing brook which paralleled the trail leading to the Big Hole Basin, was born to Ollokot and Aihits Palojami, Fairland, the first male child in our family.

Despite the struggle and difficulties of the Lolo, the child was healthy and strong. The next day Ollokot stood with the child before the camp. Ollokot looked to me and then to Aihits Palojami.

"The child will be called Tuekakas, as were our fathers before him."

Story Teller:

Slowly regaining strength and confidence, the Nez Perce move south through the Bitterroot Valley to the Big Hole basin, the land of their traditional friends, the Flatheads. The whites they encounter along the way seem to appreciate the courtesy of the Nez Perce who pay immediately for the supplies they purchase from the white trading posts.

The beauty of the fish-filled, alluvial Big Hole River with its clear water and excellent camping sites is enticing and many wish to establish a permanent summer camp.

Others have dreams and premonition of death. Those who fear the dream-perfect peace of the Big Hole are few, but outspoken.

> *Brothers and sisters,*
> *I speak to you!*
> *In a dream last night I saw myself killed.*
> *I will be killed soon!*
> *I do not care. I am willing to die.*
> *First, I will kill some soldiers.*
> *I shall not turn back from death. We are*
> *all going to die.*

Wahlitits, the Nez Perce.

Today the markers and monuments reveal the truth of those whose wyakins warned of the dangers of complacency—recording the deaths of the courageous who fought for their families and traditions and the courageous who believed they fought for their country.

Twenty-nine soldiers die in the attack on the Nez Perce camp. Forty more are wounded.

Six soldiers receive the Metal of Honor for their roles in the Big Hole attack. On the site a massive monument is erected by the army to honor the soldiers who fought and died there.

Two smaller monuments are placed by citizens in memory of the ninety Nez Perce, many of them women and children, who were killed.

"IN MEMORY OF THE INDIANS, INFANTS, CHILDREN, WOMEN, AND OLD MEN WHO WERE WOUNDED AND KILLED NEAR THIS BATTLEFIELD BY WHITE SOLDIERS, AUGUST, 9, 1877."

X. The Big Hole
August 9, 1877

In the early dawn light of August in the foothills of the Montana Bitterroots the strength of the Nez Perce is broken. On the battlefield of the Big Hole fell the legendary hero, Rainbow. A few hours later his long time companion and friend, a warrior of greater cunning and equal renown, the free-spirited Five Wounds died. Also among those to fall at the Big Hole were Natalekin, the old herdsman who blundered against the advancing soldiers and whose life at least provided us a minute or two warning, Hahtalekin, the Palouse headman, and Wahlitits, the young boy whose raid of frustration and revenge started the war, but who had quickly become one of our best warriors. By Wahlitits' side died his young wife, Telnayas, who seized his fallen gun and fired it until her own warrior death. Zya Temoni, my messenger to Howard at the Clearwater, was killed by mistake by one of our own rifles. Sarpis Illpilp, the cousin and companion of Wahlitits, died far in advance of our main lines and his body lay exposed in the hot sun for most of the day until his father, Yellow Bull, offered a handsome reward for the recovery of his corpse.

From the Wallowa these died: the powerful Tahwis Tokaitat, Big Horn Bow; Peopeo Ipsewahk, Lone Bird, who twice announced the danger of the Big Hole Basin in dreams of his impending death; and Two Moons, who fell mortally wounded bringing away the infant Tuekakas after first Aihits Palojami and then Toma Alwawonmi, sister and wife, died in the first savage assault of the troops.

The Asotin band lost two of its best men in the young Black Eagle, nephew of Looking Glass and the faithful Peopeo Tholekt who died shortly after the successful attack on the howitzer.

The small band of Husishusis Kute lost its headman, the son called Husishusis Kute after the famous orator father who died at the Clearwater. White Bird lost, in addition to Sarpis Illpilp, seven other principal warriors including the trouble-makers Tomahas and Watahipe who, in the end, fought bravely.

Many more were to be counted among the dead at the Big Hole. In the confusion and grief that overwhelmed the placid camp of the Big Hole we were never to know the total extent of our losses. In the chaos and panic of the still dark camp soldiers and warriors and women and children screamed and ran blindly, directionless. Families were disrupted so that it would be months before many people were accounted for. Some were simply to disappear, dead or lost to us forever. Only with the warriors was it possible to be exact: eighteen of our best men died at the Big Hole. Two of these, Rainbow and Five Wounds, had stood with Ollokot at the very forefront of our defense. In addition to the experienced men, five of our young boy-warriors were killed—boys who would have normally been learning the skills of their fathers in the highland plateau of the Salmon, Snake, and Clearwater, but who now fought beside their older brothers and fathers for the lives of their families.

Whatever the loss to our warriors at the Big Hole, it was the women and children who suffered most and died by the hands of the man called Gibbon. Twenty women and almost thirty children were killed in the tents of our summer camp when the soldiers came for the first time to the very lodges of the Nez Perce.

The Big Hole, Hin-mah-too-yah-lat-kekht, called Joseph, will remember forever. The shouts and the screams are with me always. The suffering and dying in the early morning darkness of the Big Hole camp was my responsibility: it came directly from my indecisiveness and hesitation. I alone might have opposed Looking Glass and have broken the lethargic quiet camp. Had I risen to speak in council, had I insisted boldly enough that the Nez Perce must move, must keep constant vigilance, had I done any of these things I might have passed life without the memories of the shouts and screams and suffering wrought by the soldiers who fought beside the tents of the Nez Perce that hazy, hot August dawn.

But I did not oppose Looking Glass, did not exercise the authority entrusted to me, even though around me I could sense the growing anxiety as day by day we remained immobile in camp by the Big Hole creek.

To those who counsel otherwise, Looking Glass restates his argument, "Between the whites of this country and the Nez Perce, there is no quarrel."

"Here they have," Looking Glass would continue, charmed and convinced by his own arguments, "here they have another governor, a different headman and a different military man."

The warriors heard Looking Glass; they listened to his opinion. He was Allalimya Takanin, son of Meiway, the great chief. The headsmen and warriors listened because he said what most wanted to hear. We had been driven from our positions at the Clearwater River, fled, passing with anguish and increasing exhaustion over the Lolo trail to this exile in a distant land. So the words of Looking Glass were comforting when he spoke of our alliance with the Asbionne, the fierce warriors of the Crow. They heard his arguments that we should stay in camp and rest and allow the horses to graze and grow strong and find fresh meat for ourselves. The people heard these things and agreed to them because they were tired and there was no other place to go.

Joseph, too, heard the arguments of Looking Glass. A more stationary camp would allow time to complete the new lodges, to kill and dry meat, to pasture the horses so that they could regain the lost flesh and strength necessary for our survival. The camp at the Big Hole might allow the Nez Perce to become a people again, to reestablish and reorient our lodges and families, to decide where we might seek permanent refuge in or near our homeland.

So I allowed myself the persuasive words of Looking Glass. I, too, wanted to believe. I, too, like White Bird and Toohoolhoolzote, the latter strangely silent and withdrawn since the Clearwater, allowed Looking Glass to have his way. It was the easy thing to do. He was Allalimya Takanin, son of Apash Wyakaikt, the greatest war-chief of the Nez Perce. So we all heard him, allowed him his way, because he was positive he was right, and I could not be certain he was wrong.

We took the easy way and for this, because of this, the Nimpau were broken. It was a thing a man, a chief should have foreseen and prevented. Yet the camp and the quiet domestic repair and reorientation were things that I accepted with a type of blind faith. It was possible, as Looking Glass argued, that there was a boundary to Howard's pursuit, or that he might simply grow tired and give up. He had driven us away from the land the whites wished to claim as their own: why would he follow a people he could neither defeat nor capture? We left him far back on the Lolo, Looking Glass reassured. Perhaps the mountain pass had been too much for him; perhaps his great army of axe men had given up their ropes and pulleys and had turned back, conceding the Lolo trail too difficult for a supply-encumbered military detachment.

While the Nez Perce rested, the telegram, the instrument our older people call the talking wire, a thing that in retrospect it is evident that no Nez Perce ever fully understood or anticipated adequately, delivered the orders which set against us a man called Gibbon. As we sat in camp leisurely calculating the speed and progress of Howard to the west of us, Gibbon, with a dangerous combination of fearlessness and ambition, moved against us from the north.

We had been in camp in the Big Hole Basin less than a week when Gibbon attacked us.

Of his presence we had no knowledge. The full heat of late summer had come to this lower and drier Montana place slowing our activity, lulling our watch. Yet, the mornings, evenings, and nights were pleasant enough and on the evening of the fifth day in the Big Hole Camp, a more or less spontaneous celebration had begun. Hototo, called Lean Elk or Poker Joe, the part Nez Perce, part French adventurer who had joined us soon after we came into the Montana territory, was to take Keletauw, daughter of the Palouse headman, Hahtalekin, as his second wife. In the cooler evening dusk, while Lean Elk and Hahtalekin disputed, half-seriously, the quality of the horses brought as dowry, an informal celebration had begun—the first diversion of any consequence we had had since before the late winter day in the Wallowa when Howard brought to us a definite demand and date for our removal to the reservation at Lapwai.

Looking Glass arrived at the lodge of Hahtalekin immediately after the evening meal. He had caught his small, prancing pony, the one he rode into our camp that first day, for the journey of less than a hundred yards. Upon his head was perched his favorite hat, the feather-decorated felt hat he had of a river boat drummer at the point the whites had come to call Lewiston. Dismounting, Looking Glass called out his greetings and brought up his gift, a small metal pan. Hahtalekin, Hohots, and Looking Glass sat down to smoke; several others stopped as well and soon, with improvised reed flutes and hastily repaired drum frames, the wedding dance began.

Even Ollokot, I became aware as I made my usual rounds, had joined the celebration. He sat with his wife, Aihits Palojami, and the son, young Tuekakas, born during our passage through the Bitterroot Valley. Around them moved the two older girls who vied for the infant's attention. As I went through the camp I was pleased, thinking that whatever the best course of action might be, at least our camp here had the advantage that it allowed those like Ollokot who had fought for months rest and quietude and that we could not help being stronger for a pause which renewed unity and spirit.

I was glad for the rest and unity, even as I made my last check of the night by following the flat lowland of the Big Hole stream along for perhaps a mile. As I moved and studied both the open prairie to my south and the sloping foothills to the north whose partially tree-covered slopes ran down to the brush which guarded both the stream bank and the northern perimeter of our camp, I was aware again that while our camp permitted unobstructed views to the south and west, the probable route of Howard if he should come so far, the treed sides of the hills to our north sloped down into the heart of the camp itself. But again Looking Glass had prevailed: there was no water or shade if we pulled back from the creek bank and it would little profit us to huddle like cattle in the open plain unless attack was imminent and then the camp should be broken anyway.

So I stood in the full dark before the moon rose and listened. From the plains behind me and from the slopes in front of me there came no sound at all—a clue, which in the clarity of reflection, now screams warning against the disaster that even at that moment built for my people in the shadows of the timber above me. The total silence should have been a warning—as possibly was the dog which barked steadily somewhere near the outskirts of the camp. But I chose to attribute the silence to the sounds of the dance-celebration which were new to the Big Hole valley and would alter the normal night sounds of the creek basin.

Even the persistent barking of a single dog meant little to me. The camp was full of dogs and any one of them, or all of them, might turn out to launch a howling, barking, joyous attack on, say, a horned toad, or an old man returning from a trip to relieve himself, or, in some instances, the most virile and fiercest attack might be launched against absolutely nothing at all. My greatest curiosity about that particular incident, even now knowing its full and disastrous results, was why only one dog barked, though it is now evident that the barking came from the area of White Bird's camp which was farthest to the northwest, closest to the point from which in a few hours Gibbon would bring two hundred armed men into the sleeping camp of the Nez Perce with the simple order: "Destroy."

Through the anguish of suffering, through the comprehension time permits, comes truth. Truth at the Big Hole lay in the prophetic dreams of those who spoke their troubled hearts, cried out their fears about this pleasant basin where in earlier and better times the Nez Perce camped with the gods and sought with compassion the buffalo, fought with vigor and blood-letting passion the Bannock and the Plegman.

It was the troubled sleep of Ollokot which first spoke the foreboding of his spirit for this peaceful camp:

The dark trees and fertile grass and solitude of this valley cry out warning to the Nez Perce.

The troubled spirits of time speak to our spirits and warn us to leave this land.

Here there is something, some evil force I cannot name, nor see, which moves against our very being.

Wahlitits, the young man who has gained courage and age since the raid which set us against Howard, dreams the dream of his own death:

From the forest of black walks in silence the man of death.

Above the trailing garment of grey-white which covers him is the dried buffalo head of death.

Death is in the wasted eyes of the buffalo skull.

He who looks on death can but join.

Wahlitits, looks into the face of death.

I do not care.

I will go with the buffalo ghost for here there is evil and death for all.

The Nez Perce will die in this troubled valley.

The spirits, the Wyakins, breathe into the open and sunlit air the subtle odor of danger. Hear the follower of Toohoolhoolzote, Peopeo Ipsewahk, who looks to the hills and speaks only of moving, of hurry and speed away from this place which once harbored our spirits:

Here is our defeat.

Here the white will walk among our tepees with the club and the torch.

I see no men who wake to stop him.

Here is as well the troubled countenance of the warrior Rainbow, the great Wahchumyus, who sits before his lodge in silence, who walks into the night unarmed, who stands for hours in the dark becoming almost a part of the earth he touches. Behind him, in the distance with the long rifle, is Five Wounds who studies his friend and is himself troubled.

So it is not that we had no warning that some force hovered over us in the Big Hole camp. Yet this did not stop the celebration Looking Glass had begun. It was as if Fate had come, cloaking, overwhelming the Nez Perce and there was nothing any man could do to counteract the forces at work on the camp. We believed so. We were tired, exhausted by months of constant flight.

Ollokot, brother, the Nez Perce, warrior spirit of my own being and flesh floats in my consciousness in many forms and images. Many are indistinct, for a man in time becomes careless and insensitive to those around him. A few are distinct, clear as though the dark camp of Miles with its myriad glowing campfires does not exist and reality is the full day's sun where Ollokot lives and waits, a boy of twelve, when he has come alone to meet me as I return from the mountain where I sought the Wyakin, the spirit and harmony of my life. Before me in the distance he stands on the foothill knoll with the hobbled horses. He waits without anxiety, calm, controlled as I ascend finally the knoll on which he stands. Before me in the noon-day's sun he waits, already at twelve my height and size though not yet my weight, confident, dispassionate, mastering even then the self-sufficiency, the discipline of mind and body which will create determination and self-confidence, unmatched by any man I have ever known.

Ollokot stands in my mind now in the camp of Miles as he did six weeks ago before Gibbon drove into our camp. I remember him twice in the Big Hole camp.

The first memory is that of the man who stood before his campfire and looked to the slopes above us where the children later admitted they saw white men standing, wrapped in grey blankets with only their eyes showing, looking out, into, the camp of the Nez Perce. The sight frightened the children and caused them to stay within the camp, though they said nothing—as one who avoids the words in fear that speaking the words will bring an event to be. Ollokot looked to the slopes and ridges above us, but saw nothing. Instead, he turned to the cradle board before them, near the fire in the cooling night air, and, picking up the infant Tuekakas, extended his hand to the fawn spirit Aihits Palojami, the sister whom I loved as though she had been born into my family. Together they walked to the village center where the people had come together before the lodge of Hahtalekin.

A second image of Ollokot stands, burns in my mind. And this is Ollokot as the troops have come into our village. Of the time sequence I am not sure, for what I remember of the Big Hole that terrible morning is that I was suddenly awake, covered with the cold sweat of dreams. About me, around me there were screams and shouting and groans, and, occasionally, the flat explosion of gunfire. Instantaneously the flap of my tent was ripped open—it may have been that the movement of the flap awoke me, or that the fore-shortened explosion of my childhood name, "Tuyuku," which Ollokot probably spoke before or as he ripped back the flap awoke me—but whatever the sequence Ollokot was before me in the faint light of the tiny lodge fire, framed by the blackness behind him. He was fully armed and—the only time in my life I was to see him adorned in any way—wildly painted. The flickering light reflected, made more sinister the bright vermillion hue of his face, made more ghostly the dull green bar which framed his eyes and nose and trailed diagonally down across his cheeks and jaws in narrow bars. Similar bars streaked and lined his forehead.

"Fight." He said but the single word, thrust to me the Henry rifle that was our father's, and was gone.

So in the pre-dawn darkness of late summer the Nez Perce fought beside and for the lodges which held our families. Before me, in the distance, but visible as I came from my tent, was a unit of six or seven soldiers. Behind them I could hear the sounds and cursing as another line of men waded the slippery, chestdeep creek. With no apparent design the men swept along the single line of lodges which stood between my lodge and the creek. Most at least continued along the line, but one stopped almost directly before me, selected, somehow, the lodge of my Wallowan, Lahpeealoot, Geese Three Times Lighting on Water, a fine, brave young warrior killed in the Clearwater fight. Quickly, frantically, the young soldier—I could distinguish the blondish hair which came almost to his shoulders as I moved cautiously closer—attacked the old canvas of the newly remade and resewn tent of the woman of Lahpeealoot. With time-detached inertia, I watched his effort to push the tent over. Failing this he instantly brought up the rifle he carried and, turning the bayonet on its side, managed to rip upward and apart one section forming an opening a man might walk through. With amazement and horror—I was now less than a dozen paces away, though the blond-haired soldier, intent on the tent before him remained unaware of my presence—I saw the white man enter the tent I knew to be defenseless, housing only Knoonemie, the woman of the dead Lahpeealoot, their three small sons and an old woman of Looking Glass' band, a remote relative taken in, after the death of Lahpeealoot and the flight from the Clearwater when the old woman's own nephew and wife abandoned her and our camp in an effort to blend back, unnoticed, into the treaty faction at Lapwai.

I was there, watching, disbelievingly compliant, when the blonde, uniformed white drove apart the folded soft canvas shrouds and forced his entry into the warm and unprotected tent's center. *Incredulously now I stand, mute and motionless as before me the hard, uniformed arms are raised and the torso twists, turns, strikes downward into the core of my existence the club-like rifle: the butt of the rifle itself time-frozen in my mind forever, suspended in inalterable slow motion above the pad which holds the half-senseless woman and the startled children. Slowly, malevolently the arch is continued but IT CAN NOT FALL, cannot strike, cannot complete this act, so malicious, so senseless, so destructive—for it should not be, cannot be for it should not be. Somewhere here there is dream and illusion which will fade way, resolve itself and the sun and the sound of the birds and the clean, untouched air of the mountains and the taste, mouth-aching cold, of the highland streams and the physical confidence and vigor of youth will return. It cannot be. It should not be. Slowly, surely, the rifle continues its arch downward. Calmly the sleepy woman raises her hand to dispel for me the dream neither of us believes: she reaches up as if to touch, as if to brush way the rifle itself and the hand, the fingers fold softly around the pole-strong instrument as it flashes to complete its thrush downward and fills the interior of the tent with the splashing explosion of flesh as the head and face itself receive the force from the trained lunge of the soldier.*

Quickly the club is withdrawn and the face and the blankets which cover the wife of Lahpeealoot turn, before the eye can look away, bright red.

The rifle comes up to strike again as children wake to sounds and a warm stickiness they do not understand. Finally now I can move, can cast down the rifle which will not fire and reach out for the soldier whose back is to me, unaware, until some sound I must have made, of my presence. But even as he tries to turn the old woman is moving toward him, the blade of the thin skinning knife catching momentarily the light of the fire.

The smoke and the sound of the rifle exploding within the confines of the tent cloak the brief, temporary union of the bodies, the frail form of the old woman and the rigid, military taut profile of the soldier, cloak the union and obscure the crumpling collapse of the woman, spent, deflated, like the toys of the whites, as the bayonet comes back with its thin, dark stain.

But the soldier will himself die. For the complexities of circumstance and heritage and conscience are resolved in the tent of the dead warrior, Lahpeealoot, and even I am conscious of my scream, conscious briefly of the rage which consumes me as I come against the hard, violent body of the soldier, conscious of a rage which finally drives dark the mind and eyes in physical intensity that is resolved only with cramp and exhaustion when I release the limp, lifeless body of the white soldier, the stranger who came silently to the Big

Hole in the early morning darkness and without a word spoken died leaving the lodge of Lahpeealoot and the Nez Perce in sorrow.

From the tent of Lahpeealoot I move in numb horror. The exertion of my struggle calmed somewhat my personal anguish and rage, but it is evident from the sounds around me that the Nez Perce must fight better, more desperately than ever before or be destroyed. With me, from the tent of Lahpeealoot, I brought the children, carrying the two youngest while the third, a boy of six, walked, limped beside me holding the loose end of my overshirt—his ankle already swelling from the weight and force of a hob-nailed boot.

From my own lodge I brought away the terrified but still stable Toma, wife and companion spirit of happier times, and the three-year-old daughter, our only child, born to us in the last undisturbed year of the Wallowa. From her bed of age I lifted the fragile, light form of Natokolas, the grandmother whose mind dwelt now in the days before even Tuekakas when she was a girl in the highland Wallowa and Snake plateaus and the great chiefs of the Nez Perce knew of the white man only as a legend and a rumor passed in wonder by the traveling peoples of the plains to our east and the river people to our north and west.

From the lodge we fled to the bush and trees which bordered the creek to the east. Everywhere there was fear and confusion as the soldiers came to the very lodges with their smoking torches. Nowhere did there seem to be more than chance fighting. In dismay and confusion our men seemed to seek only refuge and safety for their families.

Once we reached the temporary safety of the creek bank I put down Natokolas and, leaving the children to the care of Toma and Aihits Palojami, ran immediately to the south edge of our camp to do what I could about either saving or bringing up the horses. On my way I overtook my old friend Zya Temoni who had also realized the importance of controlling the horses. With care we approached the increasingly agitated herd. Luckily, my old mare and childhood pet, Whisket, was visible, and we caught her and used her to approach and catch my speckled grey stallion called Ground Snow by little Natokolas for his molted rump and back. Mounted now, I quickly caught up a good horse for Zya Temoni and we began a circular cast to tighten and control the herd. Moments later the thin, whistling whine of bullets passed near me and to my left the blanket coat of Zya Temoni puffed dust and he slumped and slid from his horse.

Alone and with difficulty, I started the horse herd away from the camp. Soon, however, two of the older boys, mounted double on one of the camp ponies, came galloping out to help. With the herd together now and moving, I gave instructions for the boys to take them to safety on the plain and hold them together—to bring them up if I called for them, to stampede them if they were approached by anyone they did not know.

With apprehension and fear I turned the deep-bottomed speed of Ground Snow back to the camp of the Nez Perce. Even as I returned it was evident that our men had begun to stand and fight.

> White Bird, his high, piercing voice clear and distinct above the confusion, calls out for the warriors of the Nez Perce:

Fight.

Save the families. Save yourself.

In all times men have fought for their women and children.

Looking Glass, now beside White Bird adds the beautiful cadence of his strong voice:

Fight with me Nimpau.

Save the women and children.

No man in all time has forced his will upon the women and children of the Nez Perce.

And so as the first light of dawn began to break over the Big Hole Basin the warriors of the Nez Perce confused, disoriented, and afraid at first, began to form themselves around the headmen who stood their ground to rally them and the warriors who, with Ollokot and Rainbow and Five Wounds, had thrown themselves against the center of Gibbon's advancing line.

Even as the troops continued their advance into the center and west of our camp, burning and killing almost as they pleased, the warriors of the Nez Perce returned from the gullies and ravines of the creek bank to the east where they had carried their families. As they returned they fell against the eastern most segment of Gibbon's line, a line that did not reach quite across our camp. Piecemeal this line crumbled and broke, and the returning warriors, led now by Looking Glass, drove Gibbon's men back toward the creek and the camp's center which created a crossfire on the soldiers and caused hesitation and confusion for them for the first time since they charged our camp. This hesitation, plus the resistance which had formed around Ollokot, Five Wounds, Hototo, and many of our strong younger men in the center of the camp finally halted the forward movement of the troops and began the long, desperate fight to drive the soldiers back out of our village.

But even as the troops fell back slowly from the center of the village itself, the sight of the destruction and the dead disheartened and weakened our warriors. Rainbow was no longer at the head of the Nez Perce warriors. The great warrior Wahchumyus, believed invincible by the men who fought beside him, known to be invincible by every man who had ever opposed him in contest or battle, died in the morning darkness of the Big Hole battle. From his isolated lodge Rainbow had come in the first and most frantic minutes of the attack. With his dispassionate and fearless heart he had sought the center of the charge, the greatest threat to our people, and, having found it, died, in anonymity during the frantic hand to hand struggle near the heart of our camp—fulfilling the prophecy of his wyakin spirit: invincible in battle after dawn—to find his death in the early glow before sunrise.

Five Wounds, the friend and—until the darkness and confusion of this fatal morning—the inseparable companion of Rainbow, was inconsolable. Many other warriors were dismayed, rendered almost inert by the sight of Rainbow's body. For Rainbow, in physical deed and simple courage, the greatest warrior of our time had come to represent for most of our people the favor of the spirit gods and the final safety of our people. The spirit Wyakin which stood over Rainbow was awesome, strong, and the comfort of our people. Around our camp fires, but never in his presence, the story was told again and again of the boy who grew to be the warrior we knew as Rainbow. It was said that in the desert where the boy Rainbow fled after the Blackfoot raid destroyed his family, a spirit appeared to Rainbow, a voice spoke to him through the transparent colors of a rare dry-land rainbow and said, promised, that as long as the sun shone upon Wahchumyus no man could stand against him in battle.

So the Nez Perce had come to rely upon this man, his strength, and his vision. At fourteen Rainbow could outrun any man known to the Nez Perce. In his late teens and early twenties came the strength to match the speed. And always since his appearance from the desolate plains there had been the resolution and determination of the man himself. Rainbow fought the Blackfoot with a fury that bordered on madness, but against all other enemies of our people Rainbow had a control and dispassion that made him seem almost casual in battle. After the Clearwater Ollokot himself told of the overwhelming numbers as the soldiers attempted to overrun the last warriors on the cliffs protecting the Nez Perce village. Ollokot told of his own fear and danger and told how suddenly, from somewhere the great Rainbow was beside him with the flashing two-bladed axe. Ollokot spoke with awe and pride of the cold effortless efficiency of Rainbow: the great Wahchumyus whose twisted and distorted body lay before us still under the guns and bayonets of the whites.

Soon after the recovery of Rainbow's body, Five Wounds and Ollokot led the attack which was to halt, at least temporally, Gibbon. Not long after that I left the warriors and turned to the people of the camp whose wails of mourning filled now the bottomland camp of the Big Hole Basin.

The dirge of mourning were but few, for we were few.

Without warning or premonition before me was her body. Cleaned, straightened, ash-tan in death, marred only by the warmth-less hue and the small stain near the breast where the wound had seeped through the blanket which covered her body.

There was through me calm, almost a release and peace. For Toma was of the days and youth when we walked free the trails and meadows of the Wallowa. To these meadows and plateaus she was now released and the suffering and pain, the dirt and sweat-covered despair and humiliation of a fugitive camp was a moment passed. The haste and anxiety, the moment by moment strain of the Lolo, where the primeval urge for existence, survival, masked and rendered callous the emotions of sense, were now gone.

Beyond the travois-lain body were grandmother and daughter—one, ninety; one, three—both Natokolas as were generations before them. On the ground they sat, breast to breast, cheek to cheek, hugging, clinging to each other. There were no words or tears and perhaps neither had little more than partial comprehension of the scene before them. The tears came when little Natokolas saw me, recognized me finally through the soot and dirt.

The tears came then and so came again the reality of our plight. Taking the child with me I hurried on beyond the women and old men, who scraped with hoes and hands shallow graves in the dry Montana soil, to signal the older boys to bring up the horses.

Story Teller: Stoneless Words

Story Teller sees today—as in the days past and as will be in the days to come—on the ground and in the burning teepees of the Big Hole camp, the bodies of the dead.

Story Teller laments, not the warriors who died, but the defenseless women, children, and old who were killed without passion as though they were animals.

Story Teller sees with sorrow the wounded hiding in the ravines to which they have fled and from which they must crawl to flee, still hunted.

Story Teller remembers as if today the daybreak attack of Chivington and his seven hundred men on the sleeping village of Black Kettle. Story Teller shutters: The slaughter and mutilations for entertainment and display. Cheyenne breasts and scrotums cut and taken to become tobacco pouches to flaunt in the saloons of Denver.

Story Teller remembers as today, for each day is as one for the story teller, the morning attack of Custer upon the Cheyenne and Arapaho at the Washita.

Story Teller is with the Lakota at Wounded Knee: camp of containment and slaughter. Story Teller sees the mass grave into which one hundred and fifty bodies are dumped and covered while many lie dead or wounded in the crevices to which they were able to crawl.

Story Teller walks upon the desolate, snow-covered ground of the Bear Paws, the last camp of the free Nez Perce. Story Teller sees the small open-sky shrines to the warriors and the people of the Nez Perce where those who wait have placed small charms and tobacco upon the spots where the warriors died.

At the height of a slight rise, near the depression of a hand-dug rifle-pit, is a small stone rolled vertical as marker. Around the stone are several pieces of ornamental jewelry and charms, together with a dozen or so cigarettes lain symmetrically in place. Against the stone leans a weathered wooden marker with the single word "Ollokot."

XI. Flight
August–September, 1877

The camp of Miles sleeps.

Warm, sheltered, and full-stomached, the white troops rest. With the morning sun they will service the guns, distribute the ammunition, and try again to overrun the camp of my people.

In the valley and the shadow of death I am afraid.

Our people are afraid; they are tired and their spirits are broken. The strength of our warriors is gone, the comfort of our children and the love of our parents are lost to us.

Our home is abandoned, our spirits betrayed. Now we wander directionless, governed, guided only by the force and speed of those who pursue.

For the Nez Perce have no place to go. Our old friends turn their backs. Our enemies lurk, waiting our collapse.

Howard comes without haste. He has time and a continent.

Where shall we go. How shall we survive. The Nimpau wanders, fugitive upon the earth.

Into the shallow recesses in the banks of the Big Hole creek we placed our dead, caving down the earth over them. About me in this camp of sorrow were the wails of mourning. We could do no more; there was no time.

Ollokot, warrior, brother, came to me. With his eyes and the unfinished phrases he sought my approval:

"We have the men."

"The cost is too great."

"He comes to our camp in darkness to kill the helpless."

"Few remain to us. Many stand behind him. You must come away."

So, as the camp was broken and the families fled, the warriors of the Nez Perce came finally together to hold Gibbon. Frightened, fugitive, the old and the young ran as best they could, walked, scrambled without direction. Only away —away from the camp of horror. On the earth behind us we were to leave eighty of our people: eighteen warriors, twenty-two women, twenty-seven children and thirteen of the old. With us from the Big Hole we carried over one hundred wounded.

The warriors of the Nez Perce came to stand in place, then, led by Five Wounds, began to move, one man at a time to a more protected position on the flanks of the first detachment of soldiers sent against us. Quickly the deadly fire directed against them from the side forced the soldiers to fall back from the chaotic camp to protect themselves.

Only hours after the first attack, the dead and wounded mostly located and dragged away by the families, the warriors watched helplessly as the great warrior Five Wounds put down his rifle and abandoned the protected position from which he, almost alone, had forced the troops to turn, to swing about and to make a stand. Five Wounds moved silently toward the entrenched position the white soldiers had scratched out on the banks of Big Hole Creek.

In the hush that fell over the battle, in the increasing August heat, the warriors watched as Five Wounds reached the brush of the creek bed that led to the soldiers' position. They watched, seeing nothing of Five Wounds now. As they watched and waited, bold and clear began the death song of Five Wounds. The troops watched and waited, too—fired, in anxiety, at nothing, nothing but the sound that floated down from somewhere close by. All watched, anticipated, and heard finally the war cry of Five Wounds as he hurdled the logs and trowel-scooped trench into the midst of the troops—coming, somehow, not from the creek brush where he had last been seen and where the soldiers watched, but from the side so that he closed with them and the knife flashed again and again before the cry was silenced.

Pahkatos Owyeen, Five Wounds, died, joining his friend Wahchumyus, the great Rainbow and the best of our life-blood spilled senselessly on the Montana soil of the Big Hole Basin far from our homeland.

In the Wallowa the Nez Perce camp. The cold, endless waters of the Imnaha fall through the canyons to the Snake. In mute mural before me is painted the lodge of Tuekakas. In stilled time stands the work of the camp: the salmon, split and gutted, dry on the lashed pole frames beside the lodges. The run is over, completed, and the nets and baskets and spears lie on the bank in the sun. The women gather to cut and scrape the camas; with them are Natokolas, grandmother, and Toneda, frail mother. In animated conversation they work, soundless to me. Beyond the camp, across the meadow of the Wallowa, ride Tuekakas, father, and Ollokot, brother. Upon the pacing horse of Ollokot is carried the carcass of a deer. Across his back is strung the man's bow. The rigid-held face of brother reveals nothing; the time-softened face of father is relaxed, benevolent. In tense anticipation I wait to greet them.

Toward us come the wagons of Howard, great heavy wagons which sink constantly into the brittle soil beneath them, which are constantly wrenched free by the oxstrong, obstinate mules fresh from the commissary officer who provides them, replaces them with his endless supply of campaign promissory notes. The wagons never stop, and pause only when the fresh teams are harnessed into place and the drivers changed.

Parallel, side by side with the wagons, pace the five hundred men who march with the easy slovenliness of experience and indifference. Through the lines there is occasional banter and the calculation of time.

"Ten minutes to the next break."

"Two hours to supper."

The greased and oiled boots thud endlessly into the increasingly volcanic soil.

Ahead and to the side are the cavalry troops. These men slump, lean hunchback forward in the way men of little self-concept will do when traveling great distances on horseback. The steel-shod and grain-nourished hooves measure forward tirelessly.

Farther ahead, in the distance on the plain before the troops, are the Bannocks, our despised enemy, whose numbers now reach one hundred, whose numbers will soon double. At their head is the young chief, Buffalo Horn, a dangerous and vicious man, for a Bannock, a brave man. In milling, undisciplined fashion, they ride. Turning, wheeling, frolicking, they boast of the big money they are promised. They caress as they ride the coins of the whites, coins carried in the pockets of worn and discarded uniforms provided by the whites.

The false dawn has come and gone and now the camp of Miles around me wakes. For some time in the darkness I have heard the sounds of men who stir, groan and sometimes stumble off in the darkness and cold to relieve themselves.

To one side, near the camp's center, is faintly outlined against the lightening grey sky the bugler who makes his morning call. Around me are raised the murmurs of protest, half-distinct curses. Beyond me, on the rise which overlooks the camp, the interior of Miles' tent is illuminated, the oil lamp inside creating, in contrast with the relative darkness outside, a surprising amount of light. Against the lighter sky the smoke from the tent's stove is now visible.

Names are called. Sleepy men, clutching cups of hot coffee poured from the pots which sit over the night-long fires, come to form an irregular line as they are organized to go out as replacements for the last watch, the sentries who stand guard and patrol the line Miles has formed around the camp of the Nez Perce.

From the Big Hole we fled through the land of the powerful Asaroke, the Crow, who would hear no more our spokesmen. Close upon us came the Bannock who watched our horses and stragglers. With them soon were some of the young men of the Crow, those who took from their agents the guns, the supplies free to all who would fight the Nez Perce.

The Crow we watched carefully. The Bannock were women, fools, cowards. Once before, long before Gibbon fell into our camp, the Bannock came to watch our camp. We ignored them. The warriors did not even go out against them. But the Bannock stayed, camping, here and there in the Big Hole Basin until some began to say they were spies who, although afraid to attack our camp, would provide the whites with our location and strength. So in the night Rainbow and Five Wounds went out—only through Ollokot, after they were gone, would I learn they were not in camp. The next morning there were dozens of strange horses in our herd and the Bannock were gone. It was said that they carried with them many corpse-bundles.

But Rainbow and Five Wounds were now dead and the Bannock grew stronger, grew, as the Crow joined them, braver. We could not move without the shadow of the Bannock and Crow around us. They would not oppose our passage, would not face us directly. Both fought in the old way, which was to raid in a test of courage and then withdraw. Even the Crow seemed hesitant to face openly the warriors of the Nez Perce who fought, instinctively, since the very beginning in Whitebird Canyon, to kill—as did the whites we faced. But still they hovered about us. If we let any of the old or weak wander from the center of our camp, the Bannock would appear to claim boastfully the scalp of a Nez Perce. If the horses were allowed to scatter, as they must do foraging, the Crow would swoop down to drive away what they could. Even as we moved tightly together there was little comfort for the Bannock and the Crow sometimes simply disappeared and we had to send our men to check the trail ahead, to find them, to know that they were not yet bold enough to try an ambush, a direct attack.

Even as we sent men forward we had to keep the main body of warriors in camp with the families to protect them, the horses, and the few supplies left to us, and, at the same time, send men back down the trail behind us to watch Howard who arrived to aid Gibbon at the Big Hole while the last of our warriors were still in their positions on the edge of our abandoned village.

With the Crows and Bannock constantly about us, with the burden of our old and wounded, our movement was inconstant and slow and Howard was able to bring his men up upon us from the rear. At the place called Camas Prairie Howard's cavalry came to form his camp only a few hours behind us. Here, however, the fears and visions which troubled our people since before Gibbon struck the Big Hole camp served to protect our people. The young warrior, Black Hair, cousin to White Bird, gut-wounded and in agony since the Big Hole, dreamed in his fitful sleep of a great raid where the warriors of the Nez Perce went into the sleeping camp of the soldiers and took away their guns, their horses, their supplies and even their clothes—leaving them naked and helpless in a country alien and hostile to them. Black Hair's brother, Otstatpoo, Firebody, brought the vision to the council of headmen. From this vision was to grow the night raid on Howard's camp in which Ollokot and twenty of our bravest survivors slipped past the Bannock and Crow scouts, entered the camp of Howard, now numbering over seven hundred, and brought away enough of the stock to stop Howard for two days while our people hurried to greater safety.

Yet Howard was to replace his horses and mules and renew his march to overtake us. Stress and fatigue now worked in his favor. Moreover, the tactical information which came to him was now superior. He had the Bannock and the Crow to harass us and report our every move. He had also in his camp the man called Captain John and the one called Meopkowit—Christian Nez Perce, treaty Nez Perce, to betray our thoughts and to anticipate our direction.

From the sheltered Wallowa we come to Lapwai and great council of the Nez Perce.

The Missionaries have brought to us their medicines, their goods, and the words of their spirit god. Now they bring to us again their agents and soldiers.

In place sit the preachers, Spalding and Whitman. With them is their pawn, Lawyer. In their stead speak the political agents, White and Stevens and Monteith. Behind them all is the uniformed Howard.

"Give up your old camps. Come in to us. We will care for you, share with you—for we are all brothers."

Against the white agents and the Nez Perce who, with Lawyer, receive their goods, stands the aged Toohoolhoolzote whose guttural cadence silences the council. "I belong to the land of which I came. The whites will not separate me from it, the whites will not section and divide the earth my mother."

Tuekakas, father, stands in place beside the old Dreamer: "We will live as our fathers lived; We will make no agreements, we will sign no papers to divide the earth indivisible."

Yet, the council continues. We are told agreement is reached. Hallalhotsoot, Lawyer, the white's dependent, will sign the papers for all the Nez Perce.

In trembling rage Toohoolhoolzote speaks the benediction for our people, "From the earth the Nimpau came, the earth's living shadow. Together in harmony with the spirits of this land we have walked. It is no more. Let no man speak for me. Let no man assume that he can take away the valleys and streams of my homeland. From this day the Nez Perce are two peoples. Christians, live in peace with the whites, but trouble me no more with these papers and promises."

Tuekakas, with deliberate steps, approaches the table of the whites, lifts from it the great Bible, and rips apart the book, placing the halves across each other before turning to walk silently from the council.

In the years that followed the free Nez Perce held our pledge until, finally, we were driven from our homeland and to the disaster at the Big

Hole. After the Big Hole, chance directed our flight. Chance disrupted, temporarily, Gibbon's pursuit. We fled with little plan or design to the godless land of the Yellowstone. At Camas Prairie we lashed back at Howard, from Camas Prairie we fled to a strange land of wonders. Hototo led now, guided our column, but even his descriptions did not prepare us for this incredible land where pools stand and smoke, reeking sulfur-taint, beside the pure, cold-water streams of the mountains.

In this bizarre and confusing land, which it seemed the gods created in jest and sport and then abandoned, our people—especially the young and the old left to us—were ill at ease and irritable.

But it was here, in the labyrinth of Yellowstone where even Hototo lost his way, that circumstance favored us in a manner that no one could have anticipated. Our scouts chanced upon a party of whites. Young Yellow Wolf, my nephew, found them and brought them to me.

There were four whites, three men and a woman —a man, his young sister, their mutual friend, and a guide. They had come from one of the white towns to the east to see the strange beauty of this land.

The guide, an old and garrulous man, knew, we were to learn, every detail and trail in this land for he had prospected for gold here, alone, years before most whites knew anything of the area.

With the whites we made an agreement. The old man would guide us through the almost impossible terrain to the northern pass out of the Yellowstone country, and, when we arrived on the plains to the north where Hototo could once again guide us, we would let them go in peace. To insure this safety, Joseph took into his lodge the white woman; Looking Glass and White Bird received the men.

Before me in the canted light of September is the physical, the tangible: woman-flesh. Incredible beauty, wondrous strange beauty like that of Narcissa: skin that is soft, hands that are supple. Breasts that swell intimate, lifewarm. Back that is smooth, lithe, strong. Buttocks and hips—rounded, symmetrical, malleable—flaring outward, inviting inward. Legs that create grace, form, and focus, that envelop, propel, that radiate thigh-loosened warmth, receptivity. Belly that is flat, illusive, ticklish. Abdomen that is touchsoft, muscle-girded firm, even now beginning to swell child-ripe. Vagina, shielded, protected, finally offered sweet-wet, luring irresistible all forces of being to union, to unison, to completion, to creation.

Eyes which reflect, project spirit and soul essence.

Forms: light, cream-white, sun-touched gold, soft auburn hair.

Forms: smooth copper, beauty of hue and uniformity, faultless form, supple beauty, flowing dark hair that envelops and shields and severs forever the matters of the world.

Eyes which are spirit and soul, which receive and accept and love. A soul and spirit which speaks the beatitudes of passivity, of restricted, settled harmony. A soul and spirit which represent the veracities and joys age-old: the freedom of the earth and the skies and waters, the beauty of the mountains and meadows unmanspoiled.

Eyes and spirits and flesh which compel man and order his existence, mold his carriage, form his conduct, create the void-urge so that no matter how or where he propels himself toward acceptance and union—and so creates the greatest man-agony, the most grievous man-error and folly as he denies in his fantasies the spirit of his fathers.

And so Joseph sits complacent, compliant, dreams of beauty: the Wallowa, dreams of beauty, loin-ache: Narcissa Whitman, dreams of beauty: Toma Alwawonmi, Springtime. Dreams of beauty, ponders action and achieves nothing. Caught passive in the transition between worlds, Nimpau-White, Joseph waits. Bound now he waits Miles, waited at Lapwai the woman-goddess Narcissa, waited on the Clearwater and at the Big Hole, Looking Glass. Waits, sits passive and powerless—for the strength of the Nez Perce is gone. The chance and the opportunity of the Nez Perce, whatever they were, are gone and now there is only suffering. Suffering and waiting. Joseph waits, hopes still—not for freedom or power or happiness—but hopes to relieve as best he can, temporarily, the ache, to relieve for the span of a meal or two the children's hunger. This, finally, even Joseph will do, can do.

We took the whites with us, held our bargain—Joseph himself coming to stop the bitter young warriors who harassed the white men, Joseph himself taking into his lodge the white woman, shielding her, assuaging as best I could her fright and terror; distinguishing, finally, that the woman before me, flesh-ripe and mature, was not Narcissa, that Miles was not Howard, and that neither Miles nor Howard were in spirit or form the benevolent Lewis or the plain-spoken Clark. Here in the shadows of summer, in the fading light of September, the core of my ambivalence was loosened and the woman-goddess Narcissa, the flesh that overwhelmed intellect, became, finally, not white woman, not white, but woman.

So the words of Narcissa and the legends about Lewis and Clark came finally to stand beside the deeds and the conduct of the present. The words and the papers were set aside and behind them were greed: the ambition for fame, the grasping for land-wealth.

I received the woman, sheltered her as I would have Natokolas, little daughter, received, sheltered, and protected. We took all of the whites and moved on, leaving forever the dry Montana basin of the Big Hole, leaving forever the great strength of the Nez Perce, the warriors Wahchumyus and Pahkatos Owyeen. Left forever in the shallow soil the form of Aihits Palojami, Fairland, sister. Left forever the form of Toma Alwawonmi, Springtime. Wife and mother. Gentle, resolute spirit that walks still with me in youth upon the banks of the Imnaha, hears and feels with me the rushing waters, sees with me the soaring eagle, feels with me, knows with me love: man-woman, man-child, man-land.

So I sit and wait, observe the waking camp, see the troops called into place. I wait the order that will bring me to Miles—or that will send again the troops against the destitute camp of my people.

The Prophecy of Smohalla

The Earth is My Mother.

Her dress is torn. Her hair is cut and wrapped in bundles. Her flesh is sectioned and fenced. Her flesh is ripped and torn to receive alien seed. Her bosom is violated for the yellow metal.

The spirit of those come to exploit and consume and foul is wrong.

The Sun and the Moon will respond. The Waters and the Wind will respond. The Fire and the Ice will respond.

The Nimpau will return to the Earth. The ground will shake with the weight of our horses. The morning light will warm the creatures who return with the Nimpau. The morning sounds will be the trilling of the women, the songs of the birds, the bugle of the elk, and the grunt of the buffalo.

At noon the warriors ride. They warriors chant: NIMPAU NIMPAU NIMPAU NIMPAU.

The Whites and those with them who violate the sanctity of my Mother, the Earth, will be driven back to the Fire and Ice beyond the edge of the Earth never to return.

Saith Smohalla, who has this vision from the Dream Spirits who speak Truth.

XII. The Bear Paws
October 5, 1877

The haze of the sun's southern cast has stood against the horizon for nearly an hour now, and through the camp of Miles there is the sound and smell of meat frying and the odor of bread and coffee. Already I know that I will be brought again to Miles, for the sergeant who is often around Miles has come and cut the ropes from my ankles. The soldiers watch but continue their eating as I make my way to the fire, there to flex slowly the numb, stiff bound hands to the warmth, there to stand—afraid to kneel or squat for greater warmth, afraid that in the stiffness of cold and hunger and fatigue I will lose my balance and fall.

The snow and sleet are gone and through the cold, wintery glare I can see to the north the camp of the Nez Perce. Here and there occasionally is the shadowy from of movement, though the distance is too great to recognize further detail. A thin smoke streak indicates a fire, though I cannot imagine where the fuel has come from. To the east of the Nez Perce camp, on a hill at its outskirts, stands a solitary figure, a figure I will learn in time was Looking Glass.

Hardly have the soldiers around me finished eating and returned, hunched with their coffee against the cold, when the sergeant comes for me. Abruptly, without comment or apparent emotion, he cuts away the remaining ropes and motions for me to come with him.

"The General will see you now." Abruptly come the only words he speaks, words which indicate openly anger and hostility.

As we walk up the slight hill to the tent of Miles, I see the man himself some seventy yards away, silhouetted against the snow-covered Bear Paws, relieving himself as he looks down into and studies the Nez Perce camp before him.

"The General says to tell you the food is for you," the sergeant states as we reach the tent of Miles.

"He says for you to eat now and the two of you will talk when he gets back."

In the tent of Miles, at the end of his great wooden writing table, is a plate heaped with the fatback and biscuits I had watched the soldiers eat earlier. A large tin cup of black coffee smokes beside it. The sergeant who today escorted me alone stands back and moves through the door, closing again the cold weather flap to aid the little black stove that glows red along its seams with heat. Without consideration or dilemma I go straight to the food and begin to eat, forcing entire biscuits and whole slabs of meat—food with substance, almost tasteless for it is volume I crave—into my mouth at one time, burning my hands and mouth with the scalding coffee, eating without pausing everything on the plate before me, wiping with the last of the bread the grease itself from the plate, relishing to the last, measured swallow the coffee which I had not tasted since the Big Hole camp, giving myself over entirely to what I knew I could not share, need not consider sharing.

Only when I finished did I pause to look around again to study the details of the tent where I had spent my first hours in the soldiers' camp. The great table was still across one end of the tent, The wash basin was in its place, the table around it water-stained. Behind the basin, hung from the pole of the tent, was a mirror I had not noticed before, but essentially that was all. There was no gun, nor any object of interest except a huge trunk near the wall of the tent. Outside, though I could not see him, I knew the sergeant stood.

Since there was little I could do but wait, I went over to the stove and, basking in its warmth, squatted, knelt as close as its heat allowed. As I waited random memories of our flight came to me: the refusal of my messenger by Howard long ago at the Clearwater,
the exhausting skirmishes after the Yellowstone, above all the fatigue brought upon us by the space and distance of the treeless plains of this place—so different from the fertile bottom lands and rushing rivers of our homeland.

I must have slept, strangely a restful and dreamless sleep, for Miles was in the tent, his man standing over me before I knew or heard anything. Slightly disoriented, embarrassed for sleep before one who is awake, I rose to face Miles. He was seated casually on the end of the table where my food had been. The sergeant held, I noticed now, the empty bowl and cup in his hand. There was something calm, at peace or rest now in Miles that I had not seen before. Less forceful and apprehensive, he seemed more certain of himself. He was smoking a pipe, something I had not seen him do before.

"I have decided to let you go, Joseph." There was no buildup, no threat or plea.

"I'm going to turn you loose and let you talk to your people about surrender. We are all around you; there is no choice."

With this he stopped and sat in silence, smoking. I waited for some time, straight, erect, anticipating the proposition or threat that I expected with his announcement. But none came. Finally I spoke, addressing him directly, using again his language.

"Let us return to our homeland, to the Wallowa, and I will do what I can to persuade my people.

"Bring in your arms, and I will do what I can to insure your return to Nez Perce land." Miles' response was quick, positive, incredible.

"Bring your people in; they have suffered enough."

Perhaps it was the reference to suffering; perhaps it was some more elusive quality inherent in the tone and words themselves, but, as quickly as it came, the suggestion that we might return to the Wallowa was subtly undercut. The old ambiguities, momentarily dismissed, flared again to stomach-tight intensity, the manipulations of a man who spoke sympathetically of suffering and yet led his troops into an unprepared, unwarned village with surprise and overwhelming strength.

I stood and looked into his face and there was nothing more. Finally, I turned and moved quickly out of the tent toward the picket line where my horse was tethered. The sergeant was soon with me, walking in hurried steps just behind me to make obvious, I suppose, the fact that I was free to go.

As I reclaimed my horse and moved through the camp, through this small army of soldiers Miles had brought with him somehow, from somewhere, to come down upon us as we camped within sight of the border we sought, as we waited the answer of our entreaties to the Sioux, a sense and awareness of personal failure came upon me as it had never before, even in the darkest hours after the Big Hole disaster. For I knew ultimately, as I mounted and began my ride to the last free camp of the Nez Perce, that whatever befell the Nez Perce, the land and the people which are one, that whatever happened to us now—to the warriors and boys and young women who crouched in the cold rifle pits of the Bear Paws camp—to the silent and hungry who huddled together for warmth in the ravines—that all of this was ultimately, as Miles said, my responsibility for I alone might have made it different. History and Fate had been within my hands had I chosen to act, had I the courage and conviction to assume voluntarily the responsibility that in the end no man may avoid.

Long ago on the Snake River, after the raid of Wahlitits, I chose to take my people away from Howard. I knew then that Howard would hang the three who, with Wahlitits, had raised their hands against the whites, but I knew then that he would do no more; I knew that the stern and rigid code which drove him, which made him blind at times to the facts before his face, would have then controlled and restricted his action. So I, Joseph, the man of peace and logic, qualities taught to me at Lapwai by Narcissa Whitman, chose not to give up the men, chose not to bend to the power of the whites—

even where I knew reason and logic dictated that very action. I chose instead to believe the camp reacted beyond my control and influence because of the pride I had and because somehow the surrender of Wahlitits and his two companions was finally, irrevocably, the surrender of the Wallowa which I had accepted as my trust from the forbears and spirits who had walked the land before me.

I chose again at Whitebird Canyon.

I chose to ride out under a flag of truce pretending to negotiate while I knew in my heart the whites, these whites, who were not Howard but were attendant officers, would only fight. I knew as I sat awaiting their progress down the canyon trail that I lured them under the guns of the warriors and I knew in reality I lured them to their deaths. And yet even at the time I knew profit would not come of it. I knew in my heart that Howard and those who stood above him would not say —because we fought and defeated them once —"excuse us," "sorry." "We underestimated your determination; return if you wish to your village and lands."

I chose and abnegated my responsibilities utterly and completely when the arrogant and foolish Looking Glass rode his prancing pony into our camp. I think even as the man came I knew subconsciously what I would do. Looking Glass was a man of personal courage and he was the son of the great Apash Wyakaikt, the Asotin chief and peer that even Tuekakas called "Meiway," the great chief. What I did was easy. I allowed Looking Glass to take to himself whatever authority and responsibility he wanted. There were times when I raised my voice against him, but at no time did I oppose him with my spirit. At no time did I position myself directly against him; at no time did I go to those I knew would listen with care and argue the danger of Looking Glass's position. I did not do this because Looking Glass was exactly the man I sought; he was a man who had an opinion and a set of ideas and the name and reputation which might make possible his ambition. And he was a man who sought the fame and recognition of leadership, a man willing to make the decisions that, in reality, I may have known even then that I should make, but found excuses and avoided.

And so I sat and played with the children before the doorway of my lodge at the Clearwater, while Looking Glass assured everyone that the camp was secure. After Howard turned away my messenger, I followed, with reservation and misgivings, the hurried and fearsome flight from the Clearwater River through the Lolo into the Montana territory. With increasing anguish I sat in the camp at the Big Hole Basin while Looking Glass assured us that the war was over, that Howard would not follow us here and that the whites of Montana were his friends and would not move against us.

With light jokes and studied non-commitment I turned away those who came to me privately in fear of the leadership of Looking Glass. On the Lolo after the Clearwater battle I heard but did not act on the suggestion Five Wounds, with Rainbow and Ollokot standing silently behind him, brought to me. I turned away the idea that we move quickly straight to Canada through the country of our oldest and best friends, the Flatheads. This would move us still further away from the Wallowa and I was unwilling to confront Looking Glass.

So I went with the Nez Perce to the camp at the Big Hole where many of us died. I went with Looking Glass into the heart of a country I did not know and moved almost every day away from Wallowa, the land for which we fought. I allowed my family and my people to go with Looking Glass and in this was my greatest personal abnegation. For each day and each step of the way I knew that my own family, Toma, spirit companion of youth, the children, Natokolas, Ollokot and his family would follow me wherever I chose. At the same time I knew most, if not all, the Wallowans would follow me as they had Tuekakas. Even beyond this I suspected Toohoolhoolzote would come with my band if the choice was between Looking Glass and the man he still called "Young Tuekakas." White Bird, my first ally, was in fact the only headman in doubt. White Bird might follow me; he might follow Looking Glass, or he might come with neither of us but make a move straight away by himself. No one, not even Five Wounds, knew the heart of White Bird—except that he would act as he chose, that he would move as the mood struck him.

The forms in the camp become more distinct. From the back of my walking horse I can see and recognize the men and women who stand, rifle in hand, behind the earthen mounds, those who had shouted in joy at my emergence from the camp of Miles, but who now stand silently. Silent and motionless too are the old people and the children in the background, frozen, motionless, and inert, as though a mural drawn, formed by some force which would study the emotions and the passions of human suffering.

And so it is these people still in the distance before my slow pacing horse whom I have led to suffering and deprivation when I followed Looking Glass into the heart of the Crow country where Gibbon fell upon us and ruined both his strength and our own. More than the physical strength lost—a momentary setback for the white, a thwarting, temporarily, of the aspiration for rank and fame for the man, Gibbon, who sought in the dark and against the sleeping families of the Nez Perce his own glory—Joseph created the circumstance at the Big Hole which destroyed the spirit and resilience of the Nez Perce. For at the Big Hole camp, Joseph and no other, allowed Looking Glass to hold the camp, allowed Looking Glass to sit in place while Gibbon, the agent of Howard, came against the sleeping tents of the Nez Perce. Joseph here forced the Nez Perce warrior to fight in desperation and against superior strength to save his very family. Joseph allowed at the Big Hole the death of Rainbow and Five Wounds, put the unwarned warrior between his family and the bayonet of the soldier. Joseph sacrificed the Nez Perce warrior who would drive at whatever cost, with whatever fear, any man from his tent. Joseph, who could have done better, did not. Joseph allowed the destruction, moved finally in rage and frustration too late to save the eighty members of our tribe who died at the Big Hole, moved, walked directionless, too inept to console those whose husbands and wives and children and parents lay upon the shallow Montana soil far from the salmon-shining streams and meadowlands which were the home of the Nez Perce.

It is the irony and decree of Fate that a man must live with what he creates, must live with the knowledge and the recognition of what might have been and is not—is not because of his lack of courage. The circumstance of the Nimpau, the Nez Perce, would have been different had not Joseph, this tattered scarecrow figure bound upright upon a pacing, tight-reined horse, abnegated the responsibility that was his. All the cleverness, all the intensity during and after the battle of the Big Hole are to no avail. The escape from the Big Hole, the successful fencing which kept the increasing Bannock and Crow mercenaries away from our families—implemented by Ollokot and his warriors—is no more than the reaction, finally, of a man who must defend his own lodge. The raid on Howard's horse herd, a maneuver spawned of necessity in the place called Camas Meadows as Howard pressed forward upon us, is but the execution of the plan of another, the dream of another—the young warrior Otstatpoo, Firebody—achieved by others, Ollokot, Looking Glass, and a few handpicked warriors.

A man, even a man as Joseph, may know that he, himself, held the people in place only days after the horse raid when at the Targhee Pass into the Yellowstone country Howard had succeeded in blocking our escape by sending the man Bacon with his cavalry on a wild, frantic ride that placed the horse troops across our path. Joseph and the Nez Perce held our place while Bacon stood before us and Howard marched continually against our rear. We held our place. We stood in the bush away from the trail, concealing as best we could the horses and travois and people. We sat in silence and avoided each other's eyes while the body dripped wet with anxiety and the infantry of Howard marched nearer. We held our courage and Bacon broke, galloping madly to the south and a distant pass, thinking we had changed our route. We held our voices which would cry in relief when

Bacon departed because Howard was upon us. We held our silence and in haste began to move through the pass while the sound of Bacon's horses could still be heard and the troops of Howard could be no more than a forced march away.

A man who seeks self-gratification, self-esteem, might console himself with the knowledge that as we moved finally out of the Yellowstone country, having, in the maze of this beautiful, godless land, temporarily escaped Howard, my plan alone lured the hostile man Sturgis and his troops from the mouth of the Clark Fort River Pass which we must use and sent him galloping to the east and the Shoshone River Pass.

Even later, at Cow Island, I controlled, with Ollokot, the warriors, brought the people away with the supplies we desperately needed, avoided the small garrison of soldiers and preserved our people.

From the moment at the Big Hole when Ollokot burst into my lodge and picked up my own gun, thrusting it into my hands with the single word "fight," I did no less than any man could do. With the Bannock and Crow mercenaries, with the horse raid at Camas Meadows, at Targhee Pass, and again as we approached the Clark Fort Pass I did what had to be done. At Targhee Pass, the most desperate circumstance after the Big Hole battle, there was, in reality, no freedom of action. We had no place to go, so we held our place, and anxiety and ambition—the very characteristics which enabled Bacon to entrap us—forced him to rush away to the south at the last moment.

I, Hin-mah-too-yah-lat-kekht, properly called Joseph, carry to my people now close before me, the knowledge which will rest upon me until the day I depart this life. I know that the ambiguities and uncertainties of my heart permitted the set of circumstances which has deprived the Nez Perce of his land and his freedom. Whatever might have been is not now, for Joseph did not act when his action might have fulfilled his soft-worded pledge to Tuekakas and, inherently, his obligation to both his forbears who inhabited the Wallowa in trust and to the spirits who created the land and erected from it its shadow-image, the Nimpau.

Yet Fate, Circumstance, and Time allowed us even then, after the Big Hole and the Yellowstone, the illusion of freedom, the possibility of escape. From the Clark Fort Pass and the evasion of Sturgis the path before us was relatively open, though increasingly desolate and barren, as we broke away from the mountains and passes to the open, arid plains that stretched uninterrupted, save for the Bear Paws, to the strange and magical invisible line the whites had drawn between themselves, calling one—the one to the north, the only place on earth it seemed might offer safety, refuge, and restitution—Canada.

Quickly, distinctly, day by day and hour by hour it grew colder and our problems increased. The tents and lodges, after the forced retreat at the Clearwater and the disaster at the Big Hole, were inadequate shelter from the wind and the rain—when there is rain in this increasingly arid land. The supplies of dried fish and camas flour were exhausted on the trail of the Lolo and never replenished. Day by day we came to depend on the random foraging of the boys and women. When we broke into the open plains it was possible at least to believe that we could see physically our immediate safety and that Howard would not fall into our camp before we knew it or could react, but the very openness of the terrain restricted the game. There is no buffalo, and the plains offer little else except the occasional antelope which leaves himself open to one of our marksmen—but the antelope are elusive and fleet and infrequent for a camp of still six hundred people.

Equally important is the condition of the horses which have sustained us and have carried us time and time again beyond the tireless, grain-fed horses of the cavalry troops. In the Wallowa the horses stood firm and healthy; their coats shone and the mares dropped colts as vigorous and as strong as their dams. The Lolo, with its terrain and infrequent meadow, was the first obstacle to affect the strength of the herd for all were weakened and some were lost for good. The grassland of the Bitterroot Valley and the pasture of the Big Hole camp restored somewhat the lost flesh, but neither provided the time or sustenance to reestablish the bottom and strength which our fine ponies once had. Now, in the cold and increasing snow we have little to maintain the horses upon which our safety depends. Still, behind us in continued forced marches comes the cavalry of Howard, men and horses hardened now, experienced now, sustained by the slow, but endless mule trains which carry food and grain.

Each new day brings more cold and snow which will kill and cover even the sparse buffalo grass the horses consume, upon which our slowing movement depends. The seventeen-hundred-mile, six-month flight has wasted animal and spirit and has left both open and vulnerable to the cold and hunger and destitution that comes when flesh is tired and simple rest and food and peace under any conditions would be a quietude acceptable, even sought.

And thus we reached the Bear Paws where the people of the Nez Perce now hail me, reach out silently to me with their eyes, searching for an answer to a question they will not phrase after years of anxiety and months of flight and the numbing effect of hundreds of shallow graves by the side of the trail while the column does not slow—neither that which flees nor that which pursues. They reach out to me with the strength that remains from courage, courage which sustains a force that goes beyond food and shelter and comes finally to a bewildered halt only in the face of a child's cold, hungry face.

We reached the Bear Paws and sat in our hungry and shelterless camp while the runners went out to Sitting Bull, asking consideration of our similar plight and safe conduct into his land away from the troops who pursue, asking a setting aside of the old animosities and a union of spirit and force as our flight and our battle demands in dignity and in acknowledgment of the common enemy who would destroy us both.

And so we sit, motionless after so long, waiting a place to flee while the horse troops of the man we learn to call Miles march from their log buildings and oat-filled stalls on a lark of a few days, a march which carries them across our route, to cut, as Howard instructs, finally, irrevocably, the path we might have followed to freedom and so complete the journey, achieve the point and line of safety we can see even now in the distance. As we sit Miles marches, hurries, against our unprepared camp with his four hundred men, lives to bring out half of his detached cavalry , still three men to our one, lives to surround our people and our spirit and force us to sit longer in hunger and cold while Howard marches constantly with his seven hundred to end forever the days when the Nez Perce walks free the earth with the spirits who created it and peopled it for his sustenance and his use.

Now, as before, the hands and eyes of my people are raised up to me.

HEAR ME MY CHIEFS

Random together now are the thoughts which are a man's being. *In the valley of the shadows there is hunger and cold and rain and fear. The man-child glides in the time-dismembered ease of youth and energy over the paths and trails of the Wallowa seeking with compassion and veneration the spirit, the Wyakin, which will guide his life. Hazy, small, infinitesimally small in the distance below, in the smoke-blue haze of absolute clarity, is the union of the Imnaha and the Snake. Beyond, rushing to union, are the Salmon and the Clearwater. Above, soars the eagle with man's heart, a silent heart filled with love beyond speech, filled with love beyond even thought, filled, fused to the dispassionate and permanent beauty that surrounds him.*

HEAR ME MY CHIEFS, FOR I AM TIRED.

In the mountains of beauty and desolation the thunder rolls through all things. The child who is man watches in wonder the lightening as it walks hotly through the air, feels, is shaken by the thunder which rides through the valley, floats up the mountain sides, and curls back in amplified echo to buffet soul and spirit, to absolve man-pride in the rain and now again snow, bringing reverence, giving promise.

HEAR ME MY CHIEFS. I AM TIRED: MY HEART IS SICK AND SAD.

A man's, a chief's life is no more than he does. It is no part of what he thinks. In trust the land and the people came from old Tuekakas, the spirit of father who lies on his death bed in the smoky lodge at the foot of the Wallowa range overlooking the infathomable depth of the crystalline Wallowa lake. To Hin-mah-too-yah-lat-kekht, Thunder Traveling from Loftier Mountain Heights, came the Wallowa valley and the people who are, as I am, but the shadow projection of the Earth our Mother. To me came the Wallowa, not to use or abuse, but to hold in trust in veneration of the father before me raised from this earth, returned to it, to hold in sacred trust for the son who would follow and know also the teeming untouched beauty, know the rush of the Imnaha, the turbulence of the Snake, know in spirit the flight of the eagle and the song of the thrasher, know and fear the roar of the grizzly.

A man must be what his time and place demands of him. He must make a choice and take a stand and allow himself the dignity of error. For a man can be only wrong... and he may be right. Again and again the singsong of Spalding and the untouchable beauty of the

Whitman woman reach out to my body and mind with the beatitudes of abnegation and irresponsibility. With ease and comfort I hear the words of Howard whose superior force means, I choose to believe, there is no choice to protect my people and their homes while even as I sit, hearing the dictated terms of promises, in the background is the age-touched form of Toohoolhoolzote who chants the dirge and the hymn of our people, the argument, the chant which points out the safety and the inaccessibility of the Snake Canyon where the virtues and integrity of our people might be sustained until we outlast the white and can return again to the highland plateaus, our home, can live again as the spirits who walk the earth intended, can watch in restitution the earth itself shedding the last vestiges of the whites' temporary wood houses and water ditches.

HEAR ME MY CHIEFS: HEAR ME THOSE WHO REMAIN WITH ME ALIVE IN THIS WORLD. I AM TIRED: MY HEART IS SICK AND SAD.

Those who fought with us are now dead. Looking Glass, whose hauteur and persuasiveness and name provided the direction than an introspective man would shirk, is dead. He has followed the greatest men of the Nez Perce; Rainbow is dead. Dead with him is Five Wounds.

He who led the young men is dead.

While these men lived, while Rainbow stood before the lodges of the Nez Perce, while Five Wounds and Ollokot stood beside him, no man might in the light of day come with impunity into the camp of the Nez Perce. The war cry of Rainbow shatters no more the hearts of those who oppose us. The laughter of Five Wounds no longer controls the tone of the camp. The dedication, the proud strength, the careful husbandry of Ollokot, no longer guide the Nez Perce warriors.

HE WHO LED THE YOUNG MEN IS NOW DEAD. *In the time-distilled moments that belong to a man, that are taken from the flow of his conscious life by some peculiarity or quirk of circumstance or fate, the form and image and spirit of my brother I am permitted to see and love. Ollokot was the flesh that is my flesh. The acceptance, the faith which credits to age—if it is a single year or a dozen years—some greater wisdom, some greater knowledge and power, some concept of elevation beyond and above the boy-man trial of physical strength, can create the greatest of animosities, can create as well the greatest of human loves. Ollokot stands silent on the knoll awaiting my return from the mountains. He is my brother and my flesh and our spirits are one, reaching only temporarily into different spheres. He is my champion and protector as if the roles were reversed and I were the younger, the weaker. Few oppose me as I pass the ambiguity of youth and adolescence for there is with me Ollokot and most fear the intensity of Ollokot, Ollokot who may finally in maturity lack the overwhelming physical strength of Rainbow—a warrior whose very size and perfect physique fails to warn fully the inhuman force he commands—Ollokot, who has not all of Five Wounds' cunning perception and constant ability to turn with each movement the effort of an adversary into foolish and wasted motion, but Ollokot, who has beyond either the dedication and conviction far beyond simple mindedness: the conviction of resolution and dedication so that to oppose Ollokot is to face a man who does not believe that any man may ultimately prevail against him, for no man can overpower him, for no man can outlast him.*

HE WHO LED THE YOUNG MEN IS NOW DEAD. He, with whom I had perfect harmony and total belief is now dead. The random bullet of the high-powered rifle strikes arbitrarily, shatters the soft flesh, denies the spirit opportunity to harden and resist. He who believed in me is now dead. Ollokot waited and watched the antics of Looking Glass, defended with Rainbow and Five Wounds the Nez Perce while he who is called Joseph created and extended the ambiguity of his heritage, urged peace and restraint, opposed war and feared all three. Ollokot fought, while Joseph sat in front of his lodge and heard Looking Glass, while Joseph waited until there was no choice, waited too late to do the best he could, waited too late to save the best of his people, waited two hours too long to avoid the charge of a man who saw himself already in the pages of history, waited, hesitated even at the moment he might have crossed the invisible border to cultivate the formal introduction to Sitting Bull who might well have his own problems and be totally indifferent to four hundred women and children, to one hundred Nez Perce warriors, who were no threat to him.

HE WHO LED THE YOUNG MEN IS NOW DEAD. HIS CHILDREN AND MINE ARE COLD AND HUNGRY. All the children of the Nez Perce are cold and hungry and fear the sounds of the day and the sounds of the night. The children of the Nez Perce cry no more. We must have time to find the children and the people who have run away to the hills for they have no blankets and no food. May I not find among the dead my own children.

HEAR ME, MY CHIEFS. HEAR ME, NEZ PERCE. I AM TIRED OF FIGHTING. OUR CHIEFS ARE KILLED. LOOKING GLASS IS DEAD. TOOHOOLHOOLZOTE IS DEAD.

THE GREAT WARRIORS ARE GONE. RAINBOW AND FIVE WOUNDS AND OLLOKOT NO LONGER STAND WITH US.

THE OLD MEN ARE ALL DEAD. ONLY HINMAHTOOYAHLATKEKHT AND WHITE BIRD REMAIN. IT IS THE YOUNG MEN WHO SAY YES OR NO IN COUNCIL.

HE WHO LED THE YOUNG MEN IS NOW DEAD.

IT IS COLD AND WE HAVE NO BLANKETS. THE LITTLE CHILDREN ARE FREEZING TO DEATH. SOME OF OUR PEOPLE HAVE RUN AWAY TO THE HILLS WHERE THEY HAVE NO BLANKETS AND NO FOOD. I WANT TIME TO LOOK FOR MY CHILDREN .... PERHAPS I SHALL FIND THEM AMONG THE DEAD.

MY CHIEFS, HEAR ME: MY HEART IS SICK AND SAD. FROM WHERE THE SUN NOW STANDS I WILL FIGHT NO MORE FOREVER.

Gone now are the ambiguities and fantasies of youth. Around me are the Nez Perce who have waited for my words and who have sunk to the cold ground with them. Nowhere is the wail of lament; nowhere are the shouts of joy. There is now only the reality of the destitute camp. In the beaten snow, the mud increases.

Around us there are the children whose eyes watch but no longer cry. At least now there can be food. We can throw down our guns and gather whatever scraps of wood and buffalo chips there are for a fire. We can take our guns out to Miles and exchange them for food for the children.

We will take the food and watch the white men, the first who have walked at will within our camp since the spirits set the Nimpau free upon the earth itself. We will take the food and watch the troops because the children are hungry and do not cry. We will eat the food and rest, remembering, in time, that we made the choices that seemed best, that we made choices of honor. We will sit and dream of the high plateaus and rivers of our homeland. We will remember the great pool on the lower Clearwater where our people gathered for the salmon runs and camas gatherings. We will wait and listen as the thunder rolls down through the valleys from the mountain heights above. And the thunder will be the hoof beats of thousands of horses as the warriors and spirits return to cleanse the earth.

Historical Characters

Spelling and pronunciation of Native American names is an effort to render the sound.

Joseph, Hin-mah-too-yah-lat-kekh*t* ("Thunder Traveling From Loftier Mountain Heights") – called Joseph or Chief Joseph by the whites. Often called Young Tuekakas by the Nimpau. Civil leader (Headsman) of the Wallowa Valley Nez Perce. Born about 1840.

Nimpau – meaning "The People" in self reference. Sahatin speaking people called "Cho-pun-nish" or "Pierced-nose people" by Shoshoni guides and Lewis and Clark. Called "Nez Perce" by early French trappers.

Wyakin – spiritual vision, guardian spirit. Reference to an individual's vision, often incorporated into his name.

Nelson A. Miles – Colonel, Brevet General. Commanded U.S. forces despatched from Ft. Lincoln, NE to intercept the Nez Perce's line of flight to Canada. Years later Miles adopted the stance of public advocate for Joseph and the Nez Perce effort to be allowed to return to their homeland.

Tuekakas – father of Hinmahtooyahlatkekht. Tuekakas was called "Joseph" by the missionaries. He was sometimes referred to as "Old Joseph" and his son "Young Joseph." Tuekakas was the principal headsman or leader of the Nez Perce in the Wallowa Valley in what is now eastern Oregon. The Nez Perce had no "chiefs" as whites used the term. Born about 1790.

Henry and Eliza Spalding – Protestant missionaries to the Nez Perce.

Marcus and Narcissa Whitman – Protestant/medical missionaries to the Nez Perce. The Whitman/ Spalding party arrived in the Nez Perce homelands in 1836; their party included the first white women and the first wheeled vehicle to cross the Continental Divide.

Ollokot – a principal warrior, "He who led the young men." Younger brother of Hinmahtooyahlatkekht.

Natokolas – grandmother of Joseph and Ollokot.

Toma Alwawonmi – ("Springtime") wife of Joseph.

Looking Glass (Sr.), Apash Wyakaikt – called "Meiway" meaning "Great Chief" in recognition of his historical influence as civil leader and war chief. Born about 1785.

Rainbow, Wahchumysus – a principal warrior.

Five Wounds, Pahkatos Owyeen – a principal warrior.

Smohalla – Wanapam spiritual leader and prophet, born about 1820, whose teachings influenced various Native American individuals and leaders. His birth name suggests "arising from the dust of earth mother."

Lawyer, Hallalhotsoot – politically astute leader of the Nez Perce at Lapwai, site of the first Protestant mission to the Nez Perce. Born about 1795.

Toohoolhoolzote – "fiery orator and proud man." Leader of Snake River area band. Considered "hostile Dreamer medicine man" by the whites. Born about 1805 (estimate).

White Bird – leader of another Snake River band. Survived flight of Nez Perce and managed, with a few followers, to slip away to Canada after Joseph's surrender at the Bear Paws.

Elijah White – Indian agent who presented (1842) Nez Perce with his list of "laws," determining that offenses against whites or white property will be punished by whites. "Whoever burns a dwelling house will be hung." Dictated that response to white offenses against Indians will be decided only by white officials.

Isaac Stevens – dynamic and ambitious, appointed both Governor of Oregon Territory and Indian agent. Stevens brought about the treaty of 1855, the principal instrument of dispossession for several tribes of the Northwest Territory, by means of complex inter and intra-tribal manipulations.

Wahlitits – young Nez Perce warrior whose attempt to revenge the murder of his father by a white man sets in motion the Nez Perce War.

Looking Glass, Allalimya Takanin – the younger Looking Glass, son of Apash Wyakaikt. Highly influential in the military strategy and direction of retreat of the Nez Perce. Born about 1832.

O.O. Howard – General, ranking military officer in the Northwest Territory.

Tecumseh, the Shawnee – organized an extensive confederacy to oppose white intrusion into Native American homelands early in the 19th century.

Perry – Captain under Howard. Routed by Nez Perce at the Battle of WhiteBird Canyon.

Seattle – Native American leader and orator from the general vicinity of present day Seattle, Washington.

Gibbon – Colonel. Directed the attack and destruction of the Nez Perce camp at Big Hole Montana. Allowed the impression that no prisoners would be taken.

Kamiakin – powerful Yakima leader who opposed Stevens and attempted to organize Columbia Plateau tribes into a confederacy. Defeated in what is called the "Yakima War of 1855."

Acknowledgements

My genuine appreciation and acknowledgement to the following:

Old friends, Wm. E Fuller and C.Trent Busch and other colleagues who had to listen and read.

Mr. Antowine Warrior for kind words and use of his painting "Young Warrior Dreaming."

NPS guides, especially L. Lula and K. Edmonds for enthusiastic and professional assistance.

Members of my family who contributed, each in his or her own way: AEW, NTW, CMW, and SLW.

Mary A. Webb for her love and support, and Joy A. Webb for her love and support and for typing "Toohoolhoolzote" several hundred times. They "put up with a lot."

Special acknowledgement to sons, Russ and Brad, who found the box, blew off the dust, converted to digital, and followed up with ms readings and suggestions.

Special recognition to Russ Webb whose software skills, editing, designs, maps, and details put all this together. He played Perkins better than I played Wolfe.

He cannot choose but hear;
And thus spake on that ancient man,

S. T. Coleridge

Biography

G. Freeman Webb comes from an agrarian tradition of many generations. His interest in land use and title concept was a focal point in a modest academic career which included graduate seminars in Native American Literature. He and his wife, Joy, now divide their time between forestry and woodworking interests in Maine and the family farm in Georgia.

www.ingramcontent.com/pod-product-compliance
Lightning Source LLC
Chambersburg PA
CBHW030817310726
48980CB00006B/531/J

* 9 7 8 0 6 1 5 4 9 2 8 5 8 *